PASSION

PASSION

EROTIC ROMANCE FOR WOMEN

EDITED BY
RACHEL KRAMER BUSSEL

CLEIS
PRESS

Published in the United States by Cleis Press, Inc., 2246 Sixth Street, Berkeley, California 94710.

Printed in the United States.
Cover design: Scott Idleman
Cover photograph: Garry Wade/Getty Images
Text design: Frank Wiedemann
Cleis Press logo art: Juana Alicia
First Edition.
10 9 8 7 6 5 4 3 2 1

ISBN: 978-1-57344-415-6

Contents

INTRODUCTION: GETTING PASSIONATE

P assion. It can mean greed, desire, affection, love or simply, emotion. You will find all of those and more in the stories contained herein. As you read these twenty stories, you too will be swept away by passion as you travel to Paris and Greece (and Beverly Hills). You'll get stuck in an elevator, take a bubble bath and a bus ride (not to mention some subway foreplay and flirting) and explore nature in some very intimate ways. You'll find couples, and couplings by men and women looking (whether they know it or not) to spice things up in the bedroom.

Here, couples at all stages of their relationships (including the very beginning) kindle their passion in various ways, from exes who reunite to young marrieds on a naughty nature walk to first timers mixing business with pleasure. When Krista in "Crave You Close" by A. M. Hartnett tells Nicky, "I'm so used to having to hold my breath," she is saying so much about their usual erotic m.o. At night, outdoors, she is free to make as much noise as she wants to.

These couples explore getting kinky, precisely because they feel intimately connected to each other. They go places, literally and figuratively, they wouldn't dare without the other. They revisit old flames and nurture new ones; indeed, sometimes the men these women crave, such as Maya does in "The Silver Belt," are not their husbands at all, but someone else, someone special, someone who is seeing them in an entirely new light. Those stories mingle with other tales of longtime lovers ignited to fiery scenes within these pages.

Passion can mean so many things, from the sexual submission of a caning to exploring new bodily territory—sexual experimentation, trying something you've fantasized about. It can mean makeup sex or role-play, a change of scenery or simply a change of thinking. It can mean looking at a lover, a husband, a boyfriend or a new boy toy with fresh eyes, sizing him up, baring yourself, daring him to come and get you.

Just as in real life, there are lovers' quarrels within these pages, slights real and imagined, as couples find tender, erotic ways to heal their hurts and become even closer. There is an element of real, raw emotion in the way love and desire can as easily tear us down as build us up that makes us appreciate each expression of romance all the more, because we know how truly special it is. I'm grateful these authors skip from playful romps to relationship-saving sex to tender memories to scorching sex scenes, together creating a book that will likely make you blush *and* make your heart swell.

As the narrator in one of my favorite pieces, "My Dark Knight" by Jacqueline Applebee, says, "I'm a not-so-hopeless romantic. I believe that chivalry still exists, I hope to find quiet nobility in the most random of places, and I believe that people who love each other can live happily ever after." She finds a dark, very sexy knight who she rescues, seduces, and then... But you'll have to read the story to find out.

Rachel Kramer Bussel
New York City

BIG-BED SEX

Donna George Storey

Have you stayed with us at the Beverly Hills Hotel before?"
The well-groomed man behind the reception desk looked
straight into my eyes and flashed his perfect teeth.

*Do I look like the kind of idiot who blows a thousand bucks
a night on a hotel room?*

That's what I wanted to say. What I actually said was, "No,
this is my first time."

"Then it will be my pleasure to show you around our hotel,"
the clerk said, scooping up the green and pink card key folder
and gliding around the desk to my side. "This way, please."

I followed him through the lobby—coral velvet chairs
arranged in a wide circle on a leafy green carpet—that was
relatively quiet early on a Thursday afternoon. He pointed out
the entrance to the famous Polo Lounge, then the route to the
storied swimming pool where countless stars had lounged in the
California sun.

I nodded and smiled, shoulders back and chin high in my best imitation of a patrician spendthrift. Slipping into the elevator behind him, I noticed the generous girth of his index finger as he pressed the button for the second floor. My gaze swept over the rest of him, discreetly: a stocky brunette not quite handsome enough for a starring role in the movies, but all the more appealing for it. I guessed he was in his late twenties or early thirties, younger than me by just a few years.

Not that it mattered. I was a happily married woman. *Very* happily married.

"We have an especially nice room for you today," he informed me cordially as we walked down the hallway, the jungle-leaf pattern on the walls illuminated by sparkling sconces.

"Very good," I murmured, still playing it cool.

He slipped the card key into the slot of room 209 and held the door for me. When I stepped inside, I literally had to bite my lip to keep my jaw from dropping. My sister—my *rich* sister—had hinted she was going to splurge on my accommodations, but this was truly the most deluxe hotel room I'd ever seen outside of the movies. A short entry hall fanned into a huge living room with a plush sofa, armchair and large flat-screen TV at one end and a marble-topped desk with an elegant chair at the other. An elaborate fruit basket presided over the glass coffee table, and vases of fresh lilies bloomed in every corner.

The clerk began his official tour, and I quickly realized I would need it. The closet door to the left of the entrance actually led into a full dressing room. Off to the left was the lavish bathroom, rich in mirrors and gleaming gold fixtures. The Jacuzzi bath was supplemented by a floor-to-ceiling glass shower stall, and I decided immediately I would try both, even though I was only staying one night. The shelves were stocked with stacks of fluffy white towels and toiletries, enough to bathe and dry the bodies of a chorus line of beauties.

"You can raise and lower the curtain this way," the clerk instructed me, pushing one of the numerous buttons on the wall. A low buzzing sound filled the room, and the pink balloon curtain above the tub slowly inched up to reveal a view of the garden in which the bungalows—the lodging of actual movie stars and moguls past and present—were hidden.

Still in shock, I didn't see the pièce de résistance until he guided me over to the desk for a quick introduction to the information folder and room service menu. Tucked away on a raised platform to the left of the sitting area was a king-sized bed, a length of gauzy material draped around the metal canopy frame like a set from *The Sheik*.

"Wow, it's like a fairy tale!" With that breathy exclamation, I showed myself for the star-struck plebian I really was.

The clerk didn't seem to mind. He smiled as if my delight made him truly happy. "Yes, this suite is one of the most charming rooms in its category. You're very lucky."

Our eyes locked. I felt a sexual *twang* between my legs.

Still smiling, he said, "Do let me know if I can do anything else for you. Our entire staff is at your service."

Only then did it occur to me to wonder if I was supposed to tip him. I had plenty of cash on me, but BRENDAN SOMMERS—I thought to check his name tag for the first time—was no bellboy. He'd merit at least a twenty if not more, but then paying him seemed somehow indecent. Or was it just my sudden urge to request an immediate and very special service involving his brawny body and that great big bed?

"I'm fine, thank you, Brendan. Thank you very much for the tour."

If he'd hesitated, I would have gone for my wallet, but he nodded, turned gracefully on his heel and disappeared.

I fell back on the sofa and finally let my mouth gape open, as it had been threatening to do for the past ten minutes. I felt like I was in a major motion picture myself and yet watching one, too, because I couldn't keep my eyes off of that mesmerizing bed. It was probably no accident that it was set above the rest of the room like a stage. In spite of the executive desk and the comfy sofa and chairs, this room obviously was made for one purpose only: wild, sweaty and very passionate sex.

The problem was, short of calling back adorable Brendan to do the honors, the only other eligible candidate for a Beverly Hills Hotel fuckfest was back in San Francisco all tied up in important client meetings. My husband, Will, had originally planned to accompany me here for my reading at Book Soup, especially after my sister offered to come out for the event and put us up at her West Coast pied-à-terre. But a suddenly convened meeting with a demanding client scuttled our L.A. getaway. I consoled myself that I'd have a chance for quality time with my sister.

The problem was, all I wanted to do now was loll about on that luscious bed—and not with a sibling.

I grabbed a pear from the fruit basket and took a bite of the yielding flesh, my gaze still fixed on the stage set before me. My sister had told me that the Beverly Hills Hotel was second only to the Chateau Marmont as a favorite assignation palace for Hollywood's many adulterers. While the real movers and shakers would surely spring for a fourth-floor suite, a minor producer or supporting-actor type had probably seen fit to blow a thousand on an afternoon's delight in this romantic boudoir.

Maybe it was a trick of the dusky light, but as I continued to stare, the ivory-colored quilt seemed to swell up, up into a mound, bunched just a little higher at midpoint. With a little more squinting, the shape resolved into two bodies, male and female, hips moving rhythmically, up and down. The sound of heavy breathing filled my ears, joined by a low feminine moan and the rustle of five-hundred-thread-count cotton sheets as the ghostly couple undulated on the broad mattress.

My cunt muscles clenched almost to the point of pain.

But it wasn't the pleasure of the starlet and her producer that filled me with such longing. What twisted my pussy into a throbbing knot of lust was the thought of what could—and would—happen on that bed if Will were here with me.

We always seemed to have extrahot sex in hotel rooms, with a special hit of shacking-up naughtiness in the budget places with the lumpy mattresses, threadbare towels and shrink-wrapped plastic cups. Whenever I could, though, I booked us rooms in rustic country inns or charming bed-and-breakfasts, because over the past seven years I'd learned an interesting fact about my husband. The bigger the bed, the better the sex, as if a grander canvas inspired him to new erotic heights.

In fact, I could plot out a timeline of red-letter days in our sex life based on the size and luxury of our rent-by-the-night beds.

It wasn't the first time we'd done it in broad daylight, when we played on the mahogany canopy bed in the plantation hotel outside of New Orleans. It was, however, the first time Will had celebrated my nude body so lovingly, undressing me slowly, stretching my limbs across the wide mattress so that I was totally vulnerable and exposed. As I stared up into the rose satin sky above me, I felt tied to the bed and to him—a purely voluntary bondage. "Keep your eyes open," he whispered as he stroked first my shoulders then the sensitive flesh of my inner arms, moving on to circle my breasts lightly with his fingertips then flick my throbbing nipples with his thumbs. Scooting down between my legs, he gazed at my secret place with such admiration and pleasure, my heart ached. "So beautiful," he said, "like a satin flower." I almost came from the heat of his gaze alone, so I was more than ready when he took me, pushing my knees up so he could go in deep. All the while he stared deep into my eyes, penetrating me that way, too, and when I came I felt like I was melting into him, body, mind and soul.

The Victorian bed-and-breakfast in Mendocino had a beautiful four-poster, and this time Will did tie my wrists to the thick posts with my panty hose. Then he sat at the edge of the bed and looked at me for a long time, his lips curved into a sly smile. I finally asked him what he planned to do next. "You tell me," he said. "Tell me exactly what you want me to do to you." He wouldn't do anything unless I spelled it out in shameless detail. Where I wanted him to touch me and with what—fingers, tongue or cock? I had to tell him how hard and how fast, too, and if I ever stopped talking, he'd stop, leaving me panting with frustration. At first I was shy, but soon enough I got so carried away I asked him to do things I'd dreamed of but never had the nerve to ask for: lube his cock in my drooling mouth then slide it between my breasts, stick one finger in my cunt and one in my ass for a two-pronged finger fuck. The slippery power play of it turned us both on, with Will ordering me to order him. When I finally came around his cock, his finger still jammed up my backside, I thought my chest was going to explode, but I still managed to dutifully inform my "slave" of my climax with a babbling string of obscenities.

The Stratford-on-Avon-style inn in Victoria, British Columbia, saw our most athletic sex, perhaps because the bed was so damned large. This time Will played no mind games, he just fucked me, sometimes slow and gentle, sometimes pounding into me like a piston. We rolled around on the mattress in every possible position—missionary with my legs trapped between his was the surprise favorite—leaving not a corner untouched by our sweat-drenched bodies. Finally he took me doggy-style, his fingers tugging on my well-sucked, pleasantly sore nipples. We both came at exactly the same time, my body swaying, lifting high above the mattress as if I were suspended in air. And I thought only Superman could fly.

After that day, we had a name for what we did: Big-Bed Sex.

And here, in tantalizing 3-D reality, was one hell of a big bed.

If Will couldn't be here, I figured at least I owed him a glimpse of what could have been, which might at least inspire him to some memorable welcome-home fucking tomorrow night. Aiming my BlackBerry at the alcove, I snapped a picture of the Arabian love nest. I took another of the Jacuzzi, realizing only then that the scalloped satin curtain over the tub bore a startling resemblance to a moist, pink vulva. Giggling as I imagined his face when he checked his email during a break, I sent both attachments with the simple subject line *BBS*. No explanation, not even a *Wish you were here ;-)*.

My husband would know exactly what I was saying.

My reading that night went well. Naturally, a biography of unsung women screenwriters of the 1930s and 1940s would be enthusiastically received in this part of the world. Afterward, my sister and I took a few of my college friends who'd come to the reading out to supper at the Polo Lounge. I passed on the thirty-eight-dollar Wagyu beef hamburger in favor of a Caesar salad and a glass of pinot noir. The food was at best mediocre, but I had to admire the complacent self-confidence of the Beverly Hills Hotel. Obviously what was good enough for Marilyn Monroe in 1960 was good enough for the less-than-stellar guests of today.

For most of the evening, I was too busy enjoying myself to dwell on the lonely night ahead. That is, until I slipped my card key in the lock and opened the door of my junior suite. Again I felt as if I'd stepped into a wonderland. The whole room was cast in golden shadow from the desk lamp and the even softer glow of the Japanese lantern beside the bed, all achingly romantic. Obviously the turndown service maid had been informed the room was occupied by a single guest tonight. The sheet, folded down on the left side of the bed only, was meant to be inviting, but instead just reminded me I was alone.

I tasted one of the bite-sized cookies set out on the porcelain plate on the nightstand—cinnamon pecan coins that melted like butter on my tongue. At least my mouth would get a hit of pleasure here tonight.

I decided to try calling Will one last time to say good night. To my annoyance, he hadn't replied to my email or responded to the two voice mail messages I left before and after the reading. He was probably busy with the meeting and then dinner with the client, but I was still hurt he hadn't bothered to check in at all. And—the thought occurred to me—if I'd inspired him with those photos, a little "big-bed" phone sex might not be a bad way to make the best of our situation.

Again the call went to his message box.

I hung up, cursing him under my breath. Polishing off the rest of the cookies in a huff, I headed to the bathroom to brush my teeth and wash my face. I decided to wear the soft terry-cloth robe to bed and discovered that it rubbed my naked flesh in a very beguiling way. Then I got the idea to masturbate myself to sleep with a superhot fantasy starring a willing Brendan who would service my every depraved desire.

Will deserved it for being such a workaholic prick.

I was just crawling into bed to get it on with Brendan when I heard the knock at the door. I expected it was my sister, stopping by with a book she'd brought for me from New York. I padded over to the entryway. There was always time to diddle myself later.

I pulled the door open—and immediately gasped, my hand

flying to my heart like that of a lady in need of smelling salts.

Standing before me in the same suit he'd put on that morning was my very own husband, looking rumpled and travel-worn and exceedingly sexy.

We fell into a hug and I drank in the scent of him: business meetings, airplanes, his own musky, masculine perfume.

"Oh, god, it's so great to see you. How did you manage to get down here?"

"How could I stay away? Where's that bed?"

"Let me show you the Jacuzzi first." I pulled him into the bathroom and flicked on the lights over the tub. "Doesn't that curtain look like a cunt?"

"It does, indeed. A nice, swollen, wet one." Will wiggled his eyebrows at me and looked around the room approvingly. "I think we'll have to try that shower, too. More than big enough for two."

"Sounds good, but first I have to show you that bed." I grabbed his hand and almost skipped into the living room.

"That's one fucking big bed," Will said, laughing. "The photo didn't do it justice."

"That thing was just made for wild sex. I can only imagine all the things that went on there."

Will put his arm around my waist. "In about fifteen minutes, you won't have to imagine anything. Let's take a quick shower and then burn that mattress to cinders."

"When do you have to be back?"

"I'm on the seven a.m. flight, but that leaves us a good five hours to play."

I laughed and dragged him over to the dressing room. "See, they provided an extra robe for me. That sweet young clerk who gave me the tour must have guessed I was the type to invite in extra company."

"All you famous authors hire gigolos to service you on the road, don't you?" Will said, loosening his tie.

I retired to the bathroom to wait for him, anxious to see him in that sexy robe. As I gazed at my flushed face in the mirror over the sink, I had to grin. I was truly the luckiest woman on earth. When we had big-bed sex, my husband always seemed to guess a desire I never even knew I had until he coaxed it forth from my fevered flesh and mind. I felt my breath come faster, my pulse quicken. What secret would he discover inside me tonight?

Just then Will stepped up behind me, the pure white of the terry cloth setting off his olive skin to perfection.

"How's my star?" he whispered, embracing me from behind.

"The lighting in here kind of makes everyone look like one, doesn't it?"

"But you really are," he said in a low, insistent voice. Our gazes met in the mirror. "And I'm the fortunate man you've chosen to service your every need."

I felt a sweet tightening between my legs. I'd swear Will had slipped inside my head and taken careful note of all my filthy fantasies about Brendan.

"Would Madame like a shower to relax her after a hard day greeting her fans? I'm well-trained in massage—and other forms of manual pleasure."

I caught my breath. *How did he know?* Of course, I could play my part just as well.

"As a matter of fact, I could use a little refreshment," I replied in my best imitation of a grande dame. "You come in the shower with me, of course. You can use those well-trained hands to wash me—everywhere."

Will went over to turn on the shower, holding his hand briefly under the spray to test the temperature. Then he came up behind me again, untied the sash of my robe and pulled it down over my shoulders.

"So beautiful," he murmured. "I'm going to enjoy my work very much tonight."

I felt another stab of lust low in my belly. Why was this turning me on so much? I'd never buy a man, never take advantage of any power I might have in real life to obtain sexual favors. But something about this absurdly luxurious room, that waiting bed, brought out my sense of entitlement. Every woman who stayed at the Beverly Hills Hotel deserved a willing servant to cater to her most selfish whim.

"Believe me, young man, I'm going to make sure you work very hard tonight," I replied with my new hauteur.

Will caught my eye and smiled then dipped his head modestly.

We stepped under the pounding spray together. I handed him the large bottle of body wash. "Spread this all over me. And remember that the dirty places need an extralong scrubbing."

"Yes, ma'am," he said, squirting a large blob of the viscous white cream onto his palm. With slow, circling strokes, he spread the soap over my shoulders, back and arms. The water washed it away as quickly as he applied it, but still he massaged me conscientiously, working his way down my back to my buttocks.

I turned to face him. "Do the front of me now."

With a submissive nod, he squeezed out another generous mess of cream and set to work on my breasts. I arched back and moaned at the sensation of his slippery hands on my sensitive nipples.

"Keep doing that. I need a good cleaning there."

"Yes, ma'am. I see this is especially relaxing for you, ma'am."

After several minutes of a very skillful massage, my clit was clamoring for equal time. "Wash me between my legs now. I definitely need to freshen up down there."

"I understand, ma'am." Will replenished his wad of soap and lathered up my pubic hair, his fingers creeping lower. Shamelessly, I spread my legs and rocked my hips, slithering back and forth over his slick hand.

And still my greedy body wanted more.

"Do your offerings include anal eroticism, young man?" I panted.

After a pause, Will answered, "It's my specialty, ma'am."

"Then wash me well there, too. I'll be curious to sample your skills when I take you to my bed."

Will's cock was already stiff, but it twitched noticeably at my latest order. Was he as turned on by this as I was?

"I expect you charge extra for a good ass-licking," I added peevishly.

"Usually I do, ma'am, but tonight I'd like to extend my complimentary services."

I almost laughed, but Will looked so earnest, I managed to stay in character. Still, when my husband slid a frothy finger up and down along the valley of my ass, I couldn't restrain a moan. He circled the tight ring of muscle gently. I gasped and moaned again. My knees were so wobbly, I had to press one hand to the glass to keep my balance.

"Perhaps you should relax in bed now, ma'am?"

"Yes, I believe I am ready to retire for the evening."

I let my valet do all the work of drying me off. He even knelt before me to towel off my legs and feet, his own body still dripping wet. Then he held my robe for me and tied the sash securely.

"Get yourself ready, then join me," I snapped and glided regally off to the living room.

Plumping up all the pillows against the center of the headboard, I pulled back the quilt and lounged back like an Egyptian queen.

A few minutes later, Will appeared at the side of the bed in his robe, his wet hair carefully combed.

I looked him up and down appraisingly. "As you know, I'm rather tired and I'm not really in the mood to be giving you directions every step of the way. So I'll leave the details to you, although I am expecting a good showing of your particular... *expertise.*"

"Yes, ma'am," Will, said, his eyes lowered. He started to climb up onto the bed.

I put a hand on his arm. "Take off that robe. I prefer to see you work in the nude."

Nodding once, Will dropped his robe to the carpet. I noticed his cock rearing up at a dizzying angle. I so wanted to suck it, but that would have to wait for another screenplay.

He stretched out beside me and leaned over to kiss one nipple and flick the other between his strong fingers. He'd done this to me a thousand times, and yet tonight I sensed a new, almost professional dedication, as if he were doing his best to please a demanding customer. His attentions paid off. My breasts seemed to swell a full cup size, they were so heavy and aching, and my pussy was drooling all over the sheets.

Finally I rested my hand on his head, nudging him downward, the way a boorish man might hint for a blow job. Will obediently kissed his way down my belly to my mons then spread my legs reverently. He lay on his belly between my thighs, his long legs dangling over the bottom of the bed.

He touched his tongue to my sweet spot.

I groaned and pushed up to him.

He teased me for a few licks then found his familiar rhythm.

I burrowed back into the pillow and sighed. At home I tried to hurry my arousal to meet his, but here I thoughtlessly abandoned myself to my own pleasure because if I wanted to, I could have him lick my pussy all night long. I must have squirmed and mewed for quite some time before Will pulled away and asked me, with great deference, to roll onto my belly so he could proceed with his "special service."

I wasn't about to refuse.

He slipped two pillows under my hips and arranged my knees just so. Then he began to kiss my buttocks, softly, moving ever closer to the crack. I pushed my ass out, opening myself for him. I felt something wet and silky probing my sensitive furrow.

"Oh, god, yes, you *are* good," I breathed. Will had pleasured me this way before, but this time felt especially dirty and delicious. In my mind I saw him kneeling behind me, dressed just like sturdy little Brendan with his good manners and his bright smile.

It was hard to beat the service at the Beverly Hills Hotel.

"Fuck me now," I ordered. Granted, I hadn't allowed him much time for a full display of his rimming skills, but this was all about what I wanted, and I wanted Will inside me when I came.

"Which position would you prefer this evening, ma'am?"

"Doggy-style, naturally," I barked.

"As you wish, ma'am." Will got up on his knees, probed me with the head of his cock then pushed all the way in. His thrusts were slow and careful, *professional*, as if he meant to maximize the sensation along every inch of my vagina.

"Would you like me to touch you in the front, ma'am?"

"Yes. And move a little faster inside me but not so fast that you come."

"Understood, ma'am," he said, his voice husky.

It usually took me a while to come this way, but I was so turned on, Will's attentions to my clit set my mind spinning and my thighs shaking.

"Faster, fuck me faster," I cried out as I felt my orgasm gather and explode around his pounding dick, rolling up my spine like a fireball. I screamed, ramming myself back onto him, milking him with each contraction. When it was over, I collapsed face-down on the mattress. My whole body was covered in sweat. Will waited until my breathing slowed before he pulled out and took me in his arms.

"Did I meet your needs satisfactorily, ma'am?" he asked sweetly.

"Indeed. You're getting a great big tip tonight, young man." I hugged him tighter, noting his slick cock, still rock hard, pressing against my thigh. "But tell me what you want now," I said in my own voice, as I closed my hand around him.

Will sighed at my touch but shifted ever so slightly away. "I thought I'd save myself for the second round. I'd feel lacking in my duty if I didn't provide Madame with at least two orgasms tonight."

I laughed, but I wasn't surprised. This was Big-Bed Sex. And it was only going to get better.

MY DARK KNIGHT

Jacqueline Applebee

’m a not-so-hopeless romantic. I believe that chivalry still exists, I hope to find quiet nobility in the most random of places, and I believe that people who love each other can live happily ever after. I’ve been let down by men in the past and have dated too many who thought that women were only useful in bed, who didn’t want anything to do with me in the morning. Despite all of this, I’m still a dreamer, a wisher and a lover of flights of fancy. However, I never believed in knights in shining armor, not until I met Omar. The knights of old that I’d seen in films and read about in books never looked like him; Omar was lean, with gorgeous ebony skin and sweet brown eyes.

I had seen him at an organic café in Hackney, East London, a few times, always rushing around behind the counter busily helping out. We had exchanged no more than a handful of words, and I’m sure he never remembered me when I visited for chocolate cake and coffee. It took me three trips and several portions of sticky pudding before I learned his name.

He wasn't there when I arrived on Wednesday after work, so I sat feeling decidedly lonely as I waited for my food to arrive. The café was crowded and hot; the weather in East London was humid and sticky. An upright fan pushed warm air over me, and I wondered why on earth I had come here today. Of course, I knew why; it was to see Omar.

I felt like a schoolgirl longing after someone unattainable; I had written his name in my address pad, even though I had no idea where he lived. I thought of him when I should have kept my mind on other things, and I longed to be close to him. I'm supposed to be a sensible woman, but whenever I thought of Omar, I seemed to lose all the sense that I was born with.

I ached for him to touch me. I had spent too many nights fantasizing about that tall good-looking man. He would hold me tightly as he kissed me on the hollow of my collarbone. He would lick slow strokes up my throat, while his wide hands reached lower to my breasts to squeeze.... I could feel myself growing aroused where I sat, and I remembered that this was a public place; they probably wouldn't appreciate me moaning and groaning at my table.

My frothy coffee arrived first. I enjoyed the strong aroma before taking a sip. It was so good that by the time my dark chocolate cake arrived, I had almost finished my beverage. The waitress gave me a funny look as she placed my cake in front of me. I shrugged; the world was full of odd folk. As she walked back to the counter, I realized that Omar had arrived. He did a double take as he looked over at me. I flushed, although I didn't know why I was feeling like that; I had longed for him to notice me, and now he had. He made his way to my table and leaned over to collect my empty coffee cup. I watched, mesmerized, as a bead of sweat rolled down his hot skin, tantalizingly slowly. I wanted to reach out and trace it with my fingertips. Omar caught me staring. I felt the blood rush to my cheeks once more.

"How are you doing?" he asked pleasantly. I took a breath before smiling back up at him. I was about to say something witty and flirtatious, when someone else called out his name. He raised his arm in a wave before turning back to me.

"It's good to see you again, Philomena."

"Olivia," I corrected him quickly. "My name is Olivia."

This time it was his turn to look embarrassed. I watched his retreating form as he trotted behind the counter to serve another customer, and I sighed. That's what I was to him, I mused; I was just another customer. But he was not just another waiter; he was so much more to me. I just wished that I could let him know that.

I replayed our brief meeting in my head as I licked gooey chocolate off the back of my teaspoon. Why hadn't I noticed the little tattoo of a shield on his arm before, or that he smelled like cakes and bread and sweet treats? And then I noticed something on the spoon; my reflection looked strange. I started with horror, seeing that I was now sporting a milky moustache above my lips; the froth stood out on my brown skin. I realized that I must have done that while gulping down my coffee. What must Omar have thought? I quickly wiped the foam from my mouth with a grimace.

I was shaken from my self-pitying thoughts as an elderly man entered the café, propelled along by a big spotty dog. I'm scared of dogs, and this one looked particularly mean, so I drew myself up and sat rigid as it approached me.

"Hey, you can't bring a dog in here!" Omar called out to the old man.

"Alfie always let me bring her in," the man retorted, waving his walking stick defiantly. By now, the dog was sniffing around my table. The creature looked up at me and then barked loudly.

I willed the beast to go away, but as I've said before, chivalry is not dead. Omar took hold of the dog's leash and led it away outside. I could see him secure the dog to a post outside the café, and then he ran back inside to return with a bowl of water for the mutt.

"Now, you know Alfie isn't in charge anymore. This is my café, and if you want to eat here, you'll play by my rules."

The old man made a complaining noise, but he sat down. I breathed a sigh of relief. It was only then that I realized that I was shaking. I took another deep breath and exhaled slowly, willing my body to calm down. What a day I was having! First I had made a fool of myself with the coffee, and now I was trembling like a scared child.

"Are you okay, Olivia?" Omar's voice was the soothing balm that my body needed. I felt myself relax instantly. "I'm sorry about the old fella and his dog," he said, trying to catch my eye, but I stared down at the table instead.

"I'm fine," I lied quietly. "I think I'd better go."

Omar's hand on my shoulder was firm but gentle as he said, "At least let me get you a cup of chamomile tea. It will calm those jitters in a snap."

I stood and stepped out of his grasp. My feet carried me out of the front door. I willed myself to not turn around and see Omar's disappointed face as I left. I inched past the dog that was still drinking from the bowl, and I scampered down the road.

By the time I reached the train station, my heart had stopped pounding, and I was trying my best to put on a brave face. It was only when sweet brown eyes looked into mine that I realized Omar was standing in front of me. He sat down on the bench beside me. We remained silent for a moment as the evening commuters walked around us.

"I didn't want you to leave like that," Omar started. "I mean, I wanted you to know that I'm so sorry for what happened. I wanted to make it up to you."

"It's all right," I mumbled.

"No, it's not. You're a good customer, and it's always nice to see you. I would hate it if you felt driven away."

"I'm hardly a good customer," I retorted. "All I ever have is coffee and pudding."

"I'm not talking about what you eat," he said with a grin. "I've noticed you, how you are always polite, how you always tip the staff generously, and..." He faltered for a moment before continuing. "Olivia, you are one hot lady!" he exclaimed.

"Thank you. It's been a while since anyone called me hot."

"Baby, you're sizzling." Omar held my hand as he spoke. "Come back with me, Olivia."

"Where?"

"I live above the café. It's a real sweet pad."

I found it difficult to breathe; could he seriously be asking me what I thought he was? Suddenly the station announcer called out my train. If I took it, I could be home in twenty minutes; safe, secure but ultimately alone. I realized that Omar was still looking at me hopefully.

"I've come on too strong, haven't I?" he asked quietly.

"No, you're just right." I was lying of course; Omar was more than just right, he was perfect. "Sure, I'll come back," I said, and I watched in wonder as Omar's face lit up. He stood instantly, and, still holding my hand, he pulled me out of the station.

It was getting dark by the time we arrived. Omar took me around the back of the building and ushered me up the twisting metal stairs to a private entrance. As he walked ahead of me, I had to do a reality check to ensure that I wasn't hallucinating, but as he scooted ahead of me to pick up a discarded sweater from the floor, I knew that this was real.

Omar showed me into a large, dark room, but as he flicked on the light switch, I gaped in wonder at what I saw. The room was decorated in medieval paraphernalia. A flag displaying a coat of arms had been turned into flowing curtains, several wooden shields were mounted on the walls, and in a corner stood a complete suit of armor, impressively shiny.

I snapped my mouth shut as I took in the decorations, and I caught Omar watching me.

"You must think I'm weird, but I'm really into the whole reenactment scene."

"I don't think you're weird, it's just a bit unexpected," I explained, but Omar looked at me warily. "I just never believed I'd meet a knight in shining armor." It was true, I'd heard of reenactment fans, but I'd always pictured them as geeky white boys running around a field, hitting each other with wooden swords. "Hey, are you a black knight?" I asked jokingly.

Omar rolled his eyes, although he still smiled. "Sure I am. Why do you think they called it the Dark Ages?" I hit his arm playfully as he continued. "The armor is European, but there were plenty of knights in Africa; the ancient kingdom of Bornu and Sokoto had armored soldiers on horseback who were feared throughout the land." He closed the distance between us as his voice dropped. "But I like the whole age of chivalry, the romance and the adventure that English knights embodied," he murmured against me. "My fair princess," he whispered, and then no more words were said as we kissed. Everything I had ever dreamt about Omar was eclipsed as his adventurous mouth pressed against mine. His tongue touched me, swept over my teeth and sucked on my lips. I found myself making contented noises as he held me tight. This was better than any fantasy I could have.

I felt the heat of the evening as Omar's hands stroked my back. I felt sweaty, a little disheveled but completely wonderful. I pulled off my top and stepped out of my shoes. Omar looked lovingly at my breasts before he kissed first one and then the other through the lace of my bra. He then dragged his T-shirt off, messing up his short hair as he did. I wondered briefly what he must look like wearing the armor.

"Bed," he whispered urgently. I nodded my head.

Omar held me about the waist, and then he shocked the life out of me as he lifted me up and put me over his shoulder. The whole room seemed to tip upside down as I was carried bodily to the bedroom.

Omar carefully let me down, and I lay giggling and panting on top of the bed. I shuffled out of my skirt and watched as Omar pulled down his trousers. I've seen a naked man before, but as Omar disrobed, I suddenly felt incredibly shy. He was so visibly turned on that I couldn't tear my eyes away from his cock.

"I've got some protection," he said shyly. "I didn't want to assume, but I thought it best." Omar opened his hand and produced a little foil packet. He may have enjoyed being a knight of old, but he was a thoroughly modern man.

Omar clutched at my backside. "I've been longing to feel this," he said, giving my bum a squeeze. "I've wanted to stroke it, lick it and spank it," he said with a hoarse voice. I was completely surprised at his admission; I'd never thought my backside was anything special. I'd certainly never had anyone want to spank it before.

"You can, if you like," I whispered, nervously looking up at him. "You can spank me." Omar smiled, but he looked a little wary.

"Are you sure?" he asked. I nodded, and his smile grew

wider. "I'll just do it a little. I promise you'll love it." I went to turn over, but he stopped me and directed me over his knees. I'd never been spanked before. I wondered how silly I must look, but Omar's murmurs reassured me. The first slap made me squeak; I held on to his legs for support. The next few slaps did feel intense, but they also made me feel warm and tingly. When he stopped after ten strokes, I actually wanted him to continue; it felt really good. But I could feel Omar's erection poking me in the belly; he was getting harder the more he spanked me.

I twisted around, kissing him as I maneuvered myself up to face him. His lips and tongue were hungry; he devoured me, making me even hotter than I'd been previously. He moved his whole body against me, pressing deliciously, with burning flesh sliding against flesh. His fingers disappeared between my legs, and soon I felt pulsing sensations emanating from my pussy. The hot, slippery touches made me undulate beneath him. I arched up and writhed as he touched me diligently. I clutched at him as I quickly reached my climax, surprised at the speed and intensity of the sensations that Omar awoke in me. I lay breathless and happy, but then I felt something else pressing against me, and this time it wasn't his fingers. I opened myself to accommodate his generous length and sighed as he plunged inside. Omar kept repeating my name as he moved, his hips impacting mine every time I heard, "Olivia." I held him as he tensed above me, and I smiled when I saw the look on his face.

"You know I do this for all our regular customers," he said with a chuckle.

We slept in the warm room; the windows were open, but the evening's heat made me feel so tired that I dozed off quickly. I dreamt of Omar decked out in his suit of armor, riding a big horse, with me holding him from behind as we raced across the English countryside.

* * *

When I awoke, I found myself alone in the big bed. I cannot describe how my heart sank at the realization that Omar was gone. I looked in the bathroom, the kitchen and the living room, but they were all empty. I received the message, loud and clear; I should leave before he got back. Omar was no different from all the other men I had known, and that was the most depressing thing of all.

The suit of armor seemed to mock me as I dressed in the living room. I had to hunt to find my shoes, and as I searched for them, I tried not to look at the suit. I tidied my hair as best as I could; I refused to go to the bathroom to look in the mirror. I didn't want to see my reflection; I wanted to ignore the silly woman who should have known better than to get mixed up with someone like Omar. I fought to hold in tears as I realized that I was just a conquest for him; just a one-night stand.

I strode up to the armor and felt all my disappointment suddenly boil up inside me, transforming into hot rage. I took off one of my shoes, and I hit it against the chest plate, sobbing as I struck it again and again. The whole suit of armor trembled, and then one piece detached and fell off. As I stepped away from the molded metal, another piece joined it, noisily clanging to the wooden floor. It didn't take me long to realize what was about to happen, but by then it was too late, as the entire suit toppled down with a deafening crash. I stared at the heap of metal in shock; there was no way I could put it back together.

Omar dashed into the room. I yelped in surprise at his entrance. "Are you okay?" he asked breathlessly, looking from the armor to me and back again.

"I'm sorry," I mumbled and stepped away to stand at a distance. "It was an accident."

Omar peered closer at the heap on the floor, and then he

picked up my shoe. "What's going on?"

"I thought you didn't want me here. When I woke up alone, I thought you wanted me gone."

"Now why would you think something like that?" he asked, shaking his head. "Do you know how long I've imagined just being with you?

I looked at his honest face, and something woke up inside me. Why had I jumped to such a conclusion? I suddenly felt terrible for wrecking his suit of armor. I stepped into Omar's embrace.

"You are beautiful, Olivia," he stated. "I want to be with you, believe me, on my honor as a knight."

I hugged him hard as he said that, but he continued with a chuckle, "I just went downstairs to get breakfast."

He held my hand and kissed it, and then he kissed me on the lips. He tasted of coffee, dark chocolate and summertime in London.

"Stay with me?" he asked when we finally came up for breath. "Be my princess."

I kept my eyes closed as I nodded in agreement, but I could sense his smile even if I couldn't see it. I felt myself being moved backward; soon the backs of my knees bumped into a sofa. Omar pressed me down, sweeping my legs open in a smooth movement. Before I even had time to realize what was happening, he'd pressed his face into my crotch, tugging my knickers down with his teeth. I helped him out by raising my bottom and slid the offending article down to my ankles.

"Stay," he whispered into my thigh. He splayed my lips open with his thumbs, and then he bent his head and licked across my clitoris. After last night's festivities, I was a little sensitive; I almost jumped off the sofa as I felt myself respond. Omar held me down, nudging my legs apart wider. His head was lost between my legs, bobbing hungrily and making loud slurping noises. He pushed a finger inside my pussy, twisting it slowly before adding another. I wanted to howl from the sensations he raised in me, but I bit my lip, silently grinding myself against him instead. Omar pressed me farther back onto the sofa, lifting my legs so that they wrapped around his shoulders. He removed his sticky fingers from my pussy and circled them over my asshole. I froze for a moment; Omar looked up at me, his face glistening from my juices. "Is this okay?" he asked, panting. I relaxed, sighed out loud and nodded my head. Omar grinned at me, and then he gently pushed a finger into my ass. I shivered at the strange invasion; it was something I'd never experienced before, but it felt so amazing, I urged him on.

"Please," I begged. "Please, please, don't stop!"

He added another finger, and my whole world turned to blinding white. If Omar was a knight, then he had well and truly conquered this lady.

I still had work to go to, but I returned to the café after that. I spent the night with Omar and the next night and the next. He soon got me interested in reenactment, and it wasn't long before I had a few medieval gowns made for myself. We spent many happy weekends visiting various sites throughout England, and we always presented ourselves as the princess with her dark knight. We stood out as the only black participants wherever we went, but Omar and I were always made to feel welcome at the events. We always had a great time with the geeky white boys and girls. And in case you're wondering, we lived happily ever after, too.

DEAR IN THE HEADLIGHTS

Angela Caperton

Low beams bathed me, and I felt every lumen glitter on the lacy black bra and garter belt I wore under an open trench coat. The cool autumn air brushed my cheeks and tickled my bare belly, but it couldn't cool me. Daniel stood beside his car, illuminated by the dome light inside it, and his expression turned from stunned surprise to primal lust when he saw what I was wearing.

My hips swayed as I walked toward him. The coattails floated around my long legs, the coat's wide lapels slapped against the swell of my breasts, and in that moment, I was Aphrodite and Anita Berber, Mae West and Ishtar.

My pussy, shaved and bare between the garter bands, shamelessly drawing his gaze, creamed with desire as I made the little journey, stopping just beyond his reach, spotlighted. I smiled, inviting him to do whatever he wanted with me, and I felt the night quicken with blood calling to blood, deferred ecstasy anticipating fulfillment.

In the moment before he touched me, I knew the night would

be everything we wanted it to be, yet only an hour earlier, Fate had seemed determined to keep us apart.

Earlier that evening, as I leaned close to the mirror to paint wine-colored lipstick on my lips, all I could think about was the plan. The lip color was yummy—and a perfect complement to the black-plum satin of the obscenely short cocktail dress I wore. I'd never dreamed I'd spend so much on a piece of clothing that barely qualified as covering, but tonight demanded it—and wearing the tight, sexy dress, the silk stockings and the burgundy-accented black garter and bra hit all the right buttons in me. Tonight was about seduction and romance, a deliberate exploitation of all the things Daniel enjoyed. I wanted to have him panting before he ever opened a car door for me.

Yes, tonight was about seduction to the point of mutual madness, followed by crazed, hungry—no, *starving*—fucking.

Five months. I'm almost embarrassed to say it. It'd been five months since Daniel and I had done the dirty. Sure, we've been married for ten years, but that hasn't diminished our desire for sex. If anything, we've gotten a lot better at finding that magical common ground where pleasure reaches a whole new plateau, with mind-blowing orgasms that are the endpoint of delightful little odysseys. Given how good we were at reducing each other to mutually spent, happy goo, it was a tragedy how rarely we had the opportunity.

Daniel was a software engineer with major clients on both coasts, and I worked as a consulting nutritionist for a medical firm serving hospitals and businesses across the country. We both traveled constantly on our own, like comets in wide orbit, and on those lucky occasions when our paths intersected, we tried not to kill each other from the sheer frenzy of our need. This was nothing either of us had wanted, but it had happened all the same.

This separation had been uncommonly long and, until tonight, when I was putting myself together, I hadn't realized how much I missed him and wanted him.

As I finished my makeup, I glanced at the wall clock in the bedroom: 7:20. I drew a deep breath and shoved back at my rising anxiety. Daniel had landed an hour ago. He wasn't late to pick me up, not yet. He was probably pulling up the drive even as I grabbed my beaded clutch from the closet. Yes, by the time I stuffed my lipstick and driver's license into the delicate bag, he'd be walking through the door, trudging up the steps and stripping off his conservative tie and day-wrinkled blue shirt before entering the shower.

No worries at all.

Action: that's what I needed. I willed the muscles in my shoulders and neck to relax. Daniel's arrival would work wonders no masseuse could ever achieve, but until then, I was on my own. I sat down in front of my laptop and punched up the Hilton's website. After confirming our suite for the night, I gave in to curiosity and opened my email. There was plenty of spam to ignore—worthless seminars and promises to boost my presence on the Web—but among the weeds, two flowers, a confirmation from Sojourn Equity and a bid request from Aclar Laser. Lasers. Engineers. I couldn't help but envision a small dismal room full of vending machines as the sole nutritional source for such a company. Health and welfare for Aclar wasn't going to be an easy sell, but if I got the contract it would be gold.

Aclar was in Minnesota.

Minnesota. Great. Maybe Daniel and I could fuck at the airport as I headed north and he headed south—we might never qualify as Mile High, but Horny Workaholics, we had that nomination nailed.

I forced myself away from the laptop and went downstairs. I

would greet Daniel with a twirl, glorying in the sexy cut of the dress and the heat of his gaze on me and then gladly indulge in a long, promising kiss. I had to keep my cool though. This wasn't a night for sprinting—this night was meant to be a marathon, a slow building, the rising notes and power of a crescendo, so when we finally, *finally*, reached the door of our suite, a single miss-swipe of the card key might turn into a voracious public orgy in the hall, with hands, lips; wet, slapping flesh and teeth. I could almost feel Daniel's cock hard in his trousers then inside me, the lacy garter torn away, bruising me with the ferocity of his assault on my clothing. The small trickle between my legs spoke volumes. If so simple a fantasy could draw out my juices, I was well past desperate.

I jumped when the phone rang, the burning visions in my brain suddenly gone like steam in the Arctic, although the slick between my legs was fair evidence of where my thoughts had been.

I reached for the phone, the ball of anxiety puffing in my stomach like a soufflé. Not Daniel. Not Daniel. Not Daniel.

"Hello?" I squeezed my eyes shut.

"Cass…" Daniel. Fuck. The reality ripped through me and my fantasies shredded in the awkward silence.

"Oh, Daniel, no." I tried to keep the accusation and the whine from my voice, and even if I did manage that, there was no concealing the sting of disappointment.

"Oh, my dear, I'm so sorry—" Daniel began, his voice heavy and sheepish.

"Daniel, I don't care if Markman's servers explode, not tonight! We've planned this date for weeks." The whine leaked out in the spewed resentment. No appetizers drenched in enough butter to stop a horse's heart, no ridiculously priced French champagne, no dancing or romantic walk in the park before checking in at the Hilton on the lake. No hot spontaneous sex against a tree or in an elevator. The weight of his tone slammed the reality home. Date night was dead.

"No, dear, not this time. It's not Markman or Sullivan. I'm on Five Mile. There was something in the road and I swerved and spun. The passenger side of the car is hanging over the ditch, and I can't get out. I think I'm stuck on Mr. Rollin's culvert. I called the auto club, but they won't be here for at least two hours. Cass…"

I closed my eyes, stomping on my directed accusation with the heel of concern. "You're okay? You're not hurt, are you?"

"I'm fine, Cass. It looked like a tree limb, or something. No blowout, but I can't get the car back onto the road."

My throat tightened. What was Fate's fucking problem with us having a date? Was it illegal after ten years of marriage?

I nodded, understanding Daniel's situation even while my throat tightened and tears began to simmer at the back of my eyes. "I'll be here, Daniel."

"I'm sorry, Cass. Pack my bag? We can still check into the Hilton."

More unobserved nodding. "I'll get it together." With that, I hung up the phone, knowing my disappointment must have been as thick on my tongue as the frosting on a gourmet cupcake.

Fuck. Fuck. Fuck.

Who could I blame? Not Daniel, not even Markman, those fuckers who had innocently condemned me to see Bruce Springsteen by myself while Daniel saved them from a virus one of their paralegals had downloaded along with an alleged Ashton Kutcher sex video.

Wallowing—that would have been the simplest trap to fall into. I had a good wallowing wine, too, a white with the faintest hint of pity dusting the crisp pop of spicy cynicism.

But. But… I glanced at the clock. Even if the auto club's estimate was off, maybe the night wasn't a complete loss. Maybe this was a test on some cosmic level. My lips twitched at the corners, the creamy, plum lipstick a dyed conspirator. Test? Bring it on. My college roommate used to say that I was a bitch when it came to tests—they never, ever won.

I tossed the receiver onto the table and went to the closet.

Fuck Fate. It was *my* night.

I rolled my Eos onto the barely distinguishable shoulder of Five Mile Road, the hard-packed dirt wider than some city streets. The lights of Daniel's Acura flashed on, pinning me. He emerged from his car, squinting against my headlights. I put my car in neutral and set the parking brake before exiting. The night air whispered a kiss on my face as the dust from the road rose around the hood like silent, moody birds.

"Cass?" Daniel inquired, his voice full of questions.

The tie of my calf-length coat fluttered against my momentum, the buttons cool on my belly and thigh. I closed the door of my car and walked toward Daniel, the coat opening at the front, the lacy bra and garter, the sexy silk stockings held tenuously in place shining in the mellow glow of the Acura's headlights, my trimmed pussy in a starring role. I took grateful steps on the hard-packed road, the dirt firm enough to keep my four-inch heels from turning seduction into a pratfall.

His surprised expression flooded my soul with delight, the silky stockings and sexy underwear truly becoming part of me, the trappings of intrigue and mystery, of whispered power that reminded me with a blast of pure arousal why I loved him. The harsh light of our combined headlights gave his eyes a glisten of gold, molten and ready. His smile widened with mischief as he processed and accepted my approach.

I let my hips swing with the surge of my lust, savored the

stroke of the garter against my waist, shivered with sweet delight as the cool evening air tried to chastise the wet truth of my pussy. I stayed focused on Daniel's face for those dozen steps, his gaze freely devouring, his slightly parted lips balm to my feminine ego as I basked in his very male appreciation.

He leaned against the fender of his car, a puppet awaiting the twitch of my finger. I battled hard to keep my face passive even as passion and power danced a duet in my heart.

"Oh, dear," Daniel said in a voice dry as the rising road dust, his hands outstretched.

I stopped just beyond his grasp, the coat open, exposing bare skin and lacy, sexy elegance. "I understand you have a flat?" The bulge in Daniel's pants ticked like a clock hand.

He chuckled, then ran his hand through his hair as he half folded over himself and shook his head. He righted himself and moved quickly as a cat to band my back in the steel vise of his arm. "Flat? I don't think so." He pressed his hips into mine, the length of his cock hard, full and hot through the material of his trousers.

Months of frustration, the hours of preparation for my orchestrated seduction, dissolved like sugar in hot water as his hand caressed my thigh, his thumb slipping expertly under the thin strap of the garter belt.

"Auto club will be here soon," he breathed onto my throat before his lips sealed the pulsing vein there.

"Soon is not now, Danny boy," I whispered against his ear as I unzipped and freed his wonderful cock.

"Cass…" he groaned against my lips and then kissed me, his hands hot and possessive against my stomach, my hips. Exhilaration surged through me. Flesh and soul, two lives melded into one; reduced down to now, this heat, this flash, this eternal bond of body and mind.

His teeth sank into the juncture of my throat and shoulder, and I threw back my head, eyes closed against the glare of my headlights. My fingers tightened around his rigid cock, the veins and silky skin deliciously familiar to me. I knew this flesh, I'd dined on it; had it pressed against my thighs, my ass and my pussy. And inside, dear god in heaven, inside me. It throbbed in my hand, the silky pearl at the head inspiring my mouth to water. I knew his taste, had savored his cock in my mouth, but now was not the time. No, auto club be damned, I was going to do nothing less than fuck my husband.

Daniel growled—growled! And I flooded, the sound so primal, so focused. He wanted, and he wanted me.

He gripped my arms, pulling them over my head, pushing me back against the hood of his Acura, my coat riding up, the warm metal pleasant on my bare ass. He clasped my wrists in his hand, tight, bruising, his weight pinning me against the waxed metal of his car. He kicked my legs apart, the action rough and thrilling, and then he dropped his trousers and boxers. Yes, I could have freed myself, I could have struggled and gotten away, but that wasn't what I wanted. No, I wanted what Daniel wanted; I wanted his fierce, noncomputerized, instinct-ruled body and brain directing his hands, engorging his cock, closing his teeth into my neck, kissing me breathless.

"Cassie," he groaned against my throat as he reached down, stroked my pussy lips and circled my clit, his sharp intake of breath a song of advent.

"Wicked woman," he chuckled as I drenched his fingers, the creamy slickness built from the anticipation of our forfeited date night and even more from the imminence of this moment, wanton, raw, wild and exposed. Daniel, my wonderful, computer-geek husband, was going to fuck me on the hood of his car on a public road.

Wet truly didn't begin to describe the condition of my pussy.

There was no ceremony, no tender gropes or simpering words. He forced my thighs apart with his free hand, stroked my slit with the head of his cock once—for orientation if I had to guess—and slid hard, fast and thick into my hole.

The shock loosed a gasp from my throat, the delicious bolt of the invasion nearly bringing me to orgasm. Yes, yes, yes! Finally! Five months of nothing and then this…

He thrust, jarringly, deep, the second push into me almost painful with its force, but it was also amazingly erotic, wholly selfish and, paradoxically, the purest expression of unconditional love I had ever felt. He fucked me. This wasn't sweet or even seduction, it was crazed, animalistic and wholly about need— his need, my need, his cock spitting me; pounding into me, hot, wet; a pointed purpose that he and I both demanded. I wrapped my legs around him, pulling him into me. One hand gripping my wrists, my knuckles grazing the arm of the windshield wipers, he used his other to tear my bra aside so he could expose my nipples to the cool air and to his mouth.

Teeth and tongue assaulted, his greedy suckling a perfect counterrhythm to his demanding thrust and I quickly, eagerly found myself on the short, steep climb to orgasm. My body craved his weight, cherished his nearly violent thrusts, his taking, taking, taking, my nipples aching, the wet, hard heat of his cock driving me to come.

Three, two, instinct recognized the sharp, hard slam into me, the slap of his balls against my ass. The clarion call rang in my ears as I panted, arched, challenged the night, dared Fate to deny this moment. One, one majestic perfect slide of flesh, of desire, of glorious, wanton lust, and I flew beyond the earth, the moon, floated a moment suspended on the whim of the universe before the shattering, glorious explosion of sense, sensibility, rhyme and vision. I came in a brilliant flash, more powerfully than I could ever remember coming before, and Daniel's howling cries and spasming final thrusts redoubled the ecstasy of the moment.

Panting, dripping, Daniel's weight pressing me into the hood of his car, I stared beyond the crest of his head now nestled at my neck. Stars, bright pinpoints, shimmered in the cooling night. I shivered as Daniel released my wrists and kissed me tenderly, lovingly.

The rumble of a truck reached us over our ragged breathing. "That's probably the auto club," Daniel said, his hands sliding over my ass, squeezing as he thrust into me, his cock softer but still eager.

I nipped the pulse of his throat as my ass slipped in the sweat and juices we'd generated. I grinned, then chuckled and squeezed my legs around Daniel. "Yes, it probably is. You should make sure you have your story straight." I tightened my pussy muscles and thoroughly enjoyed the deep resonance of his snarl.

He pinned my arms at my side and with effort withdrew, even as he bit my nipple and toyed with it like a terrier. New desire whipped inside me, and I knew without a doubt that the Hilton on the lake was in for a loud, boisterous occupancy.

"No story at all," Daniel said as he tucked his cock back into his trousers. "I'll just tell them of the dear I saw in my head-lights. I'm sure they've heard that one before."

I slid off the hood of his car, the shiny smear of our passion like an ornament or a trophy for all to see. I grinned and closed my coat as the tow truck chugged into position.

"Your dear," I told Daniel. "Tonight and forever. Meet you at the Hilton."

I walked back to my car while he talked to the tow truck driver, and just before I climbed in, when I was sure only Daniel was looking, I opened my coat again just for a moment.

I saw his face, beautiful in his love and lust, and then I climbed behind the wheel, executed a tight turn and headed for town.

As I drove, I couldn't stop grinning as the memory of what we'd just done replayed in my brain. I felt strong, alive, loved and desired. The separations from Daniel were awful, but the true test of our love was what we did with the moments Fate gave us.

Or the ones we fight for tooth and nail, because sometimes Fate needs a little kick in the balls.

THE CHERRY ORCHARD

Wickham Boyle

This story needs no introduction. An introduction could only be a melancholy look at leaving a beloved home, an opening akin to Chekhov's heroine touching walls and furniture, extolling the virtues of her cherry orchard and bidding adieu to life, love and happiness. Instead, when I left my home, I carefully made love in every room.

Begin at the bath. I lay and relaxed in bubbles of pear breath, while outside my windows the blossoms promising actual fruit and the coming of spring ripened. I lay in the tub so long that I began to feel an ancient longing well up from my toes and finish as a sharp metallic taste on the tip of my tongue. It is sex: the taste of bullets and speed, of crushing and embracing. It calls to me from tip to toe and I know its rhythms.

I conjure my man from the nursery where he is entrancing our children in low tones with dreams of flying dogs and colored water. He glues the children's eyes to the kingdom of Morpheus and flings opens the door to my world. Silently I draw up around his neck while bubbles slide down my arms and decorate his skin like the laurels of a conquering hero. A sweet, deep kiss comes rushing out of me, finding the back of his throat almost through to the bubbles on the other side of his neck. His face is a hedgehog of prickles, and each red poke wakes me to urgency beyond tenderness.

My hot breasts press to the cold tub, my nipples rise against the porcelain, and my hands grasp his warm back. Tiny calls emanate from next door. Babies rising from the tucks and folds of sleep, but not quite strong enough to find consciousness; they drift back to sleep. We laugh because the children have not found us this time. We continue to explore and run our hands over terrain that somehow always feels new. My man's body is so precious to me: hot with muscle, sinew and passion. We are pushed against each other, chaperoned by a tub that segregates the deep pull of legs and groin, and thus separated we return to kissing. Our tongues are slow and sure, fish on a path to spawning. The hunt, the swim and the leap are well known to us and always exciting.

With each kiss I am melting in the low bubbles, and I rise from the tub slippery in my lover's arms. Bright fire of fur lights his forearms as they circle me, and he draws me into the light. My left leg is on the lip of the bath and draws my labia apart to ache and drool onto the unfeeling ceramic edge. His right hand is around me and rolls down to my butt and into the opening folds. Fingers find their way through moist forest and hanging moss. A knowledgeable explorer with true aim, he finds my center and pushes it to volcanic. My standing leg is quivering as his swift digits jump in and out of the volcanic core, and explorers march to the rim of the cone. Tramping and touching, they leave no path untrod in the quest for the core. I am crazed, head thrown back, roiling with palpitations. I scream, "You know I can't come standing up, I can't. I'll die here!" We both laugh and he wraps my robe around me. "Get dressed, then I can have you and dinner together."

He descends to light the candles, and I emerge soft, hot and dressed. Black lacy bra, small panties already finding their way into butt and cunt to snuggle near the vibrations. With each step I feel the lacy material climb inside me, and the crenulated edges urge me on. I am tantalized at every step. My sea green silk shirt floats around me, the color of my love's eyes. The shirt's touch echoes the caress I feel buzzing from him. I am cocooned.

We drink champagne from singing crystal glasses, and each clink proclaims our love and gratitude for sleeping babies, long friendships, big dicks and sucking cunts. We gorge on food whose slippery countenance mirrors my own slip and slide. The salmon is like slices of cool sex, squeezed between our fingers and popped into each other's gullets. The butter, sweet and creamy, tops bread that follows the orange fish down to our molten centers. More bubbles, more kisses, and the room revolves with candlelight and sweet confusion. Nothing is cleared and the whipped cream appears with strawberries quick on its heels. The cream is heaped in peaks in a wide-mouthed bowl, and we suck and dip from finger to mouth. Yes, a cliché meal, but one fit for a final night in a treasured house. I am now so ready for my gob to be crammed with the solid force of a dick that will not melt and disappear.

I kiss my fine red-haired man, using the kissing to push him into a chair. I trail down his face and chest and pause to nibble his nipples, sucking them into tiny points, pencils sharpened finely by a simple tool. The tips glisten now and I continue my pursuit hotly until he tosses his head and moans, supine in the chair. My victim is pinned by lust in my lair, a willing subject waiting my ministrations, an imagined member of my seraglio coming to be serviced by the great sultana. I will oblige because without me he will ignite. And I take pity as his bright orange hair and fur shoot out from his body and remind me of the flames between us.

I roll his cock quickly into my mouth and open my throat wide, measuring my breath to take him fully down to my sweet center. I close my lips, suck and lick and roll about at ease. I am full from teasing his pink and rigid cock, which rests inside my lips and throat. I bob my head and push into his chest. I finger his nipples again and ignore his groans and pleas for speed. I am in full control. The heat and friction increase internally, and I feel a boiling in his loins. I am cooking a thick pudding, bringing a sweet dessert to a rolling boil, and I see that he cannot sustain the heat much longer. "I must pull all this fire into me; now is my time," I muse.

My hand is wrapped around the base of his cock, grasping like that of a soldier with a prized flag. I hold my mouth open and caress him, then close on his member with tongue and breath. As he gasps, my free arm flings across his chest, and I reach across his torso to dip my hand into the butter and in one move find his anus. My fingertip is barely inside when he comes, filling my mouth. He fills me with the cream from his jumping fish, and his rectum pulls me inside with each crushing contraction. I free him from my mouth and hand and rise to kiss him back into the present. Lost still to another world, he croons and strokes me as if I am a seer and have foretold great fortunes.

"What room next?" he buzzes in my ear. We kiss with the taste of him coating every crevice in my mouth. I love a mouth that tastes of my lover, and I imagine that he and every amorous traveler yearns for virtual experience of entering his or her own body through the portals of taste. Taste buds entwined, we move up the back staircase. My shirt trails behind me like a diaphanous banner, and his T-shirt is slung over his shoulder like a fresh kill. The hunter and the temptress traipse to bed.

Covers, pillows, fresh sheets are rejected as we sprawl across the end of the bed in a simple embrace. And here I lose memory, sight and aural ability; I taste him and feel me as I twirl inside him. I am lost, reduced to a tiny diver immersed in a sensational wet world. I almost don't notice his hand as it slips under my bottom, cupping me and darting in and out like a demented honeybee in a favorite garden. Swooning, I press myself to be present; I do not want to drown in sensations so sharp. I push him away and exhale. It's the fight of the orgasm: I know it wants me to submit and go with it. It wants me to ride it like a wave carrying me in the undertow. It wants me to trust it as it pops me to the surface and drags me down again and again. It will finally spit me out on the sandy shore, and I will be spent and unable to swim farther. Tonight I want the control.

My lover senses this and he repurposes himself to lead me more slowly. His hands pull my panties tighter into my crevices. One hand rubs a nipple in deft circles as it pokes against the ebony lace; the other hand fingers my interior folds. With all his kissing, lolling, rubbing and pulling, I am in a frenzy. He rips at my lingerie and my breasts fly loose into his biting mouth. My panties are pulled free and flung to the floor. He shoves me back and spreads me wider with each wave. I cannot differentiate hand from arm from thumb, and I am so open only my tiny clitoral mountain stands out as he holds back my cunt terrain.

A blind, violet fog begins to roll in, and an atavistic vision of my animal past claws at the mist. I am struck dumb as I see my orgasm bearing down hard. It's coming to overtake me, to hit me, to drown me and flip me head over heels, and then it does, turning me inside out, rolling me over and over in the sea foam, until I cry out to stop because I am blind and gasping for breath.

I am blind with sea and sand and salt and he, now the sultan, laughs. My tongue is dry and I can make no sounds, or maybe I am rendered deaf. I beg for my senses to be restored, and I am given refuge in his arms and stroked to sleep.

As dreams replace reality, I cast my eye into all the rooms of my home. Good-bye my house, my cherry floors, my pear blossoms. I will miss you, and I will carry your memory always, in my lovemaking.

AUTUMN SUITE

Suzanne V. Slate

S unday morning. We linger over our scones and coffee, letting the day take shape. It's early fall, but we can already tell the day is going to be a hot one.

At last he rises. He kisses me, strokes my hair then goes off to the sunroom to play the cello. I scan the paper, flip through the ads, half listening to him tune up and start warming up on the easy pieces. I stare at a bouquet of roses I brought in from the garden yesterday, probably the last of the season. These roses budded a long time ago and are now in full bloom. They are deep red and velvety, and I reach out to stroke them, slipping my fingers between the soft petals, thinking of nothing. I tune in and out for who knows how long.

Suddenly I snap to attention. He is playing Bach's Second Cello Suite, our favorite. It's the Prelude. The music crests, then tumbles to the depths of the instrument, over and over, like a wave. At the top of the phrase he pauses slightly, on the edge of a precipice, before diving again into the flow. Without quite realizing, I begin to breathe in rhythm to the music.

He is in fine form today, playing with soul and passion. Is he thinking what I'm thinking? Does he remember I fell in love with him over this piece?

Back in college we had the same circle of friends, all musicians, and we all bonded over Bach. At first he and I were just friends. But then one day I was wandering through the music building, looking for an empty practice room, when I heard the Second Suite coming from one of the rooms. Spellbound, I crept to the door and peered through the small window.

There he sat, facing the window, head bowed low over the cello as he played. He played from memory, eyes closed. He cradled his cello close to him, catching it between his muscular thighs, which tightened and flexed as he moved in rhythm with the music.

He and his cello were locked in a duet, a dialogue, each coaxing more beautiful sounds and more intense feelings out of the other. The cello looked as alive as it sounded, a warm ruddy brown tinged in gold. It glowed in the dim light of the room and seemed to pulsate with life. But it was he who was bringing it to life, embracing it, caressing the fingerboard, squeezing its curved body between his thighs.

He grew warm as he played. Beads of perspiration formed on his brow and gathered on the ends of his thick curly hair. At one point he jerked forward and a single drop of sweat fell onto the front of his cello. I was transfixed. It was as if the two of them were working so intensely together that the cello was sweating along with him. No—it was more like he was drawing such stirring sounds from the cello's depths, urging it to give up everything it had, that he actually made it weep with emotion. The tear dripped slowly down the cello's golden surface as he played on.

That was the moment I fell in love with him. I wanted to be embraced and enveloped by him. I wanted him to coax out my mysteries, and I wanted to give voice to his.

I waited until the Suite was nearly over, then stole away.

Later, after we'd become a couple, I told him the story. We laughed about my "cello envy," but it became part of our shared history, part of our lore.

Now, hearing him in the sunroom playing our suite, the years have fallen away and I am once again standing outside the little practice room, seeing him with new eyes, falling in love all over again. Suddenly I have to have him.

At the threshold, I pause, not wanting to interrupt. He is playing the Suite's most beautiful movement, the Sarabande. I close my eyes and lean my head against the doorway. In my mind's eye I see the bouquet of red roses on our dining table, warm and ripe, and I envision them opening slowly in time to the music. As the music possesses me, my own nether lips begin to ripen and swell.

He plays on, giving full voice to every note, paying attention to the silences. He takes his time. When he plays a chord he digs his bow deeply into the strings, and the cello growls and cries in response.

I open my eyes. He is playing from memory, eyes closed, his breathing cresting and falling with the music. I can see it in his face—he is remembering, too. Objectively, I know the years have changed us both, but when I look at him now I swear we are the same people we once were, back in that music building so long ago.

The sun pours into the room. It is hot, and he is sweating. His robe has fallen partway open, and I see the muscles in his bare thighs strain and flex as he embraces the cello. My lower belly tightens and I part my lips. As the Sarabande concludes I sigh, and my whole body relaxes and opens.

He opens his eyes and looks directly at me. We do not smile; somehow, the moment is too intense for that. Without a word he gently sets his cello on its side. Turning toward me, he holds out his arms. I walk slowly toward him, untying my robe and shedding it as I cross the room.

I part his robe and kneel between his thighs. He spreads his legs wide, opening himself to me. I take his shaft in my hands and stroke it, rubbing it slowly against my face, my breasts, my hair. I feel his buttocks flex and his thighs press against the sides of my breasts as his cock slowly ripens. I pause and look up at him.

He is staring down at me with a look of wonder in his eyes. I've seen this look before—it's the one he had the morning after our first night together in his dorm room. My breath catches in my chest, and my feelings are so intense I cannot maintain his gaze. I look down at his cock, now fully erect. A drop of precome glistens at the tip. I squeeze the shaft firmly, root to tip, and the drop rolls down the head and onto the back of my hand. I think of the drop of sweat on his cello. I lick the drop off my hand.

I need more of him. I rise and stand between his open legs. I slip the robe off his shoulders and toss it to the floor. The hot sun streams into the sunroom, bathing our bare bodies in bright golden light. We blink and squint a little in the glare. We are both dripping with sweat.

He pulls me toward him and I straddle him on the chair, wrapping my legs tightly around his hips. We embrace, kneading and stroking each other's backs, hands slipping on our damp salty skin. He runs his fingers up and down my spine, coaxing shudders and moans from me. I run my fingers through his hair, and he cups my face in his hands, stroking my cheeks and eyes. We kiss deeply, mouths fully open, drinking each other's saliva and tasting sex on our engorged lips. He flicks his tongue against my upper lip, and I gently bite his ripe lower lip. We feed on each other; we are insatiable. I cannot see the inside of his mouth, but I am envisioning its deep red hue and velvety texture behind my closed eyelids.

Sitting on him like this with my thighs wrapped around his trunk, I am fully open to him, all the way to my core. His hot cock stands stiffly upright between us, and I press against it with my clit, wetting it. I slide up and down the shaft to wet it fully, top to bottom. In response, his thigh muscles flex sharply under my ass. As we begin to rock back and forth in unison, a column of hot air wafts between us, perfuming the air with our mingled sexual scents. I am intoxicated. If he were not clinging to me so tightly, I would collapse. The Cello Suite spins and echoes in my brain; our chests rise and fall to the notes of the Sarabande still playing in our heads.

Now he raises my hips off his lap, reaching under my ass and probing my slit with his fingers. He pulls my buttocks wide apart and lowers me onto his cock. Slowly I sink down and he enters, filling me all the way. I have never felt so open or so complete. I cannot tell where I leave off and he begins. As he plunges his cock into me, I answer with my tongue, probing deeply into his mouth. We are straining to merge into each other, to get inside each other.

We flex our hips in unison, our pubic bones connecting over and over, sending shock waves through my clit with each thrust. Sweat drips off my breasts and down his chest as they press rhythmically together, still in time to the invisible music that surrounds us. I lick his neck, drinking him in. After this long delicious buildup we come together in giant waves that wash over us time and time again. I cry out, long and loud, head thrust back and eyes squeezed shut. My orgasm is an endless unfolding—my mouth, my nipples, and especially my pussy blossoming. Behind my closed eyelids I see a deep red rose opening, its tender inner petals bursting into a flower that ripens and expands forever. I feel completely turned inside out, impaled on his throbbing red cock.

He usually comes quietly, but this time he climaxes with soft keening moans, head bent over my shoulder, sweat from his hair dripping down my back like tears from his cello. His come courses into me in waves. Gradually the intensity of our rocking subsides, and we sit locked in each other's embrace, feeling our muscles relax and our breathing return to normal. We draw back and look at each other a little shyly, as if this was our first time. In some ways it feels like that. There are tears in our eyes. Tenderly, I kiss his eyelids, and he gently wipes the tears from my face. Though we usually talk and laugh during lovemaking, today we have no words to express what has passed between us.

He helps me untangle my legs from his hips and rise. I take his hand and draw him to his feet. Wordlessly, we walk to our dark bedroom and lie down together, naked, cooled by a gentle breeze from the fan. We drift off to sleep in each other's arms, breathing in unison while the closing movements of the Cello Suite echo in my head.

CONTENTIONS

Isabelle Gray

Alicia sits naked, perched on the edge of the bathtub, her legs spread wide. She holds the sharp edge of the blade between her thighs and though the straight razor isn't touching her body yet, she can feel its strength, what it could take from her, and the tension of the moment makes her heart pulse strangely. She holds her breath as she carefully guides the blade up the mound of her pussy. It makes a crisp, scraping sound as short wisps of hair fall against the porcelain of the tub. She works slowly, efficiently, occasionally splashing cold water between her thighs to wash everything away. She is making herself bare.

Drake comes home and is surrounded by darkness and an uncomfortable silence. He calls for his wife, frowns when there's no answer. Drake loosens his tie and heads upstairs, his body tense with nervous energy. He finds his wife in their bedroom. She is lying in the center of their bed. She is naked, lying flat on her back. Her waist is twisted to the side, her knees pressed together and pulled toward her. She smiles and holds her hand out.

* * *

They met in their late twenties during a contentious divorce trial where they sat across the aisle as opposing counsel. Alicia always loved to argue—it was her best and worst quality. She would argue with anyone about anything at any time. She even argued when she agreed with someone. It was the thrill of being contentious Alicia enjoyed most, and it was the thrill of being Alicia's sparring partner in the courtroom, in the bedroom, anywhere at all, Drake enjoyed most. On their first date—dinner and drinks at a new bistro downtown—Alicia and Drake argued about what to eat. He suggested small plates; she wanted meat, rare, bloody, with something starchy on the side. He suggested a designer vodka martini; she wanted the real thing—shaken and dirty, one part gin, one part vermouth, with orange bitters, chilled on ice and strained into a cold glass, garnished with three olives.

He drove her home and was willing to settle for a long kiss, lips but no tongue, hot but not too filthy. He didn't want to seem too pushy. Alicia grabbed the starched collar of his button-down shirt and pulled Drake toward her. He could smell her perfume: warm, subtle, lilacs. She traced his lips with her tongue, curled her fingers into a tight fist around his shirt. Drake held his breath, his cock stirring beneath his slacks. "I had a wonderful night," he whispered.

"Shut up," Alicia said. "It wasn't that great." She crushed her lips against his, all teeth and tongue. He moaned into her mouth, tried to relax as he felt Alicia quickly unfasten his belt, slide her small hand into his slacks, wrap her fingers around the hard length of his cock. Derek tried to slide his hand around Alicia's waist, pull her closer to him, but she released her grip on his collar, grabbed his arm with her wrist. She shook her head but remained silent. As they kissed, Alicia began sliding her hand faster and faster until Drake pulled away, his back arching, his entire body taut. He exhaled deeply and slowly sank back into his seat. Alicia pulled her hand out of his pants and slowly licked the silvery threads of come from her fingers. Drake shook his head. Before he could say a word, Alicia jumped out of the car and ran into her townhouse without looking back.

Drake called the next morning, and when he asked her out for a second date, Alicia hung up the phone. He showed up at her door three nights and two messages later with a dozen sunflowers and a bottle of Bombay Sapphire. His jeans were perfectly pressed, and there wasn't a speck of lint on his dark blue blazer. Drake smiled brightly when Alicia opened her door. He grinned as he took in the sight of her: her dark brown hair hanging just past her shoulders in heavy layers, her big blue eyes and sharp cheekbones. She wore a low-cut tank top and a pair of men's pajama pants rolled at the waist, leaving the flat of her stomach exposed. Alicia grabbed the bottle of gin.

She said, "I don't believe in romance." She tried to close the door, but Drake quickly stuck his foot in the gap.

"I can make you a believer," he said.

Alicia raised an eyebrow. She opened the bottle of gin, took a long sip, and set the bottle on the small table near the door. "That's highly doubtful. I'm not one of the faithful, worshipping at the altar of love."

Drake took her hand in his, turned the palm up and pressed his lips against the soft heel, the sensitive center, the webbing between each finger. Alicia tried to ignore the shiver at the base of her neck.

She curled her index finger against his chin. "I'm not convinced," she said.

Drake squeezed his way into her foyer. The décor in the room to his left was slick and modern—black leather couch, small coffee table, empty flower vases in geometric shapes.

He dropped to his knees and kissed just above Alicia's navel. Her body was warm and he could feel her breathing against him. She gently rested one hand on the top of his head. "You may need to learn a few tips on how to force your way into a woman's house."

Drake slid his hands beneath the hem of Alicia's tank top and up her slender torso, enjoying the lines of her body. When he reached her breasts, he gently dragged his thumbs across her nipples—small, hard, perfect. He kissed her stomach again, squeezed her breasts together. Alicia allowed herself to lean into the man kneeling before her. Drake sat back on his calves and drew his hands down Alicia's body, slowly pulling her pants down, following with his lips, kissing her thighs, her knees, her calves, and then he nudged her legs apart. Alicia kicked her pants away and opened herself to him. Drake held her ample ass, enjoying the heft of the soft curves in his hands. He pulled her to his lips, kissing the neatly trimmed mound of her pussy, squeezed her ass harder, flicked his tongue just once against her clit. Alicia flexed her toes and began running her fingers through Drake's hair. He smiled and traced each of her pussy lips with his fingers then pulled her lips apart. When his tongue found the salty soft pink, he sighed, and Alicia lifted herself up on her toes.

"I'm not enjoying this," she said, "but I want your tongue inside of me."

His cock throbbed, but Drake shook his head. "Not yet," he said.

Alicia bit her lower lip and tried to step away, but Drake held her firmly, sucking her swollen clit into his mouth. She hissed as her knees buckled. Drake held her clit against his tongue, sucking hard and fast, and the pleasure of it was so perfect, so painful, it took Alicia's breath away.

"I am hating this," she muttered through gritted teeth, spreading her legs wider.

Drake chuckled, his deep voice filling the space between them. He slid his tongue between her pussy lips to the tight, puckered edges of her cunt. He wanted to memorize the taste, the smell of her, how her thighs were hot and strong against his cheeks, how he could feel how much she wanted him, how her body betrayed her. He swirled his tongue against her opening in languorous circles as Alicia drew deeper and deeper breaths. At the exact moment he fully buried his tongue inside her, he slowly worked a finger into the tight folds of her ass. Alicia groaned loudly. She bit her lower lip and willed herself to stay silent. Drake began thrusting his tongue in and out of her cunt, and every few strokes he brought his mouth back to her clit. Every time Alicia was on the verge of coming, of riding the delicious crest of pleasure she was afforded by Drake's lips and tongue, he paused, allowing only his breath to fall against her.

When she could take it no longer, she grabbed his head and yanked it back. She looked down into his eyes. "If you don't let me come, I will never speak to you again." Drake grinned widely. He flicked his tongue against her clit again. Alicia moaned, pulled his head a little harder. "Open your mouth," she ordered. He licked her clit slower but then he obeyed, parting his lips, offering her his tongue. She stood above him and began rocking her hips, grinding her pussy against his tongue, his face, the blunt shape of his chin. Drake worked a finger deep inside her ass, enjoyed the sensation of her body clenching around him. Alicia came in a furious blur, the whole of her shaking as a soft wave of desire wound all the way up her spine.

Exhausted, Drake lay on his side, and Alicia stretched herself next to him. She grabbed his lower lip between her teeth, and then she surprised him. She kissed him softly, sweetly, tasting herself on his lips, and then she held her forehead against his for a long while, drawing lazy circles against the back of his neck with her fingernails.

Just as she was about to fall asleep, he whispered, "I would love to spend the night."

Alicia shot up and quickly pulled her pajama pants back on. She twisted her hair into a loose bun and shook her head. "You have to go," she said tightly.

Drake rolled his eyes. "You can't be serious."

Her eyes narrowed and she pointed to the door. "I'm very serious," she said. She pressed her bare foot into his stomach. "Don't stay past your welcome. It isn't polite."

He stood up and shook his head. "You're hardly one to give a lesson in manners."

She shrugged.

Drake looked at his watch, then straightened his clothes. Alicia held the door open. He leaned in to kiss her one last time but she turned, offering him only her cheek. His lips brushed against her. Just as he stepped onto her front porch, she pulled Drake back and placed a soft kiss just below his left ear. She whispered, "Thanks...for the gin."

"You're welcome," Drake grumbled. He walked down the stairs toward his car.

"See? I know how to be polite," Alicia said.

He threw a fist into the air. "I'm trying to force my way into your heart," he said. "I'm a man of faith. I can make you believe."

After she closed the door, Alicia sank to the floor, still warm from where they had just lain. She traced the memory of Drake's body next to her, her hand working in a lazy pattern over the wooden slats.

Four years. That's how long it took for Alicia to agree to

marry Drake. Every time he proposed, she countered with arguments as to why the timing wasn't right or why she couldn't commit or why their relationship would be better if they didn't try to fix something that wasn't broken. Along the way she disagreed about whether or not they should move in together, where they should live, who should cook dinner, whose family to visit for the holidays, what to wear to a costume party, where to put the new living room couch, and every disagreement pulled Drake in deeper, made him want her more.

He stands at the edge of their bed, his clothes in a wrinkled heap next to him. The room is lit by two candles on a nightstand and thin shafts of moonlight. "You look beautiful," Drake says.

"I do not," Alicia murmurs.

"Is there anything you won't argue about?"

She smiles, pats the empty space next to her. "Get over here."

He climbs onto the bed and crawls to meet her. Alicia keeps her knees twisted to the side, pressed together. Drake nuzzles his wife's neck then kisses her shoulder. "You have perfect shoulders," he says.

Alicia caresses his face, pressing the palm of her hand against his chin. "I do not."

He kisses the hollow of her throat. "You have a perfect throat."

"I do not." She holds her hand over his heart, feels the gentle thrum.

Drake covers her lips with his, and the tips of their tongues meet. "You have perfect lips," he says.

The candles flicker, the light contracts, expands. "I do not."

He brings his lips to her nipples, tracing the dusty rose areolas. He can smell her perfume, lilacs again, and he falls in love once more. From one moment to the next, distance is not necessary to make his heart grow fonder. He nips at her nipple with his teeth and she moans, her voice deep and throaty. "You have perfect breasts," he says.

"Absolutely not."

Drake squeezes his wife's breasts, enjoying the sensation of the soft flesh splaying through his fingers. She pulls her knees to the right until they're pointing to the ceiling. His hands slide up her thighs then down her calves. Alicia stretches her legs out but keeps them closed. He slides his hands back up her thighs then stops. He whistles as he feels her freshly shaven mound, perfectly smooth, bare beneath his hands. "You are perfect," he whispers hoarsely. Drake inches his way down her body, places a trail of kisses along her bikini line. He wedges his hand between her thighs, pressing his thumb against her clit, sneaks two fingers inside her where she is wet and tight and ready for him.

"On this point, we cannot argue," Drake says. He pulls his hands free and makes a happy sound as he sucks her sweet pussy juice from his fingers. He climbs atop her body, forcing her legs apart with his knees. His cock, thick and veined, juts forward, and Alicia feels it throbbing against her. "Everything, absolutely everything about you is perfect."

Alicia presses two fingers to Drake's lips. "Shhh. Make love to me."

He holds his cock near her cunt, penetrates her with just the tip. She wraps her legs around his waist, urges him to fill her. Drake pushes her arms over her head, clasps her wrists with one hand and holds her thigh with the other. Inch by inch he fills Alicia's cunt until he's buried inside her. He pauses, allows her body to stretch and open to him. He brushes a strand of dark hair from her face. "We are perfect," he says.

She looks up at her husband, her adversary, her love and

admires the intensity in his eyes. He thrusts forward, rears back, thrusts forward again. She raises her hips to meet him. He tries to remain in control, kisses her again, his lips rough against hers. She opens her mouth, accepts his tongue, feels the possessiveness in the communion, and she loves it. Alicia wrests her wrists free from his hold and wraps her arms around Drake's broad shoulders. She digs her fingernails into his back and he hisses, starts fucking her harder. "We are perfect," Drake says again. The room echoes with the sounds of their bodies coming together, pulling apart. Beads of sweat fall from Drake's forehead onto Alicia's lips and she savors the salt of him.

Alicia buries her head in the damp spread of skin between Drake's neck and shoulders. For once, she doesn't argue. "Yes, we are," she says breathlessly.

THE SILVER BELT

Lana Fox

Maya pretended she wore the silver belt because her husband had given it to her. He thought it would accentuate her slender waist and the curving jut of her hips—these, after all, were the physical features he'd first fallen in love with. "You were wearing that red dress," he always said. "I remember seeing the shape of you across the room." As soon as he'd set eyes on her bottlelike smoothness, the rest of the party had faded away. But many years later, once he'd bought her the belt, a distance invaded; she found him too silent, and he found her too loud. She longed to dance, he longed to sleep, and the belt round her waist seemed to taunt her, a weight she couldn't shake.

But oh, how she loved that belt! It was the weight of the metal—the sensation of its density around her core, pulling down upon her hips, and the way the chain mail bit into her flesh—that turned her on the most. At night, she'd remove it in front of the bedroom mirror, a stand-alone glass with an elaborate bronze edging, and she'd run her fingers around the dents the belt had left on her skin and wonder why he never looked across the room. She'd press her fingers round the sleek, silk triangle that formed the edge of her ivory briefs and lean from her lace bra teasingly, kissing the air. The problem was that though she longed for sex, she didn't want it with her husband; in fact, later she'd slide into bed silently, fearing if she woke him she'd rouse his cravings—his touch felt like a betrayal of the woman she'd become.

Truth was, at thirty-five, Maya felt old. On her face, the first wrinkles had started to appear, gracefully slight, but obvious once you knew they were there. Plus, every day she'd get the rush-hour train to work and would feel the bodies of others pressing against her; part of her knew these heightened sensations were due to the belt, which she'd taken to wearing regularly. Its sweet restriction made her feel each sensation with deeper, hotter keenness. Her hips seemed to swing more easily, and the weight of it made her feel womanly. Even her boss at the clothing store had remarked on how it suited her. "Not only does it go with your dresses," she'd told Maya, "but it complements your figure." Customers had often asked to try it on; then, when she explained that she wasn't allowed, they went to the boss and asked to have one ordered. But Maya's husband had bought the belt when he was on business in Paris, and nobody could get hold of a similar design.

One day, a black man with smooth, shining skin stopped at the clothing store to buy his sister a gift. As she led him across to the silk scarves, Maya felt his gaze heating her flesh beneath the dark dress she was wearing; she could sense his desire like a burn round her waist. When she pointed out the scarves that were arranged on the lattice, draped sensuously in reds, golds and browns, he stood behind her, breathing on her hair, his fingertips resting gently on her belt. She touched a silken,

fire-colored scarf, and with him so close she could sense its fabric
keenly, trickling through her fingers. In her ear, he whispered she
was the kind of woman a man should eat. "This belt," he said,
"I have seen you in it often. You always wear it. It flatters your
body. You're a real woman, no skin and bones. Your flesh is
heavy with knowledge."

Heavy. Yes. She felt that way.

Like a mine that's never been plumbed.

He stepped closer, leaning down on the belt, and she gasped
to feel its dig. "It's as if someone is imprisoning you," he said.
"Me, I would *take* you, and my taking would free you." And
perhaps he would have screwed her, right there in the store, with
customers milling and chattering together; she was so aroused,
she'd have let him, if her boss hadn't arrived and asked what
the hell she was doing. Still, as Maya rang up the scarf he was
buying for his sister, he leaned forward and whispered, "What
time do you finish work?"

"An hour, if I'm lucky."

"Are you married, Maya?"

"Yes." She lowered her eyes.

"Your body does not say 'married,'" he said, taking her hand.
"Your body says 'alone.' Are you alone, Maya?" Their connection sent a light jolt through her arm, and it was this hot energy
that made her tell him, "Yes."

Before she knew it, he'd stridden across to her boss and was
passing her some ten-pound notes, talking in low tones. In less
than a minute Maya was told she could leave early tonight. "Be
careful," her boss said, glancing in the man's direction. "There's
a *carnal* look in those eyes."

The man hailed a taxi and took Maya to a backstreet restaurant: a Thai place with white tablecloths and flower heads
floating in saucers of water. As she took her seat, he compli-

mented her dress, a simple black design with buttons down the front. The belt gleamed about her waist, especially weighty right now, and even her blonde ponytail that swung down the length of her back seemed heavier than usual, as if the fruit of her had ripened. She knew she was about to be unfaithful to her husband, and it was as if this fact were entirely natural—for once, she felt authentic.

Rather than sitting opposite, her date sat next to her on the seat that ran along the mirrored wall. With their thighs touching and his arm wrapped around her, he fed her shrimp crackers dipped in sweet chili sauce. She learned that his name was Art, that he'd worked in finance for years and now had earned the luxury to live an artist's life. "What sort of art do you do, Art?" she asked, giving a playful smile.

He laughed. He had incredible eyes, expressive and dark; when he spoke, his gaze seemed to pulse with his feelings, as if his words charged him. He placed a piece of chili-dipped cracker on her tongue. "I sketch," he said, "and paint. Also, I'm a poet."

She said she wished *she* were a poet.

He slid his fingers round her silver belt and with his free hand stroked gently down her jaw. Holding her gaze he told her, "You're more poem than poet. There are depths in you."

Later, when the green curry came, he fed her from chopsticks, his fingers working expertly to deliver the food to her lips. Every so often, he'd set down the chopsticks and undo one of the buttons down the front of her frock. Soon her dress was almost entirely loose, and if not for the belt she'd be exposed. He swept his warm hand across her thigh, lingering round the tops of her stockings. "You are beautiful," he told her. "I will rip off this dress and make love to you in your metal belt. You'll come so hard the floorboards will break."

Already, she was wet.

For dessert, they had fruit drizzled in sweet oil. He placed slim slices of strawberry on her tongue, cool and sweet like petals and dabbed the juice from the corners of her mouth. She writhed in the seat with her dress unbuttoned, the silver belt the only thing keeping her together, and beneath her skirt her silky briefs grew slippery, moistened by the thirst of her pussy. As he fed her, she let out little moans like a woman on the brink, and soon he was resting his hand between her thighs and she was moaning not because of the sweetness of the fruit, but because of the touch of his fingers and the closeness of his body and the smell of his cologne. "When did you last make love?" he asked, his fingers sliding upward, stroking the little clip that clasped her stocking-top. The sensation of his fingers was so perfect that she parted her thighs. She tried to remember when she'd last screwed her husband but couldn't. So instead, she answered, "Right now, it's like I've never been touched before."

He tipped his head and leaned right in, licking gently round the edge of her ear, before kissing her jaw, her neck. Beneath her skirt, his fingertips slid beneath the silk of her briefs, gliding against her sex. She arched back, her head falling against the mirrored wall and pressed the heels of her hands into the soft seat. At her ear, Art whispered what he'd do to her later, how he'd bind her wrists and fuck her in that belt so it clanked against her hips; how his huge sex would fill her, again and again; how he'd have no mercy; how her pussy would be dripping. And as he told her all this, his lips against her ear, he ran his fingertips up and down her slit so softly she started to quiver. Then he played her pussy perfectly, like the strings of a harp, whispering, "Yield to me, Maya. Give it to me." Right then, he pressed the tip of a finger between the slippery lips of her sex and, in an instant, found the perfect spot. She let out a gasp, parting her thighs,

feeling the burn as he stroked quicker, quicker. She grasped the
seat, mumbled something crazy, her lips moist, her body damp,
and, raising her hips, she let out a cry, dropping back her head.
"I'm going to fuck you, Maya," he told her, his voice a gentle
growl, "but first, I want to watch."

She raised her hips. "Don't stop."

He rubbed harder and quicker, his breathing growing raspy,
and she could feel his breath at her ear. "Maya," he moaned,
"come for me, beauty."

As if obeying, she felt her hips buck, and as the burn took her
over she was high, so high, coming on the seat, crying out her
pleasure, her knees jerking upward so they thumped the table,
making a wineglass fall, strawberries roll and the plates bounce
and skid. Her belt clanked, jumping on her hips, and the weight
of it was sublime. She came and came and came.

It felt like soaring.

As she slumped in the seat, dizzy and grateful, he took her
in his arms and crushed his lips to hers. Kissing her in a tight
embrace, he ran a hand up and down her stocking top before
letting the tips of his fingers reach inside her dress, massaging her
nipple through the satiny bra. "Good," he whispered, between
their melding kisses. "Come home with me, Maya."

When at last they looked up, a waiter was towering over
them, frowning coolly as he placed the bill on the table. Behind
him, the diners were staring across, some smirking, while others
sat in disdainful silence. "Time to leave, sir," said the waiter.
"*Now*, if you will."

Maya's face flushed as she buttoned her dress, barely believing
what she'd just given way to, but as Art placed the twenty-pound
notes on the table, he told the waiter, "She's perfect, don't you
think?"

Art insisted they walk back to his place, his arm round her

waist, the links of the belt clinking as she walked. They wandered through the bustling heart of Covent Garden, the lamplight from store windows licking across them, and Maya glanced at his dark skin and the heavy lashes framing his eyes. He told her that when she walked her hips rocked sensuously. "You walk like a beautiful whore. As if you are offering your sex." As she moved, her high heels clacking on the sidewalk, she saw what he meant: the way her hips swung beneath the heavy belt, thrusting forward as her thighs brushed together, the satin of her nylons slinky and warm. He was right, it *was* sexy the way she moved—her body had been soliciting without her even knowing!

In the busy London night, he pleasured her. Firstly, he pushed her against some iron railings, where he fell to his knees in the lamplight, sweeping aside the lace of her briefs and licking her so suddenly that the railings chimed when she clasped them and her belt clanked too when the small of her back hit the metal. His mouth against her sex was as yielding as a kiss, and his tongue made her tingle from the Thai food. A few minutes later, he led her into the doorway of a shop, one that sold furs and displayed them in the window curled about the shoulders of sleek black mannequins or pinned round their torsos, animal and plush. Here, he was gentle with her, kissing her on the mouth over and over, till their lips were utterly pliant. With a hand dipping inside the layers of coat and dress, he fondled her breasts through the silk of her bra, his fingertips grazing the lace round the edge, then glossing her nipples through the sheerness. He smelled of exotic cologne, and his breath at her ear was unsteady as he rubbed, massaged and pressed himself against her, yet when she reached for his sex he swept her wrist away and told her they must go. "Why?" she pleaded.

He cupped her face, eyes shining. "Maya, you are all a man could want. I must wait, don't you see? I must *suffer*."

"I don't have to be fought for!"

He gave a shy grin, then shook his head and collected her in his arms. As he kissed her, pressing close, she fell against the shop window, and he raised her thigh, pushing himself onto her, but just as she started grinding her sex oh-so-gently against the hardness of his own, and their kisses had grown more desperate, he pulled away again. This time, he ran into the street, hailing a cab. When the car pulled up, he opened the door for her, saying, "I must be in control."

As she climbed in, she told him, "Anything you say," and the submission in her voice made her poor sex flood. Throughout the journey, Art played a hand up and down her stockings, turning her on so much that she arched, gripping the seat...and yet his expression was utterly calm, his dark skin shining.

Art's apartment block had a gray stone exterior and was five floors high. When they arrived, she expected the building to be cold within; instead, they walked into a warm entrance hall, with long couches and a glass-topped table, laden with a vase of cream-colored tulips that were engorged, tumbling, heavy with life. They took an elevator to the top floor where he unlocked the door to his place; then, without speaking, he lifted her up in his arms and carried her quite easily across the threshold. She laughed, a stiletto dangling from the ball of her foot and the weighty belt pressing onto her stomach. When he set her down on a low, leather couch, he traced the line of her lips, saying, "I've never wanted a woman so much."

She pressed his hand onto her sex, letting her knees fall apart. "Please," she begged, smothered by the smell of his cologne. "That cab ride was too long."

He glared into her eyes, breathing hard, and soon his hand was sliding up her stockings, and he was whispering her name, his lips jerking apart. "I won't take you yet," he said. "I won't...

I must suffer." But even so, he lay across her and she felt his cock, large and hard, pushing onto her core. He kissed her neck and swept a hand inside her skirt, and before she knew it he was brushing aside her satiny briefs, then stroking along her sex. She gasped, "Oh, Art, you're so good at this." And her slit was so wet that it opened easily to the tips of his fingers like a flower that senses the tremor of an insect.

"You," he moaned, licking her jaw, "are edible, Maya." And he pressed in deeper, finding the perfect spot, which made her sink back into the cushions so her belt dug in, and buttons burst from her swelling breasts. His fingering grew more furious and he lowered his face to her bosom, kissing and gasping, licking beneath the lace of her bra.

"Take me," she begged, running her hand up and down the shape of his cock.

He groaned, as if in wondrous pain, then rose, wiping his lips with the back of his hand; when he lowered his arm a trail of drool strung from his mouth to his knuckles. Pulling her to her feet, he led her across the room, the back of his neck smelling of cologne. She wished to lick his skin, but didn't quite dare to. He longed to be in control, and she wanted—no, *needed*—to please him.

He told her to lie on a sheepskin rug over by the grate, which was filled with pillar candles he now lit from a taper. As he rose again, these glimmered in the chasm of the grate, some taller, some shorter, in shades of cream and white. They gave off the aromas of sandalwood and bay, heady, erogenous scents that filled her. He left and returned again with a piece of silky rope, the kind you might use to tie curtains or a robe. Making her lie on her side, he bound her wrists in front of her, and she shuddered as the cord bit her flesh.

"I will tell you what to do," he said.

She answered, "Yes."

He lit a long taper from the candles in the grate and wandered round the room, sleek in the dimness, lighting other candles, his shoulders slack and confident. In the low glow, Maya could see the many textures of the room: long futons were covered in ochre drapes and the floor itself was awash with rugs and skins. Some of these were pelts or fur, while others gleamed like satin. Art was clearly a man of textures. His bed was over by the wall—a mattress dressed with cushions and throws patterned with tiger stripes, suede and leather. Except for the mantelpiece and the vast prints—the sulking nudes of Mapplethorpe, the lunacies of Pollock—everything was low in that room, nothing rising higher than the waist. She could smell the scent of candles and skins—leathery, animal—a smell that knows itself.

This was so different from her own home, which smelt of the beeswax she used on the furniture and washing powder and mothballs. Her husband liked crisp sheets and plain, ironed tablecloths, shoes arranged by the door, mirrors that gleamed... even in the height of their passion, he'd only ever made love on superclean sheets. She was a neat person, but not as neat as he was, and his need for organization oppressed her. When they were first dating, they'd been carnal, devouring each other, but as soon as Maya had felt that something wasn't right he'd become too soft, treating her like she was precious. Feeling like a child, she'd been unable to come with him inside her. Recently, she'd realized that theirs was a marriage of servitude, in which they'd each become unchallenged, and nothing real burned.

Now here she was in the silver belt that both kept her and frustrated her. The cord around her wrists dug blissfully deep and as she rolled onto her back, the silver belt groaned, its weight like a metal collar, its links gripping her through the open dress. She raised a leg, which burst more buttons, and flexed her foot inside the stiletto. Candlelight danced across her body as Art returned to her side, half-undressed, his chest now dark and bare. Kneeling, he circled her ankle with the whole of his hand and drew it away, opening her thighs. He knelt between her knees, his eyes flicking across her body, and, in a soft growl, explained that he would fuck her until she could take no more: "…until you've had your fill."

Then, in sudden frenzy and without touching the belt, he began to tear the dress from her, his swelling biceps tightening as he worked, his skin gleaming as the candlelight swept across him. Soon she was half-bare in black silk lingerie edged with lace, and stockings teamed with garter belt and stilettos. He raised her bound wrists high above her head and, rubbing her nipple beneath the black silk so it pressed against the pad of his thumb, he fell on her, biting her shoulder, her neck and the cleavage that swelled from the delicate lace. He unzipped himself and fell on her wildly, entering her so swiftly that she cried out, pleading for his frenzy. Suddenly he was rutting with the power of a lion, telling her through shuddery breath that he'd often seen her in the store and had dreamed of possessing her many times but he'd held back because of the ring on her finger, glinting there, like a trap. "What changed your mind?" she asked.

"I couldn't bear how sad you looked."

The silver belt leapt on her waist as his body lunged against it, again and again, and with her bound wrists raised above her head, he pulled out of her, groaning and fell on her breasts, peeling back the lacy cups of her bra. "You're exquisite," he whispered, licking her nipple with the flat of his tongue. She glanced down at his dark, muscular back, where the skin was glossed with perspiration, then at her saliva-streaked breast, and she felt a wonderful burn in her pussy.

"Take me," she pleaded. She strained at her ropes, longing

to touch her clit, but this only caused them to dig more deeply. "Art, I need you inside me!" Instead, he made her raise her head so he could unknot her ponytail; then, when her blonde hair fell about her shoulders, the lines of his face grew soft.

"Maya, you move me," he murmured, parting her thighs and moaning as he filled her again. Now, he burst into a frenzy of fucking that made the whole floor creak. He grasped the belt against her waist, restricting the silver plates, and with his free hand splayed on her breast he leaned his weight right onto her, slamming his cock into her slit over and over, staring down at her pussy, which was slick beneath the lace of her briefs. "You're mine," he told her, saliva glossing his lips and teeth, and the beautiful buildup began to take her over, creeping through her sex, making her arch. She caught sight of the darkness of his cock as it thrust into her, and, arching her spine so the back of her head thumped against the sheepskin rug, she felt the flood of her climax and wailed with pleasure, half laughing, half sobbing, as the burn took her. He cried out himself, lunging like crazy, snarling, "Maya, oh, god…" And when he suddenly splayed a hand on her breast and leaned right onto her nipple, hips lunging ferociously, she knew he was coming inside her. He cried like a man in agony, his teeth gleaming against the roof of his mouth, and knowing he was coming in a long, hard stream, she came again, rolling her head, the smell of sex and sheepskin rising from beneath her.

Afterward, with her wrists still bound, he led her through to the bathroom where he washed her body with a natural sponge, removing her lingerie piece by piece, then bathing the slickness from her thighs and sex, but he left the belt in place, only lifting it a little to clean the perspiration from her hips. He dried her gently with a towel, then he guided her back through to the room of textures, where he asked her to kneel on his bed surrounded by candles; there, he sketched her in the silver belt, her bound wrists raised. While she basked in his attention and posed for him, proud, he quietly asked who gave her the belt, and when she replied he stared at her, pencil poised. "He gave it to you to entrap you, perhaps."

"It hurts that I must leave him."

As he sat sideways on his bed, sketching naked, the candle-light falling softly on his face, he told her the contraption was sacred. Like arousal itself, he explained, the belt was a burden, but when she yielded to true passion, it released her. "Your husband's gift was complicated, Maya. You can always be grateful for that. Finally, you've obeyed your instincts, becoming faithful to the woman you are."

"I never thought sex was important," she said.

He gave her an instant look of surprise, which grew to a smile. "How strange, after what we just shared."

She laughed, afraid of how free she felt, so daring and real. The room around her glimmered and she felt strong within it, as if she was choosing this moment and everything beyond.

Because no one who's been bound can fail to learn true liberty. And no one who yields to shackles will pass faith by.

FIVE SENSES

Rachel Kramer Bussel

When you're together long enough, sometimes even the hottest sex starts to seem rote. Your body might respond, get wet, hard, perk up, but your mind starts to drift and once it does, it's a goner. To be honest, I never thought that would happen to me, or rather, us. We were a model couple, or at least, that's what my friends told me, especially when their marriages dissolved. We were seen sneaking kisses at parties, when we weren't sneaking out to get it on in the car or rush home.

But sometimes monotony sneaks up on you; you don't know what you're missing until it's gone, to paraphrase Joni Mitchell. That's the state that I'm in when Lawrence calls me in my studio to tell me to get ready, because that night we're going to celebrate his latest booking. He's a comedian, which means that not only is he the life of every party we go to, but that sometimes we're flush and sometimes we're eating leftover pizza and pasta. I work, too, but I'm hardly any better; I sell my homemade jewelry at flea markets and online. Each piece is handcrafted, and I spend a lot of time seeking out just the right parts. Both of us are dedicated to our crafts—and each other. It's what's bonded us in even the leanest times. When either of us does particularly well, we treat the other to dinner. That's been our ritual for years, but every ritual needs a bit of updating once in a while.

"Where are we going?" I ask him, already mentally panning my wardrobe for a dress that maybe he—or I—have forgotten about.

"We're staying in tonight, baby," he says, his husky, crooner's voice making me shiver, as it always does.

Sight

I don't really believe him, so before he gets home, I'm admiring myself in the mirror, noting the way my blood red wrap dress makes the reddish highlights in my hair stand out and the way the plunging neckline dips between my breasts, further emphasizing them. It's the same dress I was wearing when he asked me to marry him, though I'm not sure even a man as attentive as Lawrence would remember that.

The truth is, I'm so caught up in what I see in the mirror that I barely murmur a hello when I hear my man walk in the door. When Lawrence comes up behind me and puts his hands over my eyes, I grin. The room feels electrified just by having him in it, next to me. He greets me with a kiss to the back of my neck, then lets his hands drop down to my shoulders. He kneads them deeply, and though I'm tempted to drop my head forward to give him better access, I watch us in the mirror.

His skin is darker than mine by a few shades, and I've always loved how we look together, his dark chocolate against my milkier tone. He watches me watching him before moving his grip, passing down over my shoulders, making goose bumps rise on my arms. I watch as his hands cup my breasts, holding them there, heavy in his hands, and I keep watching as he peels down the dress to expose the hot pink of my lacy bra, my nipples bursting against its constraints. He peels one layer of lace down, and his eyes meet mine in the mirror. "Can't do this at a restaurant," he says as he pinches my nub while we both look on. He exposes the other nipple, and there's something so blatant about this, more so than being totally nude. My tits are hanging out from my bra, looking almost obscene, and even though it's just the two of us watching, it feels like there are more eyes on me, a roomful. "Show off these pretty breasts. You should take them out more often. Flash me when we're at one of those awful parties." I have to shut my eyes then, because what he's doing feels so good, I just can't stand it. I don't remember the last time he drew things out like this; and just like that, I realize I've been missing this, missing foreplay.

"I want to see you, too, baby," I say, reaching back for what I know has to be a giant erection beneath his jeans. Sometimes I think I love feeling his hardness all wrapped up first, knowing that I will get to unveil it—if he lets me.

Smell

I'm busy inhaling the scent of him, the tangy, salty, musky, manly scent of not just his cock and balls but his skin, his essence. "Wait," he commands. "First I want you to do something for me." I glance at him and he looks nervous. I rise so I'm staring right into his dark brown eyes. "Take a bath with me," he half asks, half tells. His eyes search mine, letting me know he doesn't think I'm unclean, but he wants something else from me. "You wait here; touch yourself and look in the mirror while I run the bath."

When was the last time he drew a bath for me? Something else I hadn't realized was missing until I heard the water tumbling into the tub I'm used to soaking in alone. I try my best to follow Lawrence's commands—I've never been able to resist orders issued in that special voice—and I watch the pinkness of my skin blossom against my touch. I stare at myself, trying to see the woman he sees, and instead of grabbing for my handy bedside vibrator, I use one hand to press my fingers inside me while the other tweaks my nipple as he had done. Just as I'm really getting into it, I hear him calling me. "Take off that dress and come in here."

I slip off the dress and let it puddle on the floor. I stare at it for a moment before stepping toward the bathroom as I unhook my bra and toss that onto the bare, glossy wood. Just as I'm in the doorway, I step out of my panties. I pause, taking in the candles dotting the room, tiny floating ones. It smells like flowers and cotton candy. I sniff loudly as I walk toward him. "Slow, baby, slow," he says as I step into the warm water. I'm not sure that's possible, but I try. We are reversing our usual order of things, that's for sure. Normally once I'm like this—ripe, juicy, ready— and he is, too, there's no stopping us. We get down and dirty right away, sometimes so fast that we're done before I've even gotten to appreciate him.

I sink into the water, surrounded by bubbles and that sweet scent. I scoop up a handful of fluff and blow it at Lawrence, laughing when he sneezes. At first I try to keep my head above water, but he insists that I sink lower, massaging my shoulders again so I have no resistance. My lips hover just above the water-line and I shut my eyes. Like that, we could be anywhere, anyone, really. I sense him shut off the lights and I hear rustling. He takes my hand and presses it against his heart, and we sit there like that, me deep in the water, inhaling the sweetness—"Vanilla," he whispers at one point when he hears me sniffing—and letting the warmth penetrate my bones. This time, I don't reach for his cock.

He kisses my forehead, long and tenderly, then down my nose and our lips meet. His tongue teases mine, coaxing it out only to shove it back in as his tongue claims my entire mouth. We both stand close to six feet tall—I've never been a shrinking violet—but when he kisses me, I do get smaller. Or maybe it's just that his mouth is so much bigger than mine, it can capture mine in a moment. I can't breathe with my mouth anymore, so I only use my nose, and now I smell him, pure Lawrence. He is kissing me and also not. His teeth are sinking into the area right around my lips, his saliva dripping onto me as I push back against the edge of the tub to press my head closer, give him more of myself. Just as I'm getting frantic, he pulls away again. "Don't move." I nod. His white shirt is drenched and he unbuttons it, giving me a view of his firm chest, the muscles not rippling but still so achingly clear, firm, just below the surface, that I clench down below.

He steps outside, dropping the shirt on the floor like I'd done with my clothes. I hear him take a few steps, then he's back to slip a blindfold over my eyes. It's padded, warm against my lids. He runs a little more hot water. The splash against my toes is louder with the blindfold on. He runs his fingers lightly between my legs, just a hint, before he walks off.

Taste

I wait, knowing he'll be back soon. He's tied me up before and walked out, just long enough to make me wonder, long enough to make me shake against my bonds, long enough for me to drip between my legs at the indignity of being spread wide open. I'm not tied up now, but I don't peek or otherwise cheat. I sink deeper and think back on our hottest moments together: sex in the snow at a ski resort; the first time, in his car; the time he added a finger along with his cock inside me, when he let me put more than a finger or two up his butt. There have been so many special moments, but they get lost in the everyday, the morning quickies, the stolen solo affairs. It's hard to interject a fantasy or foreplay when we are both so focused day and night on Making Something of Ourselves.

It seems like he's back in no time, and I shake my head to clear it as I hear him on the stairs. "Hungry?" I hear him call. Honestly, I'm not hungry by this point, not really, but Lawrence manages to rekindle an ache in my belly, aside from the one in my mouth, for his cock. I want to be hungry for whatever he has to offer.

No smells immediately waft toward me, nothing warm, stinky, steaming. "I'm gonna feed you, Kelly. Then I'm gonna eat you." I smile and then something cool is against my lips. I reach out my tongue and taste what can only be a Granny Smith apple. I open wider and the tart, sweet fruit is against my tongue, followed by a loud crunch. It tastes good, though I still can't properly say I'm hungry.

I think about how many times I've fed him; I usually nibble as I work all day—cheese, crackers, maybe a microwaved veggie burger. I can lose track of time and skip meals, and I don't really mind. I like food, but my work nourishes me. When I cook— hearty stews, lasagnas, roasted chicken—it's with Lawrence in mind. I love watching him devour what I've made.

What next hits my lips is sweet, dripping, wet. Honey. I laugh at first, because honey is what he calls the liquid that pools between my legs. "Give me some of that honey," he'll say, and if I ever have a moment of shyness, it vanishes when I hear those words. The honey trails along my tongue, not quite fully dissolving. Next are grapes, chilled, cold against my tongue. I take bite after bite, suddenly famished. "And now, dessert." I giggle as a heavenly bite of chocolate passes my lips, and now I'm grateful for the blindfold. Without it I'd be dying to feed him back. He lets me lick the chocolate off his fingers and then kisses me deep. I hear the rasp of his zipper and he breaks the kiss, only to climb into the tub with me, pinning me beneath him. The tub doesn't really fit two, that would've been overkill, but then again, we've never tried anything but standing-in-the-shower sex. I like this, like his heft, his weight; like that he's thought so much about what he wants to do to me.

Hearing

As if I've conjured it, he whispers, "I've been planning all day to seduce you, Kel. To get you frantic and wet and tight so I can fill you right up, everywhere." I shiver at "everywhere"—is he going to put his cock back there? We've talked about it, but never actually done it; one thing I love about him is how big he is, but not for that. "Yes, baby, I am going to take you all over, and you're going to like it. I'm going to get inside your sweet ass, and you're going to beg for me to do it harder, beg for more, the way you do when you have it in your mouth. That's the only way it's going to happen."

What he tells me next is what makes me crack completely open. Never mind not having any clothes on, never mind him on top of me, never mind the heat and the bubbles and being blindfolded; it's the words he whispers in my ear and those he coaxes from my mouth that do me in. "I wish I could be in all of your holes at once," he says, slipping two wide fingers into my mouth. They are smooth, smoother than my calloused ones, but not dainty. I suck them down and when his words get to be too much, I press my teeth into his fingers, just a little, just enough to let him know how much I want everything he's telling me. "I want to take out my phone and turn on the video camera and tape us, tape you riding me, those breasts bouncing. I want to watch you come with me inside you, then keep that with me at all times, so when I'm on the road or just missing you I can watch those faces you make." The head of his dick nudges my sex, but I don't dare try to make him enter me. He lifts the blindfold and stares deep into my eyes. "I'm gonna make you scream, baby, scream for my cock, scream when you ask me to come, scream because you don't know if you want me to stop or keep going." A tear bubbles up to the corner of my eye, but I don't try to stop it.

"Yes," I say, then pull him close and this time shove my tongue into his mouth. We kiss until the water's cold, then he wraps me in our softest blanket and carries me to the bed, even though my ankles are still dripping, my hair wet. He grabs a towel and pats himself dry while I watch.

Touch

I reach for him again, but he doesn't let me. Instead he turns me over and then moves me around, positions me like I'm just his plaything. I like being his plaything, like this, alone, in the bedroom. I like it when he makes me feel like I'm there for his pleasure, because in that moment, I am. Or rather, his pleasure is my pleasure, as retro as that may sound.

With my head turned to the side, my eyes closed, and him sliding my legs open into a V, I get wet, so wet I'm sure he sees and smells. He holds open my pussy lips for a moment and I wait, but all I get is a brief lick of his tongue, a quick suck on my clit, before he vanishes. I could reach down myself, he hasn't explicitly told me not to, but he doesn't have to. I know he's in charge now.

Being facedown I don't see his finger aiming before it zeros in on its target. Slick with saliva, it presses lightly against my pucker, seeking something I'm not sure I can give. I liked the idea in theory, sort of, when we were in the bath, but this is real. "Open up, Kel, let me in. You're gonna like it, I promise," he says. It sounds like a line, something guys say—but not my guy. I take a deep breath, smell the detergent embedded in the sheet, and soon there are fingers in both my holes. Then, something else: lube, but it feels different from the lube I've used on him. I bite my lip and then I make myself go limp as his finger works its way into my ass. And he's right, I *do* like it. I suck him in deeper as his other hand plunges into my natural wetness. I raise my butt into the air, urging him deeper.

I chance a peek behind me to see his face focused entirely on what he's doing. "That's it," he croons softly. I lie there with my ass in the air, as exposed as when I've been tied up—now *this* would be a picture! But somewhere along the way the thoughts and fears and doubts stop playing on a loop in my head; I know he would stop if I wanted him to. In my backward glance he lets me see his cock, flashes its hardness, its heft, its desire right at me; that makes me wild with lust, always has.

I've been with other guys, black or white, with big dicks, some bigger than Lawrence's. He, though, has the perfect package and not just down there; he is tough and tender, strong and supportive. He takes care of me and lets me take care of him, *and* he has a beautiful cock. He fingers me for another minute or two while I ponder how lucky I am to have this man in one fine package, and all of that is what I see when I finally sit up and lean over to take the head in my mouth. He maneuvers us so I somehow can suck his dick and he can lean over me and play with me back there. We work in sync until he's filling my mouth, not with his cream, but with his length, giving me all of it and starting to rock his hips back and forth. I ease off; he's telling me that he could let it happen this way, he could stand and watch me get him off with my mouth.

"No, take me there," I tell him. "I want your cock in my ass." And it's true; I do want him there, for the first time ever. It's a first for me, a place no man has ever gone before, and that fact, as much as the ache inside, propels me. I get on all fours and I hear him rip open a condom and glide one on, then I hear lube and soon he is there.

"Touch your clit, baby," he whispers, and I do, while he sinks inside. It's tight and even though he goes slowly, it's still an unusual feeling, but I soon get caught up in it, caught up in him. His words now are gibberish, mostly, or "Yes," "Tight," "Baby," but the actual words no longer matter. We've said everything we need to say, and I know he will still wake up with me every day after this. He has promised me so much, and this is another promise we are making to each other. He knows it's my first time and I know he knows and my fingers work my clit as I realize I like it, I really like it.

I can't even explain it to myself, but now I'm the one with the dirty mouth. "Fuck my ass, Lawrence. Take it; take me." He's going slowly in and out, and when he gets almost all the way out I feel an emptiness that makes me claw at the sheets and buck backward to urge him in. I give up on my clit for a little while to hold on to the headboard and he drills into me, sensing what I need. "I'm gonna come soon, Kel," he says, and that does it for me. I love how his come feels, and even if I'm not going to feel it in the usual way, I love what it represents.

"Come inside me, give it to me, all of it." I'm rattling the bed and his hands go up to my breasts, playing with my nipples, before they reach for my arms to pull me down and cover me. His lips are at the back of my neck, his breath hot and heavy in my ear as my husband fills my ass. He lets out a groan as he softens inside me, then lies there on top of me for a moment, sweat dripping down. When he pulls out and rolls me over to look at him, there is pure love shining from his eyes, along with some unshed tears. He gets up to wash off, and when he's done he shuts off all the lights before settling down before me.

Lawrence pulls me to the edge of the bed and licks me, fucking me with his tongue. I hear a noise and realize my nails have torn the sheet a little but I don't care; I only care about wrapping my legs around his head and coming—for me, for him, for us. He doesn't need any words now; his tongue does the talking. He holds me wide open and makes sure he does it exactly the way I like it, beating his tongue against me, the pressure of his strong fingers massaging me, then his teeth are against my clit, then I'm exploding. He hums against me and takes all that I'm giving him, my honey, but keeps going. And going and going. I don't dare tell him it's enough; is it ever, really? All I know is by the time he is done eating me I'm sore in a good way, my senses overloaded.

I remember how it felt when we were first together, everything heightened. Back then I'd tell my friends that it felt like I had two pussies, six hands, three brains. Now it's like that, too, as if everything I know about my body and being has been cleared out in favor of a new system that makes infinitely more sense.

Five senses? Try fifty, a hundred, a thousand. But who's counting?

THE ARCH OF TRIUMPH

Monica Day

usually ask for directions when I'm lost. But tonight, I would rather be found.

I already figured out how to take the subway to see l'Arc de Triomphe, alone. Strolled down the Champs Elysées, alone. Got a table at a chic African restaurant, alone. All while scoping out the various possibilities for company.

At the end of dinner, after several unsuccessful attempts at flirting with men at nearby tables, I ask the waiter to recommend a jazz bar. He hands me a napkin with the name of a club, the neighborhood it's in…and his name and number.

"I don't work tomorrow night," he says in his best English as he delivers his offer with my bill. For just a minute, I'm sorry that tomorrow night is too late.

There are worse places than Paris to be alone. It's my third night here, and I've grown bolder by the day. I hail a cab and ask for my destination—*en Français*.

"La Caveau en St. Michelle, s'il vous plait?"

"Oui, Madame."

It's warmer than I expect for a September night, so I drape my sweater over my arm as I get out of the cab. The sidewalks are overflowing with people out enjoying the night—groups of men arguing and watching women walk by, lovers kissing and laughing as they stroll. Five directions to choose from with tired feet is four too many—I need someone to point the way. I pick the sweetest, most approachable boy I can find. He's leaning on a short post on the sidewalk, also alone.

"Como ça va La Caveau, s'il vous plait?" Oops. It happened again. The little bit of Spanish I know collides with the little bit of French I remember from high school. *I think I asked him who is in the cave.* I feel my cheeks turn hot and red.

"Huh?"

"Pardon," I say, laughing and try again. *"Ou es Le Caveau? C'est musica? Jazz?"*

"I speak English," he confesses and we laugh. He's French-Canadian and just arrived in Paris two days ago. It is his first time in the neighborhood, too, he tells me. He can't help. A little embarrassed, I thank him and continue spelunking for my jazz cave.

Three brave but fruitless efforts later, I hear a voice behind me: "Have you found it yet?"

I spin around and there he is, grinning. I smile broadly back. We are old friends now, based on the length of time either of us has spent with anyone in this city.

"No," I tell him.

"Let me help you look."

We wander just a block before we find it. He asks if he can come with me. The man in the ticket window shifts his eyes from him to me and back again, no doubt trying to discern our story. He's in shorts, flip-flops, a T-shirt—obviously a student and a young one at that. I am in my best Paris chic...pressed slacks, strappy black heels, red halter with the requisite plunging V-neck. I figure I've got about fifteen years on him, give or take.

While the ticket-taker vacillates between accusation and admiration, I ask for two tickets and put my money under the half-moon opening in the Plexiglas. As my new friend reaches for his wallet, I quietly turn away his arm and tell him he can buy me a drink.

The man hands me the tickets but speaks to my new companion in French. For a sickening moment, I think he is saying he can't come in. I imagine there is a dress code or some other problem, maybe even an age requirement that my new friend might not meet. I briefly entertain the thought that I could end up in jail on my last night in Paris, and I wonder who I would call to come get me out.

"The band is on a break," he translates. "He says we can walk and come back if we'd prefer. It will be about a half hour."

A half-hour stroll through the winding streets of St. Michelle and two hours of jazz later, he is not just a boy on the street. His name is Eric. He is a baroque harpsichordist, here on a full scholarship for a year—all expenses paid—to study with one of the best teachers in the world.

"Do you want to know the best part of being here, though?" he asks.

"Of course I do."

"It is looking out my window every day." He goes on to describe in great detail the spires of Notre Dame...how the light changes at different times of the day and at dusk...how he can hear the people below, catch fragments of their conversations as they stroll past his window.

"It's incredible," he concludes. "I could spend the entire year looking at it every day and not get tired or bored."

"Lucky for me you decided to leave your room," I joke, as we both laugh at the unapologetic romantic dissertation that Paris seems to inspire, even in the best cynic.

"Yes, it is good to be out...and nice to talk to you."

I decide that when a forty-year-old woman attracts the undivided attention of a twenty-five-year-old man in Paris, she should remain mysterious, anonymous even. The less information shared about sticky things back home—like a recent separation that is careening into a divorce or the two little girls there who are missing me this week—the better.

Instead, I tell him of my great love for jazz, which he knows nothing about. I tell him why scat singing is so hard and how a great jazz classic is a lot like the classical pieces he plays. How each person who plays it puts their mark on it—how the music changes even as it stays the same. And we agree that improvisation is one of the highest forms of art and speculate whether heroin makes it easier to release into the unknown, even though neither of us knows the answer firsthand.

During all this chattering and listening, nothing more than the tops of our arms touch. He is attentive and polite. He watches my drink and refreshes it, thoughtful about our drinks-for-ticket agreement at the door. And I decide that perhaps the age difference has ruled out any attraction for him, but I am grateful for the company nonetheless.

As the musicians launch into their last song of the night, my glass is empty. But this time, I decline another. It's late, and I have half of Paris between me and my hotel.

Then, without touching me, without testing the waters or looking for signs of reassurance, he turns to me and says, "I would like to show you Notre Dame...outside my window."

I have just been handled by a twenty-five-year-old in shorts and flip-flops…and I didn't even see it coming.

"I would like that."

A happy silence descends between us, as we walk the four blocks to his apartment. He has been charming. I have been charmed. The surprise of it is enough for us both for now.

"We must be quiet," he explains. Oh, my. It is practically a college dormitory. There are rules against this kind of thing, consequences if he gets caught. But he is not concerned. He takes my hand and leads me through the hallway maze to this room. We giggle a little after we pass someone in the hall who politely averts his eyes as we pass.

He offers the obligatory apologies of a single man for dirty dishes, an unclean bathroom and unmade bed.

"I wasn't exactly expecting you," he laughs. I reassure him, tell him it doesn't matter. The place we came here for is not tainted by such things.

"Stand right here," he orders, as he places me in front of the window like a favorite doll in a dollhouse. And he's right. It's breathtaking. The window is open, no screens obscure the view or the breeze. He stands behind me, hands on my shoulders.

We have said enough words for tonight. After a long silence, he lifts my hair and blows on the back of my neck. He runs his hands down my arms and back up again. I am watching the clock on the tower of Notre Dame, thinking this will be fast. I have drawn all sorts of conclusions about the hunger of a man his age. The fumbling I expect next. The uncertainty. The pace.

Drifting in and out of the distilled beauty of this moment, I can't help but wonder how I will get a cab back to my hotel at this hour. Until I feel a slight tug. He is lifting the halter around my neck over my head and slowly, ever so slowly, revealing my breasts to the warm breeze outside, to the streetlamps below and ultimately, of course, to the spires of Notre Dame.

"Beauty begets beauty," he says quietly in my ear, as his hands follow the curve of my neck, circle round my shoulders, until finally, lighting a fire along every nerve on his path, they settle around the undersides of each breast.

We sit like this for a long time. The street below is empty, but I wish it wasn't. I want to been seen here, in this light, with this young man holding me up as an offering to his precious spires. I am his souvenir of Paris and he is mine. And this is the postcard moment we will each keep forever from this trip.

Ever so gently, his thumbs curl around to rub my nipples. He presses his front into my back, and I feel the outline of his hard cock against my spine. I don't realize I have stopped breathing until I hear my own sigh escape. Whatever part of me that was unwilling to surrender to the moment, to its perfection, finally lets go.

As my head tips back and finds his shoulder, as my hands reach back to find his thighs, as I dissolve completely into the slow exploration of this stranger-turned-lover, there are no more thoughts of finding cabs or leaving anytime soon. In fact, there are no thoughts at all—and absolutely no rush to get to the next inevitable moment—for either one of us.

By the time he finally turns me around to face him, there is nothing left of the boy I met earlier. There is only the man I am here with now. As he kisses me, his face is as gruff as any man's at that hour. As his lips make their descent, from my lips to neck to shoulders to cleft of breast to nipple, he savors me in the manner of a man, rather than consuming me as a boy. And in his arms, under the exploration of his touch on every part of me, I realize I don't need to hold anything back here.

At the window, I surrender to him completely, letting him slowly peel off my Paris chic without objection. He speaks only in French now, and has requested that no more English pass between us until the light of dawn. That's okay with me. I have nothing left to say.

When we finally move the few feet across the small room to the bed, my consumption of him begins. With more hunger and urgency—the hunger that drove me here in the first place—I push him back onto the bed. I feel his cock under his shorts, and a groan of delight at its substantial size and shape escapes me before I can suppress it. He laughs. I imagine I'm not the first to notice.

With great effort, I try to unwrap him with the same slow, deliberate speed of seduction he used with me. I lift his T-shirt and my eyes follow the strip of hair that begins somewhere under his shorts, stretches up the center of his torso and spreads perfectly across his chest. His body is beautiful. I would tell him if I could, but I fear what I might say in my feeble French, so I let my hands tell him instead.

I lower my torso slowly over him, until just the tips of my nipples are brushing lightly against the whole of his exposed skin, grazing over him lightly, teasing him as I make my way to his shorts. Even as I am eye level with his cock, and I'm opening his button and zipper, he keeps his hands by his sides and lets me take him how I want. I think to myself that some woman has trained him well, and I silently thank her.

It is a gorgeous cock, thick, long, hard—and all mine. I tuck myself between his legs, entwine my hair into itself so I have an unfettered view, and slowly lower myself to his groin. I rub the head of his cock along my cheeks, my lips, tracing my nose, and I breathe him into me. He says something in French that sounds like a mixture of surprise and gratitude, as his hand reaches up to gently stroke my hair.

It goes on like this for hours. We are a tumble of giving and receiving until the lines blur between the two. Many times, I think he'll come, but he doesn't until I am completely exhausted and beg for a rest. An adolescent discomfort nags at me as I drift off, wondering why he never came, what I might have done wrong.

When the first light of dawn reveals the spires once again, I am awoken sharply by his hard cock entering me suddenly from behind. I am still wet, despite napping for a couple of hours, and he slips back inside me easily. All of his slowness from the night before is gone. He has gone primal on me. Holding himself up on one hand, his other reaches around my waist and he pounds into me from behind. His coming seems to last as long as the entire night we spent building to this climax. And although he's wearing a condom, just the thought of how much fluid he's pouring into me, imagining how it would feel to have him dripping out of me, sends me into another set of spasms that mimic his, like we're singing a round.

When we finally catch our breath, dripping sweat, our sides sticking together on his cot-sized mattress, he speaks to me in English, punctuating the end of our time together.

"I'm sorry," he says.

"Sorry?" I ask. "What's there to be sorry about?"

Suddenly, I'm nervous. Facts that my body ignored through the night pop to mind. Like the fact that he's a stranger, that we didn't have a "health talk" first or my concern that he was somehow unsatisfied and regretted the evening.

"I came too soon." Expecting to see a smile on his face, I look over at him, but he's dead serious. By the light of day, he's a boy again: earnest, eager to please. I begin to reassure him, but before I get a chance, a smile breaks out across his face.

"Perhaps I can see you again before you go," he says. "I promise, I will try to last longer."

CRAVE YOU CLOSE

A. M. Hartnett

The shouting had started shortly before midnight. Krista imagined that the rest of the family simply burrowed themselves beneath their pillows and pretended not to hear it. The Neal motto seemed to be "Don't make waves," but that's what Nicky did without even trying.

She slipped from the bed they shared and twisted her dark hair into a ponytail then wrapped his heavy robe around her. She crept down the stairs, past the den where the fight had originated and squeezed through a crack in the back door to settle on the Adirondack chair at the far end of the porch.

The night was balmy, but there was a nipping breeze that crept low to the ground and whisked straight up the hem of the robe. Content to wait for him, Krista curled her legs beneath her bottom and cocooned into the toasty robe.

When they couldn't pay the rent any longer, they had traveled six hundred miles to Nicky's hometown of St. Paul to take up residence in the Neals's spacious old house. His father had helped him get a job, and what did Nicky do on the first weekend? He went out and got drunk with his childhood buddies. That morning when Kimball passed Nicky en route to the bathroom he had seen the fresh bruises on his son's face.

It was a bad start, but it would get better. Kimball would see that Nicky was serious about getting things straightened out. What was a bit of rowdy fun?

Voices carried from the open living room window. She could hear Kimball letting into Nicky. "You're supposed to start work Monday morning. What the hell is Harold going to say when you show up at the job looking like that?"

"He's not hiring me for my good looks," was Nicky's tight reply. His tone cut into Krista. She could imagine that line between his eyebrows getting deeper and his cheeks turning red as he tried to keep his temper from spilling over. On and on it went until at last Kimball's heavy footfall pounded up the old stairs.

He'd get over it, just like he'd gotten over his son running off and getting married the day after graduation. He'd gotten over their decision to have a baby when neither one of them had a job and had even wired them money so they could pay their rent. He'd get over this, too.

Moments after the fight ended the back door opened, and Nicky emerged. He sat on the top step, lit a cigarette and drew deep.

She cleared her throat and Nicky jumped. When he saw her the lines on his face disappeared, and he ran a hand through his brown hair. "I should have known."

"I got tired of waiting for you, and it's not like I could sleep with all the yelling. I didn't really want to stay up there anyway."

Nicky stuck the cigarette between his teeth and leaned back on his hands. "Is Ethan asleep?"

"Probably not. He's in the attic with his cousins having a sleepover. I heard them making all kinds of noise earlier."

"How about a drive?" he asked, his eyes to the stars and then glanced back at her. "You don't need to change."

Krista leapt barefoot on the adjacent grass while Nicky's sneakers crunched on the gravel strip leading to the little car. He rolled the car down the driveway to the main road and then they were off. It only took a moment for her to realize their destination: the lake where they had swum as children.

"Need a lift? There's probably broken glass on the ground." he asked once he cut the engine.

She rode on his back to a picnic table at the lakeside. Her head was heavy with recollection. It was here that they had first come together and dozens of times afterward.

Nicky deposited her on the edge of the table and swung around. His big hands cupped her face and held her a moment, then moved lower to grasp the lapels of the robe as he leaned in and nuzzled her. He muttered something against her skin that she didn't catch and then gasped.

"Jesus, Kris, what the hell are you wearing under here?" he said, followed by a whistle. He split open the front of his bathrobe and gawked. "Goddamn."

She had bought the nightgown with the last of her mad money and had been hiding it since they arrived. It was a dainty mix of lace and mesh that ended just above her thighs. She had left the matching panties in the shopping bag.

Krista shimmied out of the robe and leaned back on both hands. Her whole body was already lit up and heavy with need. Nicky traced the neckline of the nightie with two fingers, from one shoulder to the other and then back again.

"You look like you were hit in the face with a pair of knuckles," she said.

His grin widened. "I was."

"You just walk around all day looking for trouble, don't you?"

"You want to give me some trouble?"

"Always." She laughed and brushed his cheek with the back of her hand. As he kissed her she reached lower and began working the buttons until his flat chest was exposed to her. She splayed her hand on his warm skin and felt his heart beating.

"We're all right, aren't we?" he asked quietly.

Gooseflesh rose on her arms and legs as his breath streamed over her while he mouthed a trail along the slope of her neck. Her heart picked up the pace with every inch his moist lips explored.

"We're always all right," she said and turned her mouth to his, sucking in a quick breath before his tongue touched hers.

Holding in a moan at the back of her throat, Krista parted her legs. She took his hand and guided it along her inner thigh. His fingertips grazed the wet heat at the apex, tentative at first as he flicked his tongue in and out of her mouth. She ran her hand along his forearm and felt the hairs rising beneath her palm.

"Put your fingers inside me," she said. "Let me warm you up."

Her breath caught at the back of her throat as he filled her slowly. At the same time he planted his knee on the edge of the table and pushed himself up to hover over her. The slats beneath them creaked with the extra weight. As she went on her back, Krista draped her arms over his shoulders and sucked his hot tongue deeper into her mouth. For a moment she simply cradled the back of his head, fingers twisting in his soft, overgrown hair as he gently fucked her with two fingers. She was getting wetter and a little tingle blossomed with each pass over her G-spot.

He glanced down her body with a twisted smile. "I love it

when you dress up for me. Nail polish, makeup, pretty under-wear: I've never seen you look less than perfect in all the years I've known you."

She moaned as his fingers left her, but the separation was only so he could pull the hem of her nightie past her belly button and tug the bodice low.

Her need mounting, she curled her tongue around his and reached lower to where his cock tented the front of his track pants. She could feel the heat beneath the thin layer of fabric as she closed her hand around his shaft.

He thrust his fingers into her again and then slowly withdrew. Krista tipped her head back and bit down on her bottom lip.

"You don't have to be quiet," he said.

She tugged the drawstring at his waist. "I'm so used to having to hold my breath."

He slid his fingers between her pussy lips and rubbed the puffy flesh around her clit. His low chuckle skittered through her and sang in her blood. "Don't hold your breath. It's just you and me out here. I can make you."

Krista couldn't give in just yet. Her throat ached where she held her cry of pleasure. The tip of his finger brushed her clit and she fought to keep it all inside. Bending her legs at the knee, she pressed her bare feet to the flat surface of the table. Each time he circled the hard bead of flesh she pushed up. His touch was so light but so potent. Her pussy contracted and she felt her juices trickling.

Krista grasped the front of his pants and pulled them down. She closed her hand around his dick and ran her thumb along the tip. He groaned and his whole body vibrated.

"God, I remember the first time we came out here. No girl had ever given me a hand job before."

"That wasn't all I did." She pumped the hot length until her hand was slick with precome. "I still can't believe it."

"Believe what?"

"How far I let you go." He pinched her clit, stealing her words for a moment as the ripple of pleasure skirled through her abdomen. "I couldn't sleep that night thinking about how you'd tell all your friends and never talk to me again."

"I did tell all my friends," he said with a laugh and withdrew, "and I did call you the next morning."

He shoved his pants to his knees and splayed his hands on her thighs to spread her apart. Krista grasped him around the waist as the hard column of flesh stretched her and dug her fingernails into his hips as the fat head bumped against her G-spot. It was like a flare went off inside of her, filling her with liquid heat.

"Go slow, baby. We never get to go slow anymore," she whispered.

The light of the moon was bright enough that she could see his face. His lips were parted and his teeth were clenched together. She imagined that he mirrored the same restraint that she did. His breath coming in hard bursts, he sank down until he was balls deep. Krista slung her legs around his waist and tucked her feet into the groove at the small of his back.

He bent low until his forehead was pressed against hers. "I don't think I can go slow."

"Fuck me hard, then. I just want to scream tonight," she said in a puff of air as she clenched her inner muscles around him.

Nicky jerked, muscle going taut as her nails cut into him. He spread his legs, arched his back and started pumping.

She could see the strain on his face just before he expelled the breath he held. It was impossible to drag her gaze from his face. After so long she thought she would have gotten over him. There were mornings when she'd watch him rolling out of bed and with the sight of the muscles in his shoulders flexing, his back crisscrossed with marks from the mattress, she would be heavy and swollen in an instant.

It never went away. It just seemed to get stronger.

Each time he pulled out until only the thick head remained, Krista arched her back, ready for his next deep thrust and the slap of his balls against her ass. His features blurred and mingled with the black sky and white stars overhead. The walls of her cunt squeezed and sucked his cock. She moaned long and loud throughout the endurance of a climax that hit her so hard it seemed like it would split her in two.

Nicky pumped her twice more and then buried his cock to the hilt. The piece of the world that had shattered with her orgasm came back together, and she watched the glorious transformation come over his face. He squeezed his eyes shut, and for a moment his face twisted into a grimace while he shot his load deep inside. In an instant the same euphoria that pumped through her flooded his face. Krista couldn't take her eyes off of him as he emptied into her. He looked so vulnerable and beautiful.

She closed her arms around him as he sagged on top of her and expelled a low moan into the crook of her neck. Every one of her senses was alive, and she keenly felt everything around her, none more so than his heart bumping against his chest.

He lifted his head and just looked at her, gaze darting over every inch of her face. She smiled and slipped her hands into his hair to give the wayward tufts a tug. Nicky blinked and drew a quick breath, and then he leaned down and kissed her.

They parted and stood facing each other as he tucked himself back into his pants and Krista burrowed into the robe.

"Hey," he said and combed his fingers through his hair. "Can I buy you a burger?"

"It's late, but I'll let you split a blueberry shake with me."

She stretched her arms out, and he turned to let her climb onto his back. "Tomorrow I'll get up with you and fix up your face so you look like a million bucks."

"I don't want you using my face to mess with your makeup."

"Trust me."

He turned his head slightly and vibrated as she rubbed her cheek against his. "Don't worry about it. It'll only melt off."

At the car Krista slid down and hugged him from behind. "I'm not sorry, you know. I'm not sorry for one damn minute. I just want you to know that."

Nicky grasped her wrists and held her against his back for a moment longer. He didn't ask what she meant and she didn't elaborate. She'd seen the apology haunting his eyes ever since they'd moved back to St. Paul.

"One of these days I'll get my shit together," he said.

Krista pressed her face between his shoulder blades and quietly laughed. "It doesn't matter. I'm not going anywhere."

AN EASY GUY
TO FALL ON

Annabeth Leong

Ina wouldn't have gotten on the bus at all if not for the people behind her in line who pushed her forward. Inside, it was packed completely full, steamy with breath and body heat. The contrast from the freezing slush falling outside made her nauseous.

Seeing a space open up ahead, Ina squeezed past people to get to it, lurching unsteadily as the bus began to move. She could already feel herself sweating under her clothes. She gripped a pole for balance and took a deep breath. The air felt a few degrees cooler in that spot, relieving her nausea just that crucial bit. She unzipped her jacket and sweater, still feeling she was about to choke in the stifling hot air.

Ina peered out the foggy bus windows, trying to figure how she would know when she got to her stop. She'd moved to Boston just the week before, alone, in December, with no one to help her navigate the unfamiliar icy sidewalks as she made countless trips from her car to the cramped new apartment and back.

She thought she should be used to unfamiliar places by now,

but the misery of the morning commute washed her with loneliness so intense that she felt like a little girl again. Ina clutched the pole harder and focused on calming herself. She met the eyes of the man standing beside her. Ina remembered him boarding the bus at the same stop she had. She looked away quickly, ashamed of the tears welling up in her eyes, but soon found herself stealing quick glances in his direction.

He was hot. He was nearly six feet tall, and his business attire enhanced his body's toned, graceful lines. His thick, curly black hair was just shaggy enough to soften his serious appearance. He had warm brown eyes that sparked green from certain angles. His smooth, brown skin also seemed warm. He stood easily despite the bus's uneven motion, not bothering to hold on to anything for support.

Impossibly, more people got on the bus, forcing Ina to stand closer to the man. She smelled subtle, smoky citrus rising from his skin. Ina wanted to hear his voice.

As she struggled to stay steady on the jerking, crowded bus, she imagined burying her face against his chest and holding on tight. She took a deep breath. She knew she was thinking this way because she was overwhelmed and scared.

The bus driver slammed the brakes, flinging Ina forward. She saved herself by squeezing her hands around the pole and leaning backward. When the bus lurched just as suddenly back to full speed, she completely lost her balance, falling against the man she'd been watching, slamming the heel of her boot onto the toe of his shoe.

"Sorry!" Ina yelped. "I'm so sorry!"

His hands came around her waist as if the two of them were dancing. Holding her there until she got her feet firmly under her body, he guided her back to standing. He placed her body in a more stable position than she'd been able to find on her own.

She could still feel the heat of his hands, which hovered nearby until he was certain she was steady.

The rush of gratitude she already felt for the help and the comforting physical contact became lust when he flashed her a quick, sexy smile. "Don't worry about it." His voice was as light and smooth as his smell, his accent precise.

Ina flipped her thick, brown hair out of her eyes and smiled back, hoping he liked her full lips and curvy figure. She leaned to look out the window again, wondering if he was watching her.

"What are you looking for?" he said.

"MIT."

"It's the last stop."

She blushed.

"Are you new in town?"

Ina nodded. The bus lurched again, and the man reached out and steadied her, keeping his hands on her waist this time. She glanced at him, wanting to step back so that he could completely enfold her. He smiled apologetically, his grip loosening.

"The bus isn't always this bad. Everyone decides to take the T when the weather is miserable."

"Thanks," Ina said. She meant it from the bottom of her heart, but he seemed to take it as a brush-off. He let go of her and became a stranger again.

The next morning when Ina went out to wait for the bus, the man was waiting at her stop, finishing a donut and the last few sips of his morning coffee. They nodded at each other, but Ina wasn't sure what to say to him. After a couple minutes of silence had passed, she felt she'd lost the opportunity to say anything.

He rode the bus all the way to MIT each day. Sometimes, Ina would watch the back of his head for the entire ride, imagining what it would be like to run her hands through his coarse curls.

In late February, they stood beside each other in a small crowd at the bus stop buffeted by a chill wind that ignored Ina's jacket and broke straight through to her skin. Their usual bus was fifteen minutes late, and Ina's fingers were tingling despite her gloves. She shoved her hands into her pockets and pulled her fingers out of the gloves and into fists, hoping that tucking her frozen digits against her palms would warm them.

The man broke his usual stoicism, hopping in place a little and checking his watch. A few minutes more passed, and he turned to Ina. "Do you want to split a cab to Kendall Station?"

She did a quick calculation of the cash in her purse and grinned. "Please."

He stepped to the edge of the sidewalk and stretched out his arm, and moments later they were alone together in the backseat of a taxi, with warm air blasting into their faces. Ina stowed her gloves and held her fingers up to the streams of air coming from the front seat.

"How do you like Boston so far?" he said after a moment.

"It's good." Ina gave him a strained smile. He shifted in his seat and seemed about to drop his efforts at conversation. "I never got your name," Ina said desperately.

"Saeed Qasim."

"I'm Ina Lopez."

He nodded. The Arabic name made her wonder whether she had any chance with him. Ina had heard about cultural obstacles, but everything she knew was vague and she didn't think she could ask him now.

"I think it's strange to see the same people every day but never speak to them," Ina managed, her face feeling hot. "You were sort of the first person I met in Boston, but I don't know anything about you."

He smiled. "I work for the Cambridge office of a certain

Internet search company," he said. "I've lived in Boston for three years, but before that it was San Francisco. I went to Stanford. My parents are Saudi, but my family moved to the U.S. when I was twelve. I love zombie movies and cheap falafel." His expression turned mischievous. "I'm a Sagittarius and I like long walks on the beach...."

Ina blushed and slapped at his arm. He glanced at the spot where she'd touched him. Embarrassed, she rushed on with her own introduction. "I got my doctorate in mathematical and computational cognitive science at Purdue, but I moved here to continue my academic indentured servitude. I eat ramen about five times a week, and I have to buy my own health insurance. I can't salsa dance, but that doesn't stop me from trying."

Saeed laughed. The sound glowed with a note of delight that complemented his warm skin. "That's not much of an advertisement. You should consult with my matchmaking aunts before posting anything on Craigslist." His face took on a funny, pinched expression. "Excellent at quickly preparing frugal meals."

"The additional left foot adds stability," Ina put in.

"Yes, they would like that one." There was a heavy pause between them as Saeed looked straight into her eyes. Ina thought he might use the opportunity to ask her out on a date. Then the moment passed, and the cab pulled up on Main Street in Cambridge. She paid her share of the fare and couldn't think of any excuse to linger.

She and Saeed again reverted to behaving as if they didn't know each other. Ina had looked him up on Facebook but had decided against sending him a friend request.

Spring came. Instead of taking the bus to MIT in the mornings, Ina walked into Cambridge to enjoy the air along the

Charles River and the long-forgotten warmth of the sun.

Then one evening, Saeed got on the same bus home that she did. She wondered why she'd never run into him traveling in this direction before. Their eyes met as he scanned for empty spots. Saeed half smiled, striding toward her past available seats in the front. But instead of sitting next to Ina, he took the seat across the aisle. Not for the first time, Ina wondered whether the attraction she felt was at all mutual.

When the bus arrived at their stop, he got off just ahead of her. Something happened as he stepped onto the sidewalk, and Saeed went sprawling, the laptop case he'd been holding flying off his shoulder. Ina hurried down after him, grabbing the laptop and reaching out to help him up.

He hesitated before accepting her hand. He steadied himself on it with light pressure as he rolled gracefully to his feet. "You at least had the excuse of a moving bus," Saeed said, when she returned his laptop.

Ina shrugged. "Not even you can be perfect, I guess. Are you all right?"

Instead of answering, he stared down at her. Ina hoped her hair wasn't sticking out all over the place. "Not even I can be perfect," he repeated softly. "Why would I be perfect?"

"I just meant, you know, you're smart, you have a good job, you look great. Can't get everything right." Why did she spend half her time around this man blushing?

"Thank you," he said, his steady gaze not allowing her to make light of what she'd just confessed. His eyes looked green in the late evening sun. Saeed glanced up and down the street, as if afraid they were being watched. "Let me try to do one more thing right. Can I take you out to dinner?"

Ina's next breath in went to her head. She felt dizzy now that the moment had finally come.

"If you don't think it's appropriate, I apologize," Saeed said, his face already beginning to close.

"No! I'd love to." Ina touched his wrist. He looked at her fingers where they rested against his skin. Confused, she pulled back. Saeed paused, shook his head slightly and reached for her hand. His fingers were long and slender, his palm firm and smooth against hers.

"Where would you like to go?"

Ina finished the last sweet, creamy sip of her Thai iced tea, studying Saeed. He was brilliant, quick to understand the work she described and just as quick to make absurd jokes about it. The combination was all too rare. Mostly, she talked about her research with other postdocs, who were often too exhausted and impoverished to see humor in anything. And many men didn't want to hear about her research at all.

But Saeed was avoiding eye contact. They'd shared an appetizer of steamed vegetarian dumplings, and he'd reacted strangely the few times their hands had brushed in passing.

Now he stared out the window as an uncomfortable silence built between them. "Everything all right?" Ina said, trying to keep her voice light.

He turned his face forward and stretched his hands toward Ina's on the table without actually touching her. "The real reason I tripped," Saeed said abruptly. "I was angry at myself for walking away from you again. You haven't been riding the bus in the mornings. I got on late this evening wondering if I might see you."

She smiled and closed the distance between them. Coaxing his hands open, she stroked the skin of his palm with a fingernail. His eyelids lowered, and she noticed how long, full and dark his eyelashes were. "I wanted you to ask me out that very first day," Ina said.

"I don't... I haven't... My parents think I'm going to let them arrange a marriage for me." Ina's finger froze and Saeed laughed, lifting her hand and kissing it. "Don't worry," he said. "That's not going to happen." His expression grew grave again. "But it does mean it's not a small thing for me to be here with you."

Ina cocked her head at him. "Are you ready to get out of here? I live right around the corner. You could walk me home."

He nodded and went to the counter to pay. Ina felt another adrenaline rush. Tonight, she didn't want to let him leave. She stood and met him at the door of the tiny restaurant. He seemed determined, almost grim, as he opened the door for her and took her hand again.

The walk to her apartment was short, and they didn't speak until they stood outside her building. Ina leaned against him suddenly, as if she'd been pushed. His arms came up around her shoulders and rested there. She pressed her cheek against the buttons of his shirt, inhaling the smoky citrus smell of him. "Do you want to come upstairs?" she whispered.

She felt the shiver that passed through him at her words. Saeed touched Ina's cheek with one hand then cupped her chin. He dipped his face down toward hers and pressed their lips together. Hot spices from dinner ignited a tingling burn across Ina's lips and tongue as she opened her mouth to him. She reached up and buried her hand in his thick, black hair, pulling their bodies closer to each other.

A little moan built in the back of Ina's throat. Saeed let go and stepped back, his breath coming as fast and heavy as hers. In the porch shadows, Ina couldn't read his expression.

She retrieved her keys from her purse and led the way into the building and then her apartment. He reached for her as soon as she shut the door behind them, drowning her nervous apology for the mess against his soft, spicy lips. Ina closed her eyes. She wanted him so badly that her hands trembled.

She untucked his shirt and slid her hands inside. His skin was smooth as his lips, but she felt the hard cords of muscle just underneath. Without breaking the kiss, he unbuttoned the shirt, allowing her to run her hands up his sides and onto his chest.

As soon as his own shirt was loose, he turned to hers, pulling it up over her breasts along with her bra and hugging her tightly so that their skin met. His torso was almost hairless and deliciously warm against hers.

Saeed stroked her back in long, firm passes. He brought his lips to her earlobe and the side of her neck. Ina found the thin trail of hair leading down below the waistband of his pants and rubbed it with her thumbs. He sucked at the base of her neck as she worked her way lower.

Ina unfastened Saeed's pants and reached into his boxers to take hold of his cock. Saeed let out a moan that was almost a sob and gripped her shoulders hard. She stroked her fingernail down his length then teased her way back up to the tip, listening with satisfaction to his long groan. Smiling, she pressed her face into his hair, sliding her lips close to his ear. "I have condoms in my bedroom."

"Ina," he said brokenly. He took a deep breath and tried again, managing her name more steadily the second time. "Ina, do you always go this fast?"

"What do you mean?"

He pulled away from her. Seeing him half-dressed in the dim light coming in through the windows sent another surge of arousal through her body.

"I didn't think you would want it this way."

Ina tore her eyes from his body and looked up at his face. The anguish she saw there surprised her. "What's wrong?"

He looked out the window, tucking his swollen cock back

into his boxers and fastening his pants. Saeed turned his back, and she saw his chest expanding and contracting as he struggled for control of his breathing.

"You think I'm a slut," Ina said. Her eyes stung. She slipped out of her tangled bra and pulled her shirt down.

"No," he said. "But I wasn't expecting to treat you like one." Saeed looked at her over his shoulder, reaching a hand back in her direction. Ina stared at it without moving. He sighed. "I shouldn't have lost control like that."

"Saeed. Why did you come up here?"

"I wanted to touch you."

"Exactly." She stepped closer. "That's what I want, too. That doesn't mean you're treating me like a slut." Ina touched his shoulder and he flinched.

"I've got to go," Saeed said. "I'm sorry."

Ina crossed her arms under her breasts. "Right."

The idea of facing Saeed was too humiliating the next day and the next. Ina chose to walk both to and from the lab, taking the shorter, less appealing route now for efficiency's sake.

Friday evening, it rained in the special New England way that rendered umbrellas completely useless. The wind drove the water droplets against her and tore at her umbrella until she gave up and closed it. Reluctantly, Ina went to take the bus.

Saeed was there at the stop. His eyes opened wider when he saw her, and he seemed about to speak to her. This time, it was Ina who turned away, pretending to study the bus schedule tacked up behind a sheet of clear plastic in the inadequate shelter where they waited.

She jumped when she felt his hand graze her elbow, so lightly it could barely be called a touch. "Ina, can I buy you a coffee when we get to our neighborhood?" His voice was so soft that she could hardly make out the words.

She snapped hard eyes to his. "This didn't go well last time, remember?"

"I didn't mean to hurt you. I at least owe you an explanation," Saeed said.

She swiped furiously at her face as a tear spilled down her cheek. She nodded. "All right."

He avoided the subject of their date earlier that week for the whole ride home and for the whole time they sat in the basement coffee shop. Ina gave up trying to steer the conversation and just let herself enjoy being with him. It all would have been a pleasure if every twinge of physical attraction she felt hadn't brought a fresh sense of rejection on its heels.

He took her to dinner after coffee, and still Saeed seemed in no hurry to make good on his promise of an explanation. As she pushed away her dessert plate, Ina drilled her gaze into his. "Thanks for all this, but I'm not going with you for after-dinner drinks or dancing or whatever until we talk about the other night."

Saeed ducked his head in acknowledgment. "Why don't you walk me home, and we can talk about it at my apartment?"

"Are you serious? You wouldn't be ashamed to have a slut like me at your home?" Ina hadn't realized how angry she was until she heard the bitterness of her words.

He grimaced. "Please. I never intended—" He gave a brief shake of his head. "Please."

"I'm sorry. That wasn't fair."

He shrugged, pushed back from the table and stood. She took the hand he offered, shivering at the grace with which he guided her to her feet.

Saeed lived just a few blocks away from her but on a much

nicer street. While Ina's neighborhood was full of mouse-infested, cheap, student apartments, Saeed had an apartment on the top floor of someone's real home. Flowerpots lined the porch, and the name QASIM was painted on the mailbox.

"I rent from relatives," he explained, leading her up the stairs to his private entrance. The small apartment was overstuffed but neat, the bookshelves crammed and the walls covered with photographs and decorations. "I've never had a woman in here before," Saeed said.

"Usually, you do it at her place." Ina felt a pang of guilt when she saw the hurt that flashed across his face. She pressed her hand to her eyes. "I'm really sorry. I shouldn't—"

He sighed and flung himself into a red armchair in the center of the living room. After a pause, Ina took a seat on the couch across from him.

"Ina, I've never dated in the American way."

She stared at him, studying his handsome features for any sign of a joke. "You don't mean you're a virgin?"

He shook his head sharply. "No, in college I would hook up with girls sometimes. It was never anyone I'd have wanted to be seen with the next day."

"So what do you mean when you say you've never dated?"

"The way I was raised, it would be scandalous for us to be sitting in my living room alone together." He smiled. "I'll hear about it tomorrow from my cousin downstairs. According to my parents, I shouldn't have been out to dinner with you, I shouldn't have asked you to share that cab with me." Saeed swallowed. "I certainly shouldn't have touched you the way I did that first day. Yes, I've slept with women I didn't care about as part of my adolescent rebellion, but this thing with you is different. Or I want it to be, anyway."

Ina rose and stood next to his chair. After a moment, he

wound one arm around her waist and pulled her down to sit on the armrest. "Saeed, I don't want to be your secret or your mistake. And I don't want to feel like you disapprove of me for wanting to be with you."

He closed his eyes and pressed his face against her stomach. "I'm glad you want to be with me."

She stroked her hand through his hair. "What happened last time?"

He exhaled. "I wanted you so badly that I couldn't think straight. I didn't know what to do."

"What about now?" Ina whispered.

"I've thought about it. A lot. I still want you that way. But I also want you to be my girlfriend. Does that sound ridiculous? I could see myself telling my family about you."

"It doesn't sound ridiculous."

Saeed stood, bringing her up with him. "I believe I should choose what parts of my tradition to follow, but I did grow up a certain way. My family thinks I'm too American, and Americans always think I'm too Saudi. What about you?"

"I think you're wearing too many clothes," Ina said, wanting to test him.

Saeed's face turned serious, and she worried that he would cut their night short again. After a long moment, a slow burn of a smile spread across his face. "You're probably right." He reached to unbutton his shirt.

Ina grinned and stepped closer, brushing his hands aside. She stripped off his shirt, running fingertips and fingernails over his chest and following her hands with her lips. Saeed pulled her head up to meet one kiss then another, his tongue gentle but insistent against hers.

They were both breathless when they broke apart. He stroked down the side of her neck and across her collarbone then cupped her breast. Ina pulled off her shirt and bra. Saeed dropped to his knees and kissed and nibbled across her stomach as he teased her nipple with his fingers. She swayed a little, feeling the powerful desire that pooled between her legs.

When he reached for the button of her jeans, Ina stopped him with a hand on his wrist. "Are you sure about this, Saeed? I don't know if I'll be able to get over it if you reject me again."

He pulled her onto the floor with him, wrapping her in the exact sort of embrace she'd wanted on the day she'd met him. She breathed against him, enjoying the warmth of his body and the hard heat of his cock as it pressed against her stomach through his pants. When he moved again to take off her jeans and underwear, she let him.

"What we did the other night meant that much to you?" he said.

Ina sighed and gripped his face so that he looked into her eyes. "What are you worried about? You think this might just be a hookup to me?"

"I wouldn't want you to take advantage of me." Beneath the surface of his humor, she saw the flash of real insecurity that crossed his face. He looked younger to her now, so uncertain compared to the confident and unapproachably handsome professional man on the bus.

She stroked the side of his face, loving the sight of his big, warm eyes and the tiny curls of dark hair above his ears. "Dating is weird," Ina said. "It's just a decision. It's something more than sex because we say it is."

Saeed ran his hand down the length of her body. "No," he said. "To me, it could never be just sex with you, no matter what I decided." His fingers trailed over her thighs, found their way to her cunt and dipped inside. Ina let out a loud moan, gripping his arm.

Saeed stiffened, and Ina shook her head to clear it. "God, I'm sorry," she said. "Do we need to be quiet?"

He looked at her for a long time, his face hard to read. Then he grinned and pulled her closer. "Let them hear it."

He rolled onto her. Ina wound her legs around his waist, bucking her hips up against his erection. They both fumbled to open his pants, getting in each other's way with playful, desperate fingers. Ina peeled off his pants and underwear as soon as she could, throwing them across the room. "Do you have a condom?" she panted.

"In my pants pocket."

She groaned. Saeed kissed her and went to retrieve his clothes. He came back wearing the condom and knelt between her legs. "Is it too fast?"

"Feel how wet I am."

He settled into her arms and pushed into her. Ina arched her back at the sharp sensation of his cock pressing in deep. They were both still a moment. Even through the condom, she could feel his pulse pounding through his cock. "I'm really inside you," he said, trailing off into a groan as she angled her hips and tightened around him.

Ina moved under him, curling her pelvis up and down, pressing her clit against his pubic bone and dragging his cock against her inner walls. At first, he held himself up on his elbows and just watched her face. She tried to keep her eyes open and focus on his face above hers. The citrus smell of him grew stronger as their bodies heated together.

Then Ina's movements grew sharper and Saeed began to move, driving slow and deep into her body. She let his rhythm take over, pressing her hips up and spreading her legs wider. She couldn't stay quiet anymore, her voice rising in little sounds that became pleas and then cries.

Instead of centering on her clit, this orgasm bubbled up slowly from deep in her womb. She grabbed his shoulder blades and thrust up against him, whimpering. Every inch of him felt excruciating to her as her body softened more and more around his hard length. Saeed murmured something not in English and thrust hard. Ina breathed in as the pleasure struck her brain with shattering clarity. "Please, please, please," she gasped incoherently, her voice all breath now.

Saeed whispered her name and slipped his hands under her body, lifting her to meet his thrusts. He moved faster, every stroke drawing out the orgasm until it seemed to go on forever. When it finally passed, the excruciating sensations remained, and Ina continued to press desperately against him.

His whispers grew loud and hoarse. She clawed at him, pulling him deeper into her as her hips moved frantically to match his pace. He seemed to grow inside her. Saeed put his lips right up against her ear, letting her hear the catch in his throat and set of soft moans that accompanied his pleasure. Ina threw her head back as Saeed's increasing excitement made her come again. He joined her in orgasm.

After they caught their breath, she wrapped one arm around the back of his head, pressing her forehead against his. "Everything all right?" Ina said. "No regrets?"

"I should have taken you to my bed," he said with a rueful smile. "I think I tore my knees open on the rug."

"Next time."

"Next time," he agreed. He lifted his weight off her, gazing at her face in a way that made her heart pound. "Seriously, Ina, I'm glad. If you had never fallen on me on the bus..."

"You're an easy guy to fall on," Ina grinned, lifting herself up on one elbow.

Saeed snorted, touching her lightly to acknowledge the joke.

His hand lingered and then wandered to her breasts.

"Looks like next time might be very soon," Ina said.

"Mmm, seems likely," Saeed said, drawing her into his arms.

LINGUA FRANCA

Justine Elyot

This one is sweet. This one is medium. This one is dry. Yes? Repeat for me, please?"

"Is sweet. Is m..." He hesitates over the pronunciation, and it comes out as "meddiom."

"Medium."

"Meeeeeedium."

I cock my head at him, wondering if he is teasing, or genuinely struggling. But then I do a lot of wondering about Karel. And not all of it concerns his accent.

"That's it," I say, wishing I could sound less patronizing. His eyes are stormy; I think he truly hates me. And I really don't want to be the overbearing boss woman. I hate this role. He is older than I am, and I think he has all kinds of Polish qualifications, and it makes me incredibly uncomfortable to run through all this obvious ABC stuff with him. But I'm the bar manager. I have to do it. So I'm doing it. "And the last one?"

"Dry," he says, with a flourishing rolled *r*, tossing his head and smiling insincerely. Even his insincere smile is stunning—I can only imagine how world-illuminatingly gorgeous his sincere one must be. It would be nice to see it sometime.

"Okay, and can you run me through the mixers?"

"Gin, vodka, white rum, dark rum..." He reels them off like a catechism, and when he reaches the end I want to stick a gold star on his shirt or clap or say, "Good boy," but I know he would probably murder me, so I just smile tightly and say, "Right. Well, I've some accounts to do and the bar opens in ten minutes, so I'll leave you to it, Karel. See you later."

He says nothing, bending down to retrieve some glasses from the washer, but I catch a brief "Bye," on my exit.

It is Karel's fifth Saturday as a barman at the West Cliff Grand, and I'm no closer to knowing anything about him than I was on his first. I know that he is a man. I know that he is Polish. I know that he has the angriest, most beautiful face I have ever seen in my life. And that is all I know. Once more, the columns of pounds and pence swim before my eyes as I ask myself where he lives, what he likes, who he loves and whether he will ever say anything polysyllabic to me.

Every day (except Tuesday) we edge past each other, at the pumps or the optics or the glass washer, avoiding eyes and speaking a language that is reduced to its base elements: yes, no, right, okay, what, where, why. If I try to correct him, his eyes flash hot sparks of rage; if I compliment him, the rage is more intense still. If I try to talk to him, properly, as I have at the end of a few shifts, he checks his watch and says, "Must go, have meeting."

Tempting as it is to leave him to solo bar duties this afternoon, I know there is a big wedding reception booked, and I would be derelict in my duty. Reluctantly I shut up my ledgers, stow them in the filing cabinet and head, slow-footed and full of familiar dread, to the bar.

There is tension in every single move he makes: in the washing of a glass, the jabbing of the till buttons, the scooping up of ice. It is disquieting but riveting, and, while the bar lazes in the early part of the afternoon, I find it difficult to keep my eyes off him. I want to know him. Actually, I *want* him. I wince at the stray thought and try to bat it away, but it is stubborn. For one despairing second, I consider resigning and looking for work in another hotel, just to wean myself off this weird addiction. It is like a lesion on my skin, growing there, needing lasers to remove it and cure me.

Soon enough, the wedding guests begin to drift in—an advance party of beefy young men requiring lagers, followed by their fathers and uncles splashing out on the spirits. Swaths of vivid color among the morning-suit grays and blacks denote the presence of women, sipping at wines or cocktails with cherries.

"Oh, no, I think a Liebfraumilch might be too sweet," an elderly lady in a feathered turban is telling Karel, to his expressionless disgust. "But that other one is certainly too dry. Perhaps a sherry. Do you have Harvey's Bristol Cream?"

"Yayss," says Karel. I love his accent. I want him to talk to me. I want him to tell me about his homeland while we walk along the beach at sunset, hand in hand... Yeah, get real, Maggie. There's a whole mob of customers at the bar, and I'm completely ignoring them in favor of swooning over a man who hates me. I need to snap out of it.

I snap out of it for well over an hour, serving the postprandial bride and groom and guests until the majority of them disappear next door for the first dance and beginnings of the disco. I nod at Karel to take his break, then, thirty minutes later, I take mine on the terrace, smoking a much-needed cigarette and looking out to the darkening sea.

Back in the bar, only a few of the more hardened soaks are

lounging at the tables. As I walk through the door, I notice one of them take a pack of cigarettes and lighter from his pocket and move to spark up in the room.

"Excuse me," says Karel, in the middle of wiping a glass. "Is forbidden smoking inside."

"You what, mate?" The tone is belligerent. I bristle. This sounds like trouble. "D'you speak English? What did he say?"

The man's friends all pitch in. "Dunno. Some foreign gobble-dygook. Can you say that in English, mate?"

This is a periodic difficulty at the hotel. Somebody, usually somebody very drunk, will want to start a fight with Karel on the basis that he is Polish. Karel has handled it well up until now, but he has never faced a whole table full of these lowlifes before.

"There's a smoking area outside," I tell them, walking over to the table in an effort to place myself between it and the bar.

"Thanks, love, but we're talking to Count Dracula here." There is ribald laughter. "Come on then? You got a problem with us? You got something to say? Say it in English, boy!"

"You don't smoke in here," says Karel, his chin defiantly set. "I think is stupid—I like to smoke, too. But is forbidden." He shrugs and glares at me, as if telling me to get out of his fight.

"If you don't like our laws, boy, you can go back home." The smoker is on his feet now. No amount of ingratiating, or rationalizing or sympathizing is going to deflect him from his one avowed purpose tonight. His face is an ugly purple, and he has ripped off his tie and picked up a glass, holding it high in one hand.

"Get out! You're barred!" I cry in a hopeless attempt to preempt the next move, but there is a huge splintering of glass and then the smoker has vaulted over the table, brandishing his jagged weapon at Karel.

"Come on then! D'you want some? Show us how you fight over there."

"You really want to know?" Karel's sneer is so frightening that it would make a Roman Legion turn tail—a sober Roman Legion, that is, not one that had drunk enough to fell an ox, like these boys. No matter how much rage and loathing might be boiling in Karel's soul, he is one man against seven, and I cannot see a way out for him.

I leap for the aggressor's wrist, trying to get the broken glass from him, but he throws me off with such force that I knock my head against the bar and see stars. All the same, I rise again, determined to come to Karel's aid. Through my daze, I see that the glass has ripped his shirt and superficially cut his chest, but he is leaping over the bar, fifty suns' worth of gleam in his eyes, feet first, fists flying, and I hurl myself into the middle of it and then...I don't know.

"Stupid," is the first word I hear on returning to consciousness. I recognize the accent and thank God, or whoever else might be responsible, that Karel must still be alive. "Stupid girl."

"You can't talk to me like that. I'm your boss," I say weakly. I wince at a sudden sting on my forearm—it is witch hazel, applied by Karel, whose slowly focusing face bears down on me, looking as pissed off as ever and twice as sexy. "Where are we? Are you okay?"

"I'm okay. But you. Are you crazy?"

Crazy for you.

"Yeah. I think I am."

"I think you are. You are lucky." He is stern, not letting me draw my arm away from his flinch-inducing attentions. "This mans—they want to kill me."

"They didn't though."

"No."

I try to lift my head, peering around. We are somewhere unfamiliar, with peeling wallpaper and a jumble of bunk beds squeezed in any old how.

"Is this...what is this place?"

"I live here. You like?"

"It's not...the West Cliff Grand. Is it?"

He laughs, and it is half a real laugh. Real progress there.

"We are not in Kansas, Toto," he misquotes, seeming to relish his ability to say the line. "No, this is not the West Cliff Grand."

"How did I get here?"

"I bring you." He mimes the action of hefting a sack of flour. Not a flattering gesture, but I still strongly regret being unconscious for that particular experience.

"Then...what happened? In the bar?"

"I don't know. Perhaps they are still there. I call Security and I go, with you. They are fighting so much they don't even see." He chuckles and puts a palm over my forehead, sucking in a breath when he feels the egg-sized bump.

"Oh, my god. You just left...with me?"

"I should stay and be killed? You think?"

"I...no. I guess not."

"For myself, I don't care. They can kill me if they like. But for you...is not right. You do nothing wrong. Instead...no, except...yes, except stand in front of me. Why do you do that? So dangerous!"

"I didn't want to see you hurt."

He sits back on his heels and frowns at me, as if trying to work out if I am joking.

"I mean it! God, Karel, not everyone is a miserable bastard like you!"

His eyes widen and he stares for a few seconds before breaking into—yes!— a genuine smile. It's a little bit roguish, a little bit devilish, but it's definitely genuine.

"You try to help me because you are good person? Eh? Maggie?"

Oh, *no*. He is onto me. He knows I fancy him. And I'm sure my face is giving me away, a big fat tomato on top of my neck.

"Yes, I bloody am," I huff, trying to throw him off the scent. "I'm a good person."

"You would do the same for any man? Like the man with the glass?"

"No, not him. Because he was a violent lunatic."

"And what if I am a violent lunatic?"

"You're...not. Are you?"

"I think you're a good person, Maggie. I think you...I think I like you."

"You don't like anyone!"

"I like people who tell me the truth. Who aren't afraid. Of me, or of a man with a broken glass. I like that." One finger, slightly skinned, comes to rest beneath my earlobe, stroking it slowly. He puts his face close to mine. I can smell blood and maleness and cigarette smoke. It's a strangely intoxicating combination. "You," he whispers, his hot breath inside me, travelling along my ear canal, wrecking my chemistry for all time, "need to go to a hospital."

The Saturday night wait at Accident and Emergency is long enough for Karel to tell me his entire life story, from a boyhood spent playing in the shipyards of Gdansk at the height of martial law, to an escape to university in the post–Cold War era, to a succession of ill-paid jobs and unsuitable, crumbling apartments.

"It was the only choice. England," he says, cradling my head against his shoulder, stroking back my hair over my throbbing bump.

"You resent it, don't you?"

"I suppose. I should go to classes—but I feel like..." He shrugs, unable to find the words. "I am too..."

"Stubborn."

"What is stubborn?"

"It's what you are. And bloody-minded. And wasting your time brooding when you could be enjoying life."

He seems to take this in, or at least the last part of it; the eyes with which he fixes me are troubled.

"I should enjoy my life," he says slowly. "Yayss. Is so simple?"

Sent away from the hospital with a clear bill of health and some handy painkillers, I am suddenly too shy to make a next move. I should just get a taxi home, shouldn't I? I should call the hotel and explain my absence. I should...

"Come with me!" says Karel, and he takes my hand, leads me at a swift march across the road and onto the pine-scented Common that lines the top of the cliffs, breaking into a run as our feet hit the grass, pulling me along behind him, laughing and shouting, "Run, Maggie, let's run!"

It is late now, very late, and the Common is empty; pinecones are shattered beneath my staggering feet, and then beyond the edge of the land I can see the sea, dark midnight blue with glints of reflected moon. The funicular has closed for the night, but Karel finds the zigzagging path that descends to the beach and drags me down it after him until, breathless and giggling, we collapse into a shelter on the seafront, falling into a kiss that makes the earlier stars from my head bump seem tiny and insignificant.

The fit of his face against mine is perfect; I have to grab him round the head, plunge my fingers into his tumble of hair, pull him closer, closer, into me. He has bundled me onto his lap and

I lean back against the safety bar of his arm, letting him bend me back ever farther until I feel devoured, consumed, an extension of him. His evening stubble scrapes me raw, but I just don't care, wanting our mouths to fuse, our skins to meld, the passion that pours in from him and out from me to take permanent root in us.

I never thought those laser-keen brown eyes would be looking at me with anything but animosity; to see them glazed with desire, the pupils enormously dilated, is almost strange enough to make me shiver. I think my body is already performing that response for me, though, quite without explicit prompting, and my heart is bumping against his in a call and response pattern, our pulses synchronized. The blood rushes through me so that I cannot tell if the roar in my ears comes from my own veins or the tide washing up on the sand a hundred yards distant.

I am no longer Maggie—I am the kiss, I am the sensation, I am longing and lust and need and something that might be love. As long as he is close to me, the whole world can fade to black.

His tongue pushes at mine, and it becomes a competition, a race to prove who is the most ardent, which neither of us can win. He concedes this, breaking lips for a moment, but only so he can hold my face still between his palms and drop kisses all over my forehead, my cheeks, my ears, my nose, even my eyelids, slowly and with a reverence I have never seen before from any lover, let alone this proud, ferocious man. I want to return the gesture, because I feel that I could kiss his face all night and every night forever, but he stops me, looking seriously into me, his hands still locked beneath my ears, thumbs on cheeks.

"I am your man," he says solemnly, as if reciting a vow. "You are my woman. Is right?"

"Is...right," I echo, almost expecting him to produce a gold band from somewhere, and then, to my stunned surprise, he does something very similar. From an inside pocket, he takes a chain with a pendant depicting a white eagle and he places it around my neck.

"You are welcome in my country," he says. Does he want me to move to Poland with him? I start slightly, registering alarm. "No, don't worry!" He smiles and rolls his eyes upward, in self-reproof. "We stay here. But you are...I can't explain."

He looks angry again, but angry with himself, for his lack of language skills.

"An honorary Pole?" I hazard.

"What is honorary?"

"Oh, god, I can't really explain either. Like a Pole?"

"Yes. You are brave, like Polish. So I give you this. And also because I want you."

Simple as his way of putting things was, it stirred me deeply. It came down to that and only that. Wanting. Wanting a person for your own, wanting everything good to come to them, wanting to help everything good come to them.

"I want you, too," I tell him, and I put the eagle pendant to my lips and kiss it. He seems intensely moved by this and ducks in to kiss me once more, lingeringly, gently.

"We have said everything," he says. "I don't want to talk now. I want to...do."

"To act?"

"To do. To you." His smile curls upward into breathtaking roguery. I know exactly what he means. He can say it all with that expressive face.

"Here?" I look around. It is getting cold.

"You have keys to the bar."

"The bar!"

It only takes a few more kisses to persuade me.

The night porter is reluctant to admit us at first, but he gives up quibbling in the face of Karel's fierce look, and we find our workplace much as we left it: glass on the carpet, half-drunk spirits, a cigarette butt in one of the tumblers.

"I wonder if Security threw them out?" For some reason I whisper, as if I don't want to be caught in here.

He shrugs. "They are not important."

Instantly I am caught up in his embrace once more, my legs held up by his in case they give way, which is not unlikely. He walks me backward, painstakingly, until I fall onto one of the red plush sofas, and then he is looming over me, one hand next to my head, preventing my escape, and the other takes hold of my white uniform blouse and rips it open. A pearl button pings onto a nearby table and I gasp, part thrilled and part outraged. "Karel!"

"I sew it," he grins, then his head is down there, his hair brushing my throat while he explores my cleavage with the full force of his lips and tongue. His hand works busily at my other buttons, undoing them in a less destructive way, until my lace bra is exposed to him, and his stubble prickles downward, seeking out the overspill of my breasts.

He lures my nipples out of the cups using the tip of his tongue, licking and sucking, taking his time, savoring the flavor. I plant my fingers in his hair, which is reddish-brown and falls over his brow, plentiful and sometimes a little lank. I stroke and knead automatically, my wits absent, all of me concentrated at my nerve endings, especially those between my legs.

He seems to understand instinctively that attention is needed there. He lays me down along the length of the sofa, pulling off my skirt and burying his face in my belly while his fingers stray down beyond the elastic waistband of my knickers. They almost dance, they are so light and nimble. I arch my back and squirm, inviting him to increase the pressure and move on downward,

but he loves to tease me and watch my expression as it grows
more frantic with need, laughing softly, looking up at me through
the valley of my breasts.

"Touch me," I gasp.

"No talk," he admonishes, almost but not quite delving into
the folds of my vulva. The fingertips are barely there on my outer
lips, and I try to buck so that he is tricked into the fast-flowing
juices, but he is wise to me and simply gives my thigh a light slap,
laughing again, a laughing demon. "Okay," he says eventually,
relenting, and I ease out a low sigh at the sudden invasion of his
fingers, properly in and on and around me, pressing and pushing,
finding me more than ready for whatever he has in mind. While
his fingers work, he watches me intently, catching every nuance
of my response to him, every pained twitch, every flutter of my
eyelids. "I see what you like," he tells me, now using two fingers
to skewer me, in and out, getting coated with the evidence of my
arousal. "I like it, too. You want me? Inside?"

It seems a redundant question, given the rate at which I am
flipping about on his fingers, but I am glad that he has asked it.
He is not—as I vaguely feared—using me for some kind of sexual
revenge. My pleasure matters to him just as his does to me.

"Excuse me," he says, and I sit bolt upright, watching him
disappear to the Gents'. Oh! The condom machine!

I put a hand to my mouth, quashing a hysterical giggle. This,
I remind myself, is reality and not a fairy tale. Reality is full
of these passion-dampening moments, but it does not make the
passion any less intense. I have never wanted anyone as much
as I want Karel tonight (and, if I'm honest, for a lot longer than
tonight), and I want to hold that feeling close, living out every
laden second of it.

"Take your clothes off!" He returns to the bar with a strange
swaggering gait caused, I notice to my satisfaction, by the

straining bulge at the crotch of his black work trousers.

"What if I don't?" I flirt, shimmying out of my unbuttoned blouse all the same.

"You will," he says, throwing off his torn waistcoat and getting to work on his shirt cuffs. His face is dark with purpose and he looks magnificent, stripping down to his taut, hard body, kicking off the shiny shoes, snapping the belt through its loops, his eyes on me. I am down to knickers and bra, the red plush feeling stiff and a little scratchy against my skin. I know there will be friction, but I don't care. I just want that sexy beast right there, right on me, right now.

He skins on the condom and sits down, erection pointing to the ceiling, grabs one of my ankles and tugs at it. "Here," he says gruffly. I scramble to my knees and he pulls me by the elbow until I'm straddling him, my arms around his neck, locked into a kiss again.

"You are still dressed," he grumbles, setting my lips free, but he improvises well, pulling my knickers aside and guiding me onto the wide tip of his cock. I lower myself slowly, feeling every inch as it travels up inside me, joining me to him and him to me. Here we are now, one being, connected at the pelvis, filling each other, giving to each other, taking from each other. And so we cross the frontier, becoming real lovers, sexual partners, a couple. Karel holds me by the hips, controlling my pace, keeping it slow and sensual. He bends down to tease my nipples with his tongue, or he sucks hard at my neck, hard enough to mark it, or he moves his hands around to cup my bottom, squeezing it hard, moving me a little faster now. I love to hear the throaty sounds he makes, the little gasps of joy or growls of lust. He is a very expressive lover; I think if he knew more English he would be talking dirty to me, but for now he contents himself with grunts and squeezes and a few light slaps to my behind while his tongue finds the places that melt me with unerring skill.

He is urging me on now, and it is hard work. I have to use all the strength of my upper thighs and abdomen to keep up the pace, but it is worth it. The friction sparks hotter and hotter sensations; his eyes are great gaping black pupils of lustful distress as his grip on self-control begins to slip. He shudders and shivers beneath my energetic assault. I dip my head and suckle his neck, feeling my climax approach, and he begins to make broken, helpless noises in his throat, and then I am there, and he is there, and we are there together, one explosion of fire-cracker heat, melting through us, burning us into one.

The man who was closed is open now. I am grateful as well as blissful when I lay my head against his sweating shoulder. We hold each other until we stop trembling and our hearts begin to slow; his lips are against my hair, mine down in the delicious flesh of his swanlike neck.

"You think we have job tomorrow?" he asks idly.

"Maybe. Maybe not. But it's summer. There are jobs like this everywhere. At the fairground, on the pier, at the kiosks, in the shops. We'll be okay."

"I know we will. We will be okay. We will take care of...you and me."

"Each other," I correct. "And I'm teaching you better English. Who knows, it could get you out of these dead-end jobs."

He smiles broadly. "Which am I?" he asks. "Sweet, medium or dry?"

I laugh. "None of those. I think you're a Polish spirit, served icy cold but able to set you on fire inside."

He nods. "I like."

We kiss again, amidst the glass splinters, which are starting to sparkle in the rising sun.

THIRD TIME'S THE CHARM

Charlene Teglia

When the elevator came to a halt and the lights went out, Lynn Taylor gritted her teeth and said, "This is going too far, don't you think?"

The elevator's only other occupant snorted in the darkness. "Are you blaming me for this? Did I cause the latest stock market crash, too? Maybe this is your fault. Maybe you set this up because you want me back."

"I want you back like I want a dozen donuts. It sounds like a good idea and the initial rush is fantastic, but then I'd be left with that sick feeling and the realization that I should have had a V-8." Lynn blew out her breath and then said, "Okay, it's not your fault. It's not my fault. It's bad luck and poor building maintenance. Our only fault here is in not moving out of these apartments fast enough."

She groped forward, arms outstretched, until she found the control panel. She started hitting buttons at random in the vain hope that one of them would do something.

"Good, try to get the emergency phone," Nick said. "It should be below the buttons."

Right. I knew that, Lynn thought. She felt her way down and located the box with the phone and pulled it free. Then she swore. "No dial tone."

"No problem," he said in the calm, commanding tone of voice he was probably used to using in emergencies. "Don't panic. Do you have your cell phone with you?"

Lynn pictured her cell phone, tucked inside her briefcase, sitting on her kitchen counter. It might as well have been on Pluto. "No."

"No? Christ, Lynn, when are you going to start being more careful? I bought that for you so you wouldn't ever be stuck in a situation like this and couldn't get help."

She felt her face stretch into an evil smile. "Well, where's your cell phone, Mr. Prepared?"

"I dropped it yesterday. I was going to pick up a replacement on my way home from work and decided to stop off at the apartment first." She heard him move in the darkness and then felt his hands close over her shoulders. "Sorry. I shouldn't have said that. It's not my job to keep you safe anymore, is it?"

"It was never your job." She shouldn't have let him pull her back to rest against his chest, shouldn't have relaxed into him when he did. But old habits died hard, and Nick Logan was a very hard habit to kick. She'd tried twice during their on-again, off-again relationship over the last year and hadn't really succeeded yet.

Lynn thought about the first time she'd seen him, holding the elevator for her a few weeks after she'd moved into this building, with his short dark hair and warm brown eyes, smiling that smile she could never resist, his muscular body solid and inviting. His personality had seemed to fill the space, and she'd been drawn forward, into the elevator, into conversation and within a week, into his bedroom.

She should have taken up smoking instead. There were programs proven to break people of that habit. There was no Quit Nick Logan solution.

"You okay?" His voice was low, his mouth far too close to her ear.

"Fine." The word sounded strained, which probably told Nick entirely too much.

"You can blame me if it makes you feel better." His hands stroked gently along her arms, and Lynn knew he wasn't talking about being stuck in the elevator.

"That would be unfair. It's not your fault. It's not anybody's fault, we just want different things."

"Maybe not so different." He kissed the side of her neck, and Lynn shivered while a familiar weakness stole over her. "I want you. You still want me. That's something."

"Yes, but we can't spend our lives in bed. Sooner or later we have to deal with reality."

"Reality is overrated. And we could try." Nick's hands moved very slowly up her arms again and down over her breasts, giving her plenty of time to anticipate his touch and move away if she didn't want it.

Unfortunately, she did want it. His palms warm and sure against her nipples made her close her eyes in pleasure. But it didn't change anything. "We're too different."

"Different can be good. My parts go out, yours go in."

His "out" part was hard and distinct against her butt and Lynn couldn't help smiling. His hands moved over her breasts again, slow, gentle, warm and so familiar. So right. Why was it that every other man on the planet felt wrong in comparison?

Nobody else smiled like Nick, or made her coffee the right way, or knew how to make her laugh or just felt right being there next to her.

Yes, and nobody else can piss you off like Nick, either, Lynn reminded herself.

"I think we should try again," Nick said, and Lynn straightened up in shock.

"You have to be kidding me."

"I'm dead serious. I know where I went wrong. I'm overprotective. I leave the seat up."

Lynn snorted. "Try again."

"All right, how's this: I shut you out. My hours are crazy, my job sucks, I see terrible things and I come home and I see you and I want to keep you out of it. I don't want you to see the things I see or know about them. I want you safe and happy and so I shut you out, and I hurt you doing it. And I make you nuts being overprotective because I can't stand the thought that someday I might get a call and find out that the victim is you."

Lynn felt her jaw drop.

"I'm sorry, Lynn." The sincerity in his voice was unmistakable, his tone raw. "I know that dating a cop is the pits. I know that if you're crazy enough to marry me, the chances of making it work are terrible because the job puts a hell of a strain on relationships and the divorce rates are astronomical."

"If you're proposing, the romance is lacking," Lynn said. But she didn't move away from him. She turned in his arms and pressed her cheek against his chest, needing to be closer.

"I miss you. I need you. I know I pushed you away and it's my fault you walked, but I want another chance, Lynn. Third time's the charm. This time I intend to get it right."

She closed her eyes and let the sound of his voice, the rhythm of his heartbeat, the clean masculine scent of him and the familiar shape and feel of his body against hers fill her senses. "I miss you, too," she admitted.

He slid a hand under her chin and lifted it to meet his kiss. His mouth moved over hers, warm, tempting, seducing her into opening her mouth for his tongue. When she did, the kiss escalated from temptation to devastation. He devoured her lips, his hands hard and hot on her body as they sank together to the elevator floor.

It had been too damn long. Lynn shuddered with want and tugged at his shirt, got it loose and ran her hands under it, hungry for the feel of his bare skin. He pulled her shirt up and broke the kiss long enough to pull it over her head, rolled with her so that she was lying on her back and grazed the curve of her breast with his teeth.

She buried her fingers in his hair and moved restlessly underneath him, until he planted one knee between her legs and pressed into her. She felt swollen with need, aching for his touch to relieve the pressure.

"You feel so good." His hands moved over her, rubbing her nipples, cupping her breasts, sliding down her rib cage and her belly before hooking into the waistband of her pants. Nick lifted her up just enough to pull her pants and panties down her hips and then all the way to her ankles.

Then his hand was between her legs, cupping her mound, moving over her and Lynn made a low sound of frustration, rocking her hips into his hand in an effort to guide him where she wanted him to go.

"Is this what you need?" His voice was a dark whisper.

He parted her folds and drove two fingers into her and Lynn let out a moan. "*Yes.*"

Nick touching her, penetrating her, looming over her in the dark was enough to make her dizzy with need, frantic with heat.

His thumb rubbed over her clit and then his mouth replaced it, drawing on the sensitive nub of flesh while his fingers moved inside her, and Lynn came with a liquid rush.

"My turn." She heard his zipper lower and the fabric rustle as he worked his pants down far enough to free his cock. He stretched out beside her and tugged her on top of him. "Floor's hard. Don't want to hurt you."

"Overprotective," she said, but without heat as she spread her legs and let her knees rest on either side of his hips. Her breasts pushed into his chest, the thin fabric of her bra the only barrier between them with his shirt pulled up out of the way. His cock nudged her opening, thick and hard where she was slick and soft.

"Take me inside you, Lynn." His voice was low and rough with desire, and Lynn knew he was asking for more than sex. Now was the time to turn back if she couldn't give him the chance he wanted.

She thought about what it would mean if it was really, truly, finally over between them. No more falling into bed with him, no more waking up with him. No more Nick hard and hot inside her. No more arguments or making up. No more catching his eye and sharing a silent joke that nobody else was in on. The thought of no more Nick in her life made her cold inside, and she knew it was hopeless.

"I should have taken up smoking," she told him. Then she lifted her hips and lowered herself onto his cock, impaling her pussy, feeling him slide into her inch by inch until he filled her.

"Bad for you," he said, closing his hands over her hips and holding her still as they both took a minute to adjust. "Those things will take years off your life."

"So will you." Lynn tightened her inner muscles around his cock and laughed when he groaned.

"I think that's mutual. You're killing me." He lifted her hips slightly and thrust up into her, hard and fast and deep. "I can't go slow, Lynn."

"I don't want slow." She rocked into his thrusts, meeting him, taking him deeper, wanting him as deep inside her as he could go, and she felt the beginnings of another orgasm building.

The tension spiraled with each thrust, and she moved harder against him, wanting more pressure, and he gave it to her. She felt his cock throb and knew he was as close as she was.

The next thrust sent her off, her muscles tightening convulsively around his cock, and she came again. She felt him spurting inside her, a jet of liquid heat that heightened her pleasure and drew the orgasm out.

She collapsed on him, panting, and felt him holding her close, his lips moving over her hair, his cock still buried deep inside her.

"I love you, Lynn."

"I love you, too." She kissed his chest and cuddled into him, feeling at peace for the first time in six long, painful weeks.

"Do me a favor," he said, stroking her back. "The next time I piss you off, don't stay away so long. I had to pull a lot of strings to arrange this."

She lifted her head and stared at him, even though she knew it was useless and she couldn't see him in the dark. "You did set this up."

"You wouldn't talk to me." His hands cupped the bare curve of her ass and squeezed. "I knew you might not forgive me, you might not want to try again. I knew it might really be over. But I had to know for sure, and I couldn't think of another way to find out."

"You could have sent flowers."

"I did. You left them on my doorstep."

That was true. He'd tried repeatedly to talk to her, on the phone, in person, passing her in the hall, and she hadn't given him an opportunity. She'd been afraid that if she listened to him, she'd be drawn back into the same cycle of kissing and making up while the larger problem between them lay unresolved until the next argument brought it back to the surface.

This time was different, however. This time, the real problem that drove them apart was out in the open and acknowledged. Nick had finally opened up to her, and she knew he hadn't done that lightly.

He would still work late and miss dates, and she'd still sit up worrying until she heard from him. She didn't kid herself that it would be easy, but she knew to the depths of her soul it was worth the effort. She couldn't cut him out of her life any more than she could cut him out of her heart.

Lynn shifted on top of him and let her hands follow the line of his shoulders, luxuriating in the feel of his skin under her hands and his cock still hard inside her. "Just out of curiosity, since you arranged this private moment, how much time do we have before we're 'rescued?'"

"Long enough for you to go for thirds." Nick's mouth captured hers again, and he rocked his hips into hers in a sensual promise.

"Mmm. Good," she sighed against his lips. "I hear the third time's the charm."

RIDING WILD THINGS

Lizzy Chambers

The smell of fresh-churned dirt, stock and horses filled her nostrils as she took a final breath. Then Leigh nudged Blaire gently in the ribs, leaned forward and braced herself as the horse took off, through the chute and into the arena. Music blared and the fans screamed, but all Leigh saw was the first barrel jutting out of the ground ahead of her. Every muscle in her body was tight and controlled. Every move she made was executed perfectly to guide Blaire, and they rounded that first barrel with time to spare before heading to the second.

It was the fifth round of the National Finals Rodeo, and Leigh had every intention of moving on. She'd been working toward this for years, since she was fifteen years old and dreaming about it since she was ten, when she saw barrel racing for the first time at the Central States Division Rodeo. Dirt, sweat, horses and loud music—it was just the kind of reckless, bad-ass sort of thing Leigh had always loved. And it turned out she was a natural.

Her talent was plain for all to see as she circled the second barrel and dodged for the last. Her horsemanship was impeccable, and the audience was on its feet, roaring. If she could lead Blaire around the third barrel without slipping, they'd have the best time of the night. Leigh would be a shoe-in for round six and just a little farther down the road toward the championship. She braced herself and leaned into the turn. Together, she and Blaire nailed it, and Leigh's face split into a bright white smile as they raced back to the chute, her thick blonde braid whipping out behind her. The air felt cold and wonderful rushing against her face, cutting through her clothes and enveloping her body. She released her muscles as they crossed the finish line and experienced the peak of the ride—knowing she'd blown away her competition yet again.

Blaire slowed to a trot and Leigh relaxed, steering her lovely mare back into the enormous barn. Other rodeo competitors clapped as she returned, and someone shouted her time, 13.93 seconds. Definitely respectable. She dismounted at the trough and waited while Blaire drank.

The next half hour was filled with congratulations from her parents, her friends, her parents' friends and anyone else who'd seen her ride. It was satisfying. But everyone's compliments were eclipsed when Jake Daniels came up behind her, his low voice stirring every bone in her back.

"Nice ride, Leigh." The deep tones were unmistakable, and Leigh's smile returned, along with a noticeable flush as she turned to face him.

If there was anything she'd dreamed about half as much as being a champion barrel racer, it was this man. Jake was six-and-a-half feet tall, deeply tanned after endless days working on his daddy's ranch and beautiful, at least to Leigh. His cheeks were hard, flat planes, brushed by blond lashes that shaded bright blue eyes. But what Leigh loved best about Jake was expressed in his mouth; his ornery, wild, curling smile and also in his eyes, which were lit and alive. Jake rode bulls. Jake had a fire inside of him. Jake was everything Leigh wanted a cowboy to be, everything she'd been looking for.

She'd had her eye on him for a couple of years now. She was twenty-two, with a string of unremarkable relationships behind her. None of the men she'd been with had what it took to be with her. They'd tried to tame her, but Leigh wasn't one to be tamed. What she needed was somebody who could race alongside her, who could burn as brightly. She had a feeling Jake might be the right kind of man.

"Thanks, Daniels," She met his gaze and settled into the feeling that passed between them. It was white heat.

Jake moved a little closer. "How'd it feel?"

Leigh laughed. "I don't know if there are words for it."

"Crazy?"

"Crazy and great."

Jake nodded. "I'm gonna have a ride like that tonight."

"Yeah?"

He nodded again.

"I'll be watching."

Jake got even closer, touching her face with fingertips that felt electric. "Well," he said, low and quiet, "I sure hope so."

And then he was gone, taking Leigh's breath with him.

It took her a minute to recover. Her mind swam through all the memories she had of Jake, real and fantasy. She saw him on the back of a bull, holding on tight while the animal kicked and jumped and spun. She saw his face, bent into a fury of concentration and raw determination. And then she imagined him leaning over her with a similar daredevil expression, his hands on her body, his hips perched between her legs. Could Jake give her what other men had failed to? Leigh wondered if she'd ever find out.

She shook herself out of it and headed over to where Effie Ambers and Caroline Poole were watching the bronc riding. They were both barrel racing girls, too, and the three of them stood in a row along the gate, a group of fast-riding women in glittery, overembellished cowgirl outfits that belied their inner toughness. Each one of them was champion of her home division. Each one of them had hit the ground while barrel racing plenty of times before, eating her fair share of dirt and wincing through her fair share of cuts and bruises. Even though they were her competition, Leigh felt at home with them. They understood how it felt to need to go fast, to be in control of something so out of control.

But tonight Leigh had a hard time paying attention. She couldn't focus on the riding playing out in front of her. She didn't have any comments to make about the performances and certainly not the performers. None of the men clinging to the backs of the kicking, bucking horses could hold her attention for a second, and Effie and Caroline's bubbly conversation washed over her without effect until—

"Beer, Leigh?" Effie held a bottle out to her, and Leigh took it gratefully. The ladies clinked bottlenecks and drank, Leigh a little more quickly in an attempt to quell the burning between her legs.

Effie laughed. "What, it's not enough to beat us on the field? Ya gotta finish your brew first, too? You seem kinda distracted."

"Leigh's thinking about her boy," Caroline Poole cut in, giggling, her round freckled face lighthearted and friendly.

Leigh smiled. "No use in lying, I guess."

"I didn't know you had a man, Leigh." Effie frowned.

"I've got him picked out," Leigh nodded. "Just have to make my move."

"Jake Daniels," Caroline confirmed. "I seen 'em talking.

Looked like they was about to do more than that, too."

"Maybe later," Leigh grinned.

Effie punched her in the arm. "Girl, he's a wild one. Watch out."

"Aw, I think Jake's sweet," Caroline commented. "I been in a lot of rodeos with him, and he's always a gentleman. I don't think I ever heard of him fooling around with nobody or anything."

Leigh nodded. "He's a good guy."

"But he looks like he knows how to be bad when it's called for," Caroline added slyly. "He's fine."

Leigh nodded again. "I'll tell ya'll how it goes."

They all laughed and clinked their beers again.

"How you gonna pull it off, Leigh?" Caroline asked.

Leigh shrugged. "Wait till he's done riding. Jump him when he heads to the bathroom. Something like that."

"You don't want him to make the first move?"

"Don't really matter to me so much," Leigh admitted. "I mean, I guess that'd be nice, but I just want him, you know? I been wanting Jake for a long time."

"I hear that," Effie nodded. "Men take too damn long."

"That's the truth," Caroline agreed, and the conversation turned from Jake to men in general and their universal short-comings. An hour passed quickly, along with another beer, and the bull riding was upon them.

Leigh felt goose bumps rise to her skin, provoked by the electric current running through her entire body. She was nervous on Jake's behalf and also excited. He had the potential to do something great, to have an amazing ride like he'd said and to get on into the next round. She was impatient for his turn, restless while seven men rode before him. But then she saw him down on the other side of the arena, perched on the edge of the pen where the bull he'd been assigned bristled, getting rowdy.

She watched as he slowly eased himself onto the animal's back, winding rope around and around his hand, the only grip he'd have besides the steel clamp of his thighs around the bull's ribs.

It was finally his turn, and the arena practically went silent as the audience waited for the officials to open his gate and free the bull. After another minute of securing himself, Jake slowly raised his hand into the air and the pen was flung open. The bull exploded into the arena, the crowd exploded with noise, and in her chest, Leigh's heart exploded with anxiety and love for this crazy man taking on this dumb-ass, brave-ass feat.

The bull kicked its back legs up a few times, and at first it seemed like Jake was going to have an easy ride. But then the bull began jumping up into the air and twisting its entire body left and right, every bull-rider's worst nightmare. And Jake held fast. Leigh was too far away to see his face, but she knew he wasn't fazed. She knew that he'd been imagining this since he was a little boy and that he was ready. The crowd groaned in unison as the bull gave a particularly ugly twist-kick combo and for a moment, it seemed that Jake had lost his hold, slipping off to the side, but then he righted himself and continued to be flung back and forth on the bull's back, like a rag doll. It was misleading, the way he was so easily thrown around. It made it look as though his body was loose, relaxed. In reality, Leigh imagined that his body was wound tighter than a drum as he clung to the crazy, bucking beast.

And then it was all over. He flipped over the bull's head and landed on his backside in the dirt, a perfect place for getting gored in the gut. But the rodeo clowns were there in a heartbeat and distracted the bull away from Jake long enough for him to run off the field. As soon as he was out of harm's way he turned around to look at the clock and even from her great distance, Leigh could see the enormous smile on his face as he saw his qualifying time. Like Leigh, he was headed to the next round.

"Looks like your boy came out all right," Effie nudged her. "Gonna go celebrate all night long?"

"You bet," Leigh decided and began walking way.

Effie catcalled and Caroline hollered, "Go get yours, girl."

Leigh smiled and felt her pulse quicken, like it did whenever she was facing down a good challenge. She walked out of the arena and back into the barn, trying to decide where Jake would head first. But she didn't have to look far. She found him just outside of the barns near the trailers, and as soon as he noticed her standing in the light of doorway he took off at a sprint, his big, crazy grin still filling half his face.

"Leigh!" he crowed when he reached her, and he slipped his hands around her waist, pulling her up into his embrace. Delighted with this outcome, Leigh flung her arms around Jake's neck and pressed her face to his hair, knocking off the cowboy hat that had stayed in place throughout his entire go-round with the bull. He spun them around, still shouting his excitement at the top of his voice. And then he slowly lowered her to the ground, a new expression taking over his face. It was still exuberant, but there was an edge to it now and Leigh realized it was because they had both become aware of that white-hot heat again, blazing like hell between them. And she noticed that he hadn't let her go.

"Great ride, Jake," Leigh said, suddenly shy. But Jake was staring and she wasn't sure he'd even heard her. He leaned in close enough that she could feel his breath on her lips, coming quick and not just because he'd just finished riding.

"Leigh." His voice was husky. "Leigh."

She took one last look at his blue eyes and his handsome face, and then she closed her eyes and kissed him. He was immediately receptive. His hold around her tightened and his lips moved

under hers. They couldn't be any closer. Their noses brushed
as they kissed again and again. She unclasped her arms from
around his neck and ran her fingers across his smooth cheeks,
and then she just held him, her hands spanning from either side
of his chin to where rough, curly blond sideburns ended beneath
his ears. He rocked back and forth, still clinging to her, his hands
flexing and rubbing through the fabric of her sequined button-
down. Wherever their bodies met, heat flushed over her skin,
and it didn't take too many kisses before all she wanted was to
wrap her legs around his waist and go. She was vaguely aware
of the people who'd been standing near the trailers with Jake,
congratulating him on his ride, but then Jake was carrying her
off into the shadows and she forgot to care who saw.

His hands slid down her back and over her backside, gently
urging her pelvis into his, and now Leigh *did* pull her legs up
and wrap them around his waist. She rubbed against him fast
and hard, but he stood straight, withstanding her urgency and
reminding Leigh that he was a hard-ass bull-rider. But she bet
he'd never moaned on the back of a bull, and he was definitely
moaning now.

"Oh, Leigh, baby." Leigh felt his low voice vibrate deep in
his chest as she kissed his cheek, his neck. "Did you know I
always—I always—oh, Jesus," he groaned as she rolled her hips
over his groin. Leigh gasped, too, and then sucked hard at the
skin just beneath the sharp corner of his jaw.

And then all at once he put her down, shaking his head,
dazed.

"This ain't right," he said, out of breath. "We can't do this
here, not like this. This ain't right."

"I don't understand," Leigh stepped back as if he'd slapped
her. "Why'd you let me go on like that, then? If you didn't want
me…" She trailed off.

Jake paused a second, and then laughter rolled out his crooked smile. "Goddamn, girl. You have to know I want you. Everybody in this whole rodeo knows I want you."

"What?"

He pulled her in again, resting his cheek against her forehead, his hand fitted over the curve of her waist. "Baby, I've been crazy about you since the first time I saw you ride. Saw you take off on that horse, your hair flying and your eyes all lit up," He was rocking her again, as if they were dancing out there, in the cool night air under the moon. "Saw you and I knew I'd be crazy about you. Then we met and I saw your eyes up close." He looked at her. "Green eyes. Pretty, green eyes."

Leigh sighed, her heart beating fast and full and taking up too much room in her chest.

"So you understand why we can't do it this way. Not out here, standing in horseshit in front of everybody. I love you too much for that."

She pulled back and looked up into his face. The reckless look was gone. It was something steady looking back at her. Something real. She felt herself shudder, and Jake smiled again.

"And you know," he continued, "I got some idea how you feel after what happened just now, but if you're serious—not just hot for me right now, but kinda...kinda in love, maybe you wanna meet me at my trailer? In twenty minutes or so?"

She nodded, a soft smile stealing over her face. Jake leaned in and kissed her forehead. And then he let her go, saying, "Leigh, tonight I'm gonna love you right, the way you deserve. The way I want to."

"Glad to hear it," she laughed and started to walk away, glancing behind her to find him watching with a smile on his face like he'd just won the lottery.

As soon as she was out of his line of vision she took off at a trot for her family's camper. They were still gone, and Leigh felt confident that they'd stay gone for a while, watching the end of the bull riding and then having drinks with their friends at whatever bar everyone was headed to tonight. She ducked into the small bathroom, flipped on the light and looked over her reflection. She had dirt on her face, no doubt left there by Jake, and she smiled as she washed it off. But she didn't change out of her clothes or put on any extra makeup. If he was in any way repulsed by the way she looked now—wearing dirt from his clothes, sweat from her own outstanding, qualifying ride, and the outfit she felt most comfortable in—they'd never make it. And anyway, he'd said he loved her. That he'd first fallen in love with her when he saw her on the back of a horse. And so, twenty minutes later when she left her trailer for his, she was the same girl, with a little less dirt and a tiny bit of perfume.

The temperature had dropped even more by the time she left, and the air felt wonderful against her feverish skin. But she didn't take any time getting over there. She was ready to love him right, too, and full of energy. She only stopped just outside his trailer to look up at the stars, the millions of them that lit the sky overhead, and whisper a quiet thank you.

Only the screen door was shut when she arrived, but Leigh still knocked on the side of the camper.

"Come in," he drawled from inside and Leigh did. But she was hardly through the door of the dimly lit room before she was being swept up into a pair of strong arms and crushed by Jake's mouth against her own. Her heart beat frantically, she was so caught off guard, but she was used to being taken by surprise. Years of experience with horses had taught her how to regain ground in a hurry. She took Jake's face in her hands and took over, kissing him deeply. She ran her tongue over the sharp edges of his teeth and then withdrew, pausing momentarily. But this second was all Jake needed. He lifted her into the air, his big hands cupping her backside lovingly, one of them darting between her legs to brush her burning center and drive her wild. She struggled for a moment and then slipped her hand between their bodies, dragging her fingers over the healthy erection that was filling the left leg of his already-tight jeans.

He groaned and his grip on her slipped. They both tumbled to the floor of the tiny camper, laughing hard.

"You know what I think the problem is?" Jake said. "We're both used to trying to control the situation. Now we're gonna have to take turns here or somebody's liable to get hurt."

Leigh giggled. "Well, on that note, I'll go first!"

"You think," Jake laughed and hoisted her into the air again, cradling her against his chest as he carried her over to the little bed, hidden behind beige curtains. He dropped her gently onto the mattress and then climbed in after her. It was a neatly made little bed, sheets tucked in and a sleeping bag unfolded over the top, but Jake mussed it in a hurry as he rolled his long, broad body in next to hers.

"Since I'm in charge here, first things first," he said as he began to unbutton her shirt. Soon he had pulled it open, exposing the thin white undershirt beneath. He leaned over her and pulled the undershirt up over her belly, kissing the soft white skin beneath it, dragging his lips slowly and letting his hot breath linger. Leigh didn't need all this encouragement. She spread her legs and moved to unbutton her jeans, but Jake stopped her.

"My turn," he reminded her and returned his attentions to her stomach, even pulling down the waist of her jeans a little so he could suck at the skin over her jutting hip bone, hard enough to leave a mark.

"Come on, now," Leigh scolded. "We both know what we're here for."

"I'm here to make love to you, baby," Jake replied. "Every last inch of you."

And he did. He helped her take her shirt the rest of the way off, and then he pulled the undershirt up over her shoulders. In Leigh's whole life, no one had ever looked so pleased to see her breasts, and after a moment of admiration and soft fondling, Jake took her nipple between his lips and sucked, his tongue darting across the stiff peak at rapid speed. Her back arched and she ran an impatient hand between her legs.

"Do you, uh," Jake paused. "Do you like a little biting?"

Leigh smiled like she'd just won nationals, and Jake took her nipple in his mouth again, this time using his teeth and tugging gently. She twisted with pleasure, her pussy now drenched, and managed to fling her left leg up over Jake's hip, pulling his lower body onto hers. He obliged her this time, letting her push against him like she had outside earlier that night. She made herself dizzy with the sensation, sure she was going to come, until Jake took hold of her hips and held her still. He unbuttoned her jeans and pulled them down and off her legs. She unbuttoned his and he sat up long enough to kick them off as well.

"Let me see that chest, cowboy," Leigh insisted, and Jake pulled his shirt off over his head with a loud rip. When he climbed on top of her again, bare skin met bare skin, her nipples grazing pleasantly over his warm chest and his dick pressed tight against her pussy. He dragged his hips upward, his penis sliding between the folds of her center, and even through her underwear and his she could feel the heat of it, scorching her clit as he built their friction.

Leigh kissed and sucked at his soft bare chest while he moved, pausing only when he stopped to take their underwear off. She just watched, casually, until he made to thrust into her.

"Hold your horses," she blocked him with her hand. "My turn now."

"Leigh, baby, I'm so ready."

"My turn." She held fast.

In the scant light of the tiny table lamp, she could see that he wanted to ride her into the ground, but she needed more than that. She needed a hard, fast, wild and desperate fuck, and the only way she was going to get it was if she teased him until he was about to burst. Sure that he was watching, she spread her legs and touched her clit, tightening her abs as she moved.

"I want you to touch me like this," she said. He immediately obliged, dragging his calloused thumb from the bottom of her lips to the top, until it grazed her clit. Then he just made slow, firm circles while she writhed under him. Surprise lit his face when he sank his middle finger into her and felt her wetness. She was warm and slick and ready to take him into her body, but she wasn't going to let that happen, not yet. She pulled away from him.

"On your back," she demanded. Jake hesitated this time, giving her a wild-child look that made her wonder if her turn was over, but then he did as he was told. Leigh sat up and cupped his balls, squeezing just a little as she took the head of his erection between her lips, licking off salty precome as she did. He gasped and then groaned some variation of her name as she took the rest of him into her mouth. She bobbed her head up and down for a few seconds and then pulled back. He was grinning up at her, and she realized for the first time that there had always been something dirty about the look on his face, and it wasn't just thrill-hungry like she'd originally thought.

"You've been thinking about this for a while, haven't you?" she asked, and his smile got even bigger as he nodded.

Leigh crouched over him, her knees on either side of his hips, and with her hand she slowly guided him into her body. As she sank down onto him, she sighed with satisfaction and began to rock back and forth. The tension started building right away for her and she moved faster and faster, loving how he fit inside of her, loving the sensation of her clit against his body every time she pushed forward. When she came, she was exhausted, hardly able to sit up long enough to ride out the last sweet waves. Her arms fell to her sides and the contractions blasted through her, and when it was over she fell forward, kissing Jake's face.

But before she could even catch her breath he flipped them so that he was on top again and thrust into her, his thick cock stretching her beautifully. "You know," he whispered in her ear, "you're not the only one who rides wild things." And then he began to roll in and out of her at a breathless pace. Her shoulders slid across the soft flannel comforter as he pushed into her again and again, and she wasn't surprised when she felt herself coming alive once more, her body tensing with oncoming orgasm. She reached around and squeezed Jake's tight butt, urging him on, and then the wall broke and she moaned loud enough for the entire rodeo to hear. Shortly after, Jake let out a guttural groan and spilled his pleasure inside her body, collapsing against her, showering her face with kisses of appreciation.

He held her for a long time after that, still inside of her while he stroked the curls that had come loose from her braid during their romp.

Finally he spoke. "I want you to know that I'm not a onetime rodeo kind of guy."

Leigh pressed a kiss to his chin. "Then I guess it's a good thing I'm a repeat competitor, as well."

He smiled. "So you wanna sign on for future riding events?"

She shrugged playfully. "I suppose. What kind of cowgirl

would I be if I didn't get back on the horse?"

Jake laughed rich and loud and hugged her close, and they continued loving on into the night, both of them planning on plenty of rounds to come.

NO RISK, NO REWARD

Saskia Walker

I t was when I said good-bye to Cameron that I realized I was in love with him.

We stood together in the rustic village railway station in the heart of the Yorkshire Dales. Emotion and desire swamped me, and I could not comprehend that it was over. Cameron lifted my hands to his lips and kissed my fingers gently then smiled at me. Like a jolt of electricity straight to my center, that smile turned my desire to liquid heat. It made me think about the way he made love to me, the way he locked my gaze as he entered and filled me to capacity, refusing to let me look away from him as he claimed every part of me. It stole my equilibrium, making me vulnerable. It also made every nerve ending in my body yearn for more of what we'd had these past two weeks, but it was over.

We'd said good-bye.

"I wish you were coming with me, at least for the weekend," he whispered, and his eyes filled with mischief and suggestion.

Why had I said no? Fear of getting any more involved than

I already was, perhaps. I put my fingers to his lips, forbidding him to say more.

Beyond Cameron the platform attendant lifted his hand. It was time for him to go. He kissed me one last time and I turned away quickly, not wanting to watch him board the train, not wanting to wave good-bye.

Blinking back the emotion, I darted back through the station and into the parking lot, climbing into my Land Rover to find my own private space. That didn't help; I could still smell his cologne and I could still feel his warm, strong hand reaching over to cover mine on the steering wheel when I had parked there.

I rubbed my face and cursed myself for falling so heavily for an American who was just passing through. He'd meant to stay in Yorkshire for two days, visiting my brother while he was traveling in Europe. When we'd been introduced, two days quickly turned into two weeks. I was on summer break from my teaching job, and Nathan, my brother, had introduced us at a busy wine bar. At some point that first day Nathan left us alone. While others came and went, we talked and talked and connected at a deep level. Afterward, Cameron came home with me, instead of going back to Nathan's.

Nathan told us he knew we'd hit it off. He'd known since he first met Cameron in the States, the year before. *Yeah, right,* I thought, with a wry smile. It didn't really matter, because this wasn't something I could deny.

I sat unhappily in the Land Rover and blew my nose. Through the fence that separated the lot from the rail tracks I saw that his train was disappearing out of the station. In forty minutes it would arrive in York, and he would change to a fast, mainline train to Edinburgh, where he was attending an academic conference on Monday, before traveling on. He'd invited me to go with him for the weekend, and I was tempted, just for two more days of what we'd had. But I was already in too deep.

Still, I wanted to go. Really I did. To hell with the consequences.

My pulse raced erratically as a crazy idea flitted through my mind. The train would stop at each of the villages between here and York, and if I put my foot down I could get to York Station in around the same time. I could surprise him and show him what I was made of. It was madness, a token gesture, but an important one all the same. Now that I had identified my deeper emotions, I suddenly needed to do something about it. A heady emotional rush drove me to act, born of the incendiary mix of desire and affection I felt for him. I shoved the keys into the ignition, locked my seat belt in place and reversed out of the parking place.

Seconds later I was on the road. If I made it to York in time, we'd have another ten minutes together before he left. I laughed at myself, shaking my head at my own reflection in the rearview mirror. Why was I doing this? Because I wanted him. Cameron was the best time I'd ever had. That first night, when I invited him to crash at my place, he stopped me on the threshold, backing me against the doorjamb.

"If I come inside, I'll undress you, because I want you." He stroked my neck and then kissed it, his breath warm against my skin. "You do realize that?"

I swallowed. Deep down I knew it, but he was so forthright. I was shocked, but I wanted it, too. "Yes, I know."

As soon as the words passed my lips, his hands were all over me—demanding and masterful. His mouth claimed mine and I flared at his touch, turning into an elemental thing, all damp heat and vitality.

Moments later he lifted me from my feet, walked me inside and kicked the door shut behind us. "Which way to the bedroom?"

His voice was gruff and urgent with need as he looked down the hallway.

Unable to muster a verbal response I nodded my head and pointed at the bedroom door.

"Too late, I've spotted the sofa." He turned me into his arms, wrapped my legs around his hips and headed for my old leather chesterfield in the lounge area beyond.

My hands locked on his shoulders possessively; my sex was throbbing.

He tipped me back over the arm of the sofa and allowed my shoulders to slide down onto the cushions, so that my hips were positioned right there on the arm of the sofa, my lower legs dangling free. I laughed, breathlessly. The way he handled me, so sure and direct, made me melt. Then he parted my legs, reached under my skirt and touched me between my thighs. When he made love to me that night I was truly in heaven.

I squeezed my thighs together and blinked. Apparently I couldn't keep sex with Cameron out of my thoughts. I covered the first part of the drive to York quickly. Hope sped me on. Then I got stuck behind a tractor hauling a trailer full of hay bales. The oncoming traffic made it impossible to pass. My fingers tapped impatiently on the steering wheel while I waited for the driver to pull over and let me by. He would, hopefully, soon enough. Glancing at the clock, I could see it was going to be tight but there was still time. Making the connection was a challenge, one that I intended to rise to.

That's what Cameron had done to me. He'd changed me because he challenged me and pushed me beyond my limits. I never would have tried anything like this mad car chase before he came into my life.

"Why not?" he'd asked, when I said we couldn't possibly

have sex out on the open landscape of the Yorkshire moors.

I glanced across the heather-covered ground and along the path we had walked. "Because someone might see."

"But you want to?" He continued to stroke my pussy through my jeans.

Gasping for breath, I wriggled under his touch. "Yes."

"Do you see anyone else around?"

I looked, scanned from the rocky outcrop beyond us to the rolling hills below. "No, but someone might pass by while we're…"

It was too late. The click, click, click of my opening zipper signaled my surrender. He had his hand inside my jeans, inside my panties, and I wanted it.

"I'm willing to take the risk, if you are." His finger slid into my damp groove.

I couldn't reply. He made me come three times with his hand, until I was so desperate to have his cock inside me that I begged him to take the risk.

"I need you, Cameron."

He took one last glance around, then hauled my jeans off, flipped me over so that he was covering my back, and climbed between my thighs.

"No risk, no reward," he said as his hard cock plowed into me.

I smiled to myself as I remembered. It was his motto.

The tractor had moved aside and I was into the home straight. The traffic through the city center unnerved me, but when I saw the station up ahead and looked at the clock, I had maybe ninety seconds to spare.

I got lucky and snagged a parking place just inside. As fast as I could, I locked up the vehicle and ran into the station, scouring the information boards for the arrival of the train I wanted to be there to meet.

"This is crazy." I bit my lip. I was dizzy and high because I'd acted so impetuously. I couldn't make sense of the information I read. Then I saw it and ran to the platform.

Nothing. No train and nothing approaching. Then I saw him across the platforms, his familiar khaki jacket and faded jeans, his short-cropped blond hair and broad shoulders. In my haste I'd gone the wrong way. I was in the wrong place. Panic hit me. He was on his way to the intercity connection.

"Cameron," I hollered across the platforms, competing with the noise of the trains, the crowds and the announcements overhead.

Heads turned.

I shouted again.

Cameron drew to a halt and stared at me.

"Don't get on the train!" I grappled for a reason to hold him back—something worthy, something that made sense. "I... I'll..."

I'll what?

"I'll drive you to Edinburgh."

He peered across at me with a disbelieving grin. "Yeah?"

I nodded frantically, shouting back across the gap between us. "I'll come with you, at least for a couple of days."

He threw his backpack over his shoulder, weaving through the oncoming crowd at top speed. "Wait right there," he instructed.

Heady relief flooded me, and it morphed into an almost orgasmic rush as I watched him jog along the concourse to meet me.

Capturing me in his arms, he lifted me from my feet. "I always knew you were a wild woman, out of control underneath that cool, calm exterior."

"No, it's you." I laughed, clutching at his shoulders gratefully. "You made me do this."

"Did I? Why?" The knowledge was there in his eyes, shining brightly, but he wanted me to admit it. He set me down on my feet.

I leaned into him, crushing my breasts against his chest. "Because I want more."

"Are you sure?" He tipped my chin up with one finger, studying me intently. The whole world sped away from us. There was only us. There was only this moment.

"Absolutely. I didn't want to go home without you, so I took the only other option." I laughed softly. "Only trouble is, will two more days be enough?" I looked deep into his eyes, trying to let him know how I felt.

"We can address that." He sounded so sure. "Anything is possible. We're in charge of everything that happens for us."

Something in my chest knotted.

He touched his finger to my lips. "Damn," he added, with that mischievous smile of his. "The fact you came after me is making me so horny."

"I can tell." I wrapped my hands around his hard hips and rubbed my body up against his. The bulge of his cock through our clothes felt too good.

"Which way is the car?"

I nodded back at the exit I had torn through moments before.

He grabbed my hand and headed in that direction, moving so fast I had to jog to keep up with him. Outside, when he looked at me for directions, I pointed the way, catching my breath before heading on.

When we reached the car he snatched the keys from my hand. He dumped his backpack on the driver's seat, then opened the rear door and pointed into the backseat. "On your back, please, ma'am."

I rounded my eyes. "You can't be serious."

"I can." He wrapped his hand around my shoulder and guided me to the back door. "There's no one around right now, and if anyone turns up and gets too close, well...it'll look as if I'm loading luggage."

"Loading luggage, hmm?" I sat on the backseat and then lay down.

I was about to say more when he tugged my high heels off and threw them into the foot well. Then he shoved my skirt up around my hips and grabbed me around the back of my knees, forcing me to open and bend my legs, so that my knees were drawn up and my underwear exposed. The way he took control of my body—wow. It did all the right things. I was hot and wet and wriggling like mad, desperate to be filled by him.

He pushed his finger down one side of my panties, teasing into my damp slit. His eyebrows lifted. "Believe me, I've got some luggage to load right now."

I couldn't believe he intended to do it, right there in the parking garage. We were under a low-ceiling area, in a corner, but still...could I do it? What if someone approached a nearby car?

He pushed one finger inside me and my temperature rose, need taking over.

Hell, yes, I could do it. "Hurry," I urged. "Be quick."

"Quickie in the parking garage, huh?" He stripped my underwear the length of my legs and off and then unzipped his jeans. "You have such great ideas."

"Cheeky!" God, I loved him, and now he knew it.

He had his cock ready in his hand. I moaned. Behind the shelter of the open door he bent down and kissed me right on the clit. My back arched, my clit thrumming at the touch of his mouth, the stroke of his tongue. He lapped and suckled, sending me wild. My core clamped on itself repeatedly, wanting his hardness there.

"Cameron, please, hurry!"

He lifted his head. "You are so demanding."

"Yes," I sparred, and reached down to spread myself for him. "I drove like a bat out of hell to get here, so you better reward me."

His eyes darkened as he looked down at my offered sex. Then he was over me, his glorious cock stretching me open. As he thrust into me and slid against the slippery walls of my sex, I clenched his shaft in welcome.

"Oh, yes," he murmured, and ran his hands over my breasts through my top.

My nipples stung from the contact, aching for more than that—naked skin against naked skin. Then the crown of his cock pressed against my center and I arched and cried out, squeezing my knees tight against his hips.

"Fuck, you are so hot." He began to thrust hard and fast, working into me over and over again until he shoved me right across the seat and we were both on the brink of climax.

"Oh, no!" I thought I heard voices approaching, but mercifully they faded away into the distance. Grasping him around the back of his neck, I urged him on. "Hurry, can't stop now!"

His eyes locked with mine. "So glad you did this."

A hot tide swelled in the pit of my belly. I was closing on release with every thrust of his body. "Cameron," I whispered.

"You do know I'm crazy about you?" he asked, right then, right when we were both on the edge of orgasm.

Oh, how that hit me—it hit me where I was on fire for him.

"I feel the same," I managed to respond and tightened my grasp on his shoulders. My core contracted and went into spasm.

Relief washed over me. His cock swelled and bowed inside me, then jerked and spent.

The sound of a passing car made me half sit against him. He took the chance to kiss my neck. Over his shoulder, I could see we were safely obscured by the open vehicle door. My legs were weak from everything that had gone before, the dash to the car, the power of the orgasm. "I may have to stop along the way, my legs are weak."

He kissed my cheek, reluctantly disengaging down below. "We can take all weekend to get there." He looked deep in my eyes. "So long as we're together, nothing else matters."

I nodded and then cupped his jaw, stroking his stubble with my thumb. Who knew what would happen? Right at that moment being together was all that did matter.

"No risk, no reward," I responded, echoing his motto—the motto that I had now embraced as my own. Never had it been more true, and never had I felt more rewarded.

IF

Emerald

I breezed through the screen door in a breathless whirl. "I brought the tablecloths," I said to the bride's mother, who was busy assembling hors d'oeuvres at the kitchen counter. I set the bag from the store on the dining room table, which was already cluttered with picnic paraphernalia—except for tablecloths, which Sarah had called in a frenzy to tell me her mother had forgotten to pick up.

"Great," Janice said as she turned from the counter and gave me a hug. "Here's your name tag. Would you mind being in charge of handing those out?"

"Not at all," I said, shuffling through the stack as I stepped back out to the deck. I peeled the back off mine, labeled with my name and MAID OF HONOR in smaller letters below it, and pressed it to my dress.

"Hey, Valerie," Sarah called behind me as I reached the wooden steps. I turned as she emerged from the house and met me in a hug. "Where's Chris?"

"He wasn't feeling well this morning. He wanted me to tell you and Shawn that he's really sorry to miss your engagement party."

"I'm sorry to hear that. Tell him I hope he feels better. No big deal though about today," Sarah continued with a wave of her hand as we headed down the steps to the backyard. "This is really just to introduce the wedding party and Shawn's and my extended families to each other before all the wedding stuff starts in earnest, you know?"

I nodded as Sarah continued on to find Shawn while I veered toward the front of the house to commence my job. The guests started to arrive, and I greeted them at the driveway and directed them with their name tags to the picnic tables in the backyard. As one of the groomsmen I knew and his wife approached, I handed them their name tags before turning to the man with them.

"I'm Hayden, Shawn's best man," he said with a smile. He slipped his sunglasses off to reveal friendly slate gray eyes below his tousled dark hair.

"Oh, yes, I remember seeing your name in here." I gave him a quick smile, feeling a bit flustered as I shuffled through the stack in my hands. I knew next to nothing about the best man, except that I would be walking down the aisle with him in about six months...and that I found my face burning at the idea. Unnerved by this response, I located his name tag and handed it to him.

"Thanks," he said easily. I kept my voice light as I directed the three of them to the yard, a vague heat forming in my belly as I noted the lack of a ring on Hayden's left hand.

I turned back toward the driveway, recalling with a deep breath that I myself *was* spoken for. My eyes dropped as guilt replaced the excitement stirring in me. Chris and I weren't married, but we had been together for three years, and even if I had been feeling inexplicably restless and confused lately,

I was still monogamously committed to him.

When the last name tag had been handed out, I went to the dessert table. In a rare indulgence, I allowed myself a piece of cake and carried it to the circle of chairs occupied mostly by the bridal party. I took the empty seat directly across from Hayden and did my best to ignore the fluttering in my stomach as I turned my attention to the cake on my plate.

It was dark chocolate, with a layer of raspberries in the middle and creamy white frosting on top. I scooped up a dollop of frosting and gave it a delicate lick as I listened to Sarah talk about invitations. Nodding, I ran my tongue over my frosting-sweetened lips and glanced up to see Hayden watching me.

I blushed and looked down—though not before I caught the deliberate interest beneath his cool gaze. Breathless, I turned my attention back to Sarah as confusion formed in my core. Why was I having such a response to Hayden? I was in a serious relationship. Much as I would have jumped on this opportunity years ago when that wasn't the case, I was in no position to do so now.

When Sarah paused in her description, I jumped up and dropped my plate in the trash on the way to the food table to grab something to take inside. I didn't look back as I headed with both hands full toward the house. On the way up the wooden steps to the deck, I climbed too quickly and slipped, nearly dropping the Crock-Pot in my hands before I felt a firm grasp around my waist from behind.

"Easy," Hayden's voice said in my ear, and I got wet. It might be that I wasn't supposed to, but I did.

I steadied myself and turned around. Hayden's hands slipped from my waist, and he smiled.

I cleared my throat. "Thank you," I said. "Can I get something for you inside?"

"No, I'm just heading to the restroom. Let me get that for you," he said as he reached in front of me for the screen door.

"Thank you," I said again, aware of the adrenaline zinging through me as I set the Crock-Pot on the counter. I bit my lip as I stood still for a moment. I wondered if the fact that I felt utterly forbidden from touching Hayden—much less fucking the hell out of him, which was what I really wanted to do—was influencing how desperately I felt like I wanted to.

I went to the guest bedroom and sent Chris a text message, eager to lock myself away from people for a few moments. I waited for his reply informing me that he was feeling better before I left the room, trying not to think about Hayden happening to wander in and catch me there. As I headed back outside, I felt very grateful that he didn't.

Didn't I?

Slowly, the guests began to take their leave. The sun had turned a dark orange on the horizon, and the sky overhead was the color of smoke when I grabbed a round of gifts from a table to take inside. As I approached the wooden steps, Hayden came down them.

"It was a pleasure meeting you, Valerie," he said with a smile.

"Are you leaving?" My voice managed to stay light despite the tug I felt inside when Hayden nodded.

"Well, I would hug you if I wasn't all loaded down," I laughed as I neared him, indicating the wine-bottle-laden gift bags at my sides and feeling a wistful pull at the missed opportunity.

Hayden hadn't paused, and even as I spoke he reached me, his arm sliding seamlessly around my waist as my words evaporated. I caught my breath as he held my lower back lightly while I pressed against him for a moment.

I turned my head and barely brushed my lips against his cheek as I stepped back.

"There. I'll kiss you instead," I said, surprised by how unaffected my voice sounded.

Hayden's chuckle was barely audible. "That wasn't a kiss."

Barely moving forward, his lips touched mine so lightly it was possible those behind him on the deck wouldn't even know what was happening in the shadowy dusk around us. He backed up as silently as he had moved forward.

My breath had seemed to disappear into the growing darkness. Though I stood stock still, my lungs surged for air as I sought my voice, which seemed to have dissolved as well. Finally a whisper came out.

"Hayden."

His eyebrows rose.

The fixation in me seemed to snap, and I smiled, suddenly feeling clearer. "I want to let you know that I find myself, um, quite attracted to you."

This seemed a laughable understatement, but I stayed focused. Hayden's intense gaze was fixed on me. It showed nothing to discourage the disclosure.

"Desperately, in fact," I continued. My eyes flicked to the ground, then back up to his. "And I am not in a position to act on that at this time. Otherwise, I would have done so already."

Hayden's expression cleared, and I could see he didn't have to ask questions.

I backed up. Exhaling slowly, I said, "It was a pleasure meeting you too, Hayden. I guess I'll see you at the wedding."

He stepped away as well and smiled. "Yes. You certainly will."

He gave a wave as he turned and headed for his car. I hoisted the gift bags and walked up the wooden steps to the deck, my stomach churning, head whirling—and pussy dripping.

* * *

I found Chris on the couch under a blanket when I walked in the front door.

"How was the party?" he asked before I could say anything.

"Uh, fine," I answered. Did my voice betray me? My stomach clenched, and I reminded myself I hadn't done anything wrong.

I looked into Chris's beautiful blue eyes. I loved him so much. I had made a decision to be with him, and that was what I wanted.

Wasn't it?

"How are you feeling?" I asked, moving to sit at his side.

He sat up a little. "Better. You're beautiful." He smiled at me as he moved a wisp of hair from my face. His expression segued into concern. "What's wrong?"

I had barely noticed the tears filling my eyes. I shook my head dismissively and stood up.

"I'm going upstairs to change. Can I get you anything?"

"No, thank you," Chris said, still watching me as he eased back against the couch. "I love you."

"I love you, too." I pulled the blanket over him and smiled, leaning down to kiss his cheek before I turned and left the room.

Upstairs, I pulled off my dress and slipped out of my sandals. Why did the complication of Hayden have to come right at this time? I had been feeling unsettled and uncertain for the past several weeks as it was.

Maybe that was why.

Standing in my thong, I thought of Hayden and caught my breath. I could almost feel his hands on my waist from behind, the confidence of his arm sliding around me in the darkness. I swallowed.

Quietly, I crept to the door and closed it, then slipped off my thong and eased onto the bed. I spread my legs and remembered the little contact Hayden and I had had at the party, surprised by the force of the arousal that resulted. I dropped my fingers between my legs.

Breathing heavily, I pressed my clit, remembering the way Hayden's arm had slid around me without pause, the breathlike feeling of his lips touching mine, the hunger in his eyes when I caught him watching me lick the frosting. I was astonished by how easily I came thinking of nothing else. Twice.

I closed my eyes and imagined Hayden finding me in the guest bedroom. I could almost feel his tongue circling one nipple, then the other as he pulled my clothes off before pushing me onto the bed and shoving my legs apart as I begged him to ram his cock into me hard.

I made myself come six times. As I got up shakily and headed for the shower, my eyes fell on the name tag still stuck to the dress crumpled on the floor. My insides twisted as I remembered that what had just happened with Hayden in my fantasies could remain only there.

Two weeks later I woke in the middle of the night. Blinking sleepily, I glanced at the moonlight penetrating the blackness out the window and didn't bother checking the clock. I looked at Chris, his breathing even as he lay on his side, facing me, his hands balled into fists just under the edge of the blanket.

I had been thinking about Hayden alarmingly frequently in the weeks since I'd met him. It had been a bit surreal to feel something so encompassing that Chris had no idea about. I found the juxtaposition uncomfortable, and I had a sad feeling that Chris had no idea anything was wrong. Of course, while I knew that *something* was, I had no idea *what*. And it had been there, I knew, even before I met Hayden.

I shifted my head on the pillow and smothered a sigh. The idea of leaving Chris, leaving the relationship, seemed startling to me, and I didn't feel at all certain that was what I wanted. But why was I so captivated by Hayden?

I flipped onto my stomach and faced the other direction. Moments later I felt the bed shift and was about to turn my head when I felt Chris's form against my side, his lips dropping to the back of my neck and moving steadily to my ear. I was shocked by the goose bumps that immediately stood all over my body, by how quickly the confusion that had just seemed so paramount fell away under the heat of Chris's touch.

For a split second I felt compelled to contemplate that, but Chris made his way on top of me, his erection pressing against my ass, and my distraction evaporated. He didn't say anything, just reached up and gave my hair a little tug as my whimper got lost in the pillow. His lips nuzzled my ear then moved across my cheek and finally barely reached my lips, which he kissed lightly before returning to the intense erogenous zone of my ear.

I heard the condom wrapper and felt him shift briefly and then slip inside me, my legs together, still facedown, flat on the bed. He moved his hands to my shoulders, fucking me with a slow rhythm that seemed to fit the silence and the moonlight and the middle of the night like a door clicking quietly shut.

My eyes closed, body pressed against the mattress, I basked in the heavy warmth of Chris's weight and his cock sliding in and out of me. I gripped his fingers as he slid his hands over mine on the pillow, and he squeezed back before letting go to slide one hand under my body. I came silently and quickly, the only outward indications the audible quickening of my breath and the tensed pressure of my body against the mattress and Chris's fingers.

Chris came silently, too, his grip on my shoulder tightening.

When it was done, he reached to kiss me again, and I smiled sleepily, my eyes still closed. Chris slid off me, curling his arm around mine and pulling me into a spooning position. For a split second I felt his grip tighten in the darkness, and I had the instantaneous sense that my suspicion of his obliviousness had been misplaced. I blinked my eyes open as the grasp relaxed, and I heard Chris's breathing return to the steadiness indicating sleep.

Letting go of any attempt to grapple things into making sense, I took a deep breath and followed suit.

Shopping for bridesmaid dresses with Sarah the following weekend, I noticed that anything having to do with the wedding seemed to remind me of Hayden. I sighed as I zipped up the A-line burgundy dress and stepped out of the dressing room.

Sarah cocked her head. "Hmmm. That's nice." Her brow furrowed. "Could I see the blue one again?"

I smiled, amused by her indecision. I had tried each of her three final dress choices twice; this would be the third time for the blue one. I ducked back into the dressing room and slipped on the royal blue floor-length strapless gown. She looked up as I emerged for her inspection.

"I like that," she said as she examined me. "Do you like that one or the short black one better?"

"For a winter wedding, longer seems to make sense," I responded. "Of course, it's up to you."

Sarah nodded thoughtfully. "Oh, by the way, I asked Shawn to meet us here at two-thirty to go to the tuxedo store down the street so we can look at the tuxes that match the dresses I'm looking at. Do you mind coming with us to give your opinion?"

"Of course not." I returned to the dressing room to change back into my street clothes. As I stepped into my shoes, I heard voices outside the door and deduced that Shawn had arrived.

I opened the door, and my breath caught as I saw Shawn talking to Sarah—with Hayden standing next to him. My heart took off like a pistol firing, and for a second I couldn't speak.

Sarah turned to me. "Shawn brought Hayden with him, obviously. You guys met at the engagement party, right?" Shawn said something to her before I could answer, and she turned to him.

Hayden stood casually, his hands in the pockets of his khakis. I met his eyes, his slow smile shooting sparks through my body. I swallowed and managed a somewhat unnatural smile back.

Sarah and Shawn started toward the door, and I snapped out of my daze long enough to thank the salesperson who had helped us, before the four of us exited the store. The bride and groom fell into step with each other, leaving Hayden and me together behind them.

The intense attraction I still felt toward Hayden was undeniable. Guilt flooded through me as we made small talk, and I wondered if my voice sounded as stilted to him as it did to me. I also wondered if what had seemed to be his mutual interest was still there, or if what I had said at the party had—understandably, admittedly—erased it.

Obviously it had had no such effect on me.

As we entered the formal wear store I held back a groan, suddenly realizing that if there was one thing I didn't need the temptation of seeing Hayden in right now, it was a tuxedo. I looked around and tried to quell the simmering in my stomach as Sarah talked to the salesperson. After a brief interim of vest and tie collecting, Shawn and Hayden disappeared down the hallway to the changing rooms.

Moments later they both emerged in tuxedoes, and my insides melted a little bit. My pussy actually grew wet at the sight of Hayden in his black tuxedo and silver vest. There was a brief discussion of colors, during which I hoped my silence wasn't conspicuous, before the two men went back down the hall.

Looking at Hayden had reminded me of how I felt when I saw the decadent chocolate desserts in the bakery section of the grocery store: I was so used to depriving myself that it didn't even occur to me to buy one—I simply looked at them longingly, and every once in a while I found myself startled by the sudden and violent urge to throw aside the glass door and shove one in my mouth before I could change my mind.

"Sarah, can you give me a hand with this?" Shawn called from his dressing room.

Sarah disappeared down the hall, and reluctantly I followed her. I settled on the chair near the three-way mirror as Sarah slipped into Shawn's changing room.

Another door opened, and Hayden stepped out in the same tuxedo with a dark red vest and tie that I recognized as matching the burgundy dress I had just tried on. I stared for a moment before realizing it would be polite to acknowledge his presence rather than just salivate over it. I looked up at him and managed a smile.

"What do you think?" he asked.

I bit back exactly what I thought, which was that I wanted to fuck him senseless.

"It looks lovely," I said. "Actually…" I tried to stop myself, but my body seemed to move of its own accord as I stood and straightened his slightly crooked bowtie.

"That's better," I murmured.

The heat of his body was like a magnet—and I a helpless paper clip—as I pulled back with supreme effort. His steel gray eyes held mine, and confusion and uncertainty suddenly flooded through me so strongly my eyes almost filled with tears. I took another step back.

As I did, Hayden caught my arm, pulling me into the changing room and pushing me against the wall in a single movement. His mouth was on mine before I had time to catch my breath, much less remember to resist. My body pressed into his, cradling the erection I felt beneath his trousers.

A whimper escaped me, and abruptly I broke away, my pussy wet and throbbing as I stumbled to the other side of the tiny dressing room. I braced my hands against the wall, silently trying to catch my breath. Behind me I heard Hayden doing the same.

"I'm sorry," he whispered. I turned back to him. "Really. I know you told me. I just found you…irresistible."

Well, I certainly knew the feeling. He looked down, and I didn't doubt his contriteness.

I nodded at him, near tears. I had come very close to crossing a line.

Hayden cleared his throat and touched my arm as he opened the door for me.

"I'm very sorry, Valerie."

I smiled feebly to let him know it was all right—I knew it wasn't all his fault, after all—and passed through to the hallway.

Shawn and Sarah emerged momentarily, and I jumped. I barely noticed the conversation around me as I resisted meeting Hayden's eyes. To do so felt like it would threaten my resistance to the violent urge to push him right back into the dressing room—and shove him in my mouth before I could change my mind.

When I got home, I found myself again incessantly fantasizing about Hayden. Chris was out, and I lay on the bed and pictured Hayden and me the day of the wedding, hidden in one of the preparation rooms after the ceremony as I knelt and sucked his cock, his breathing frantic above me as he stood in his shiny black dress shoes and ebony tuxedo, shoving his hips forward and grasping the back of my head.

His insistent pumping into my mouth would make my pussy drip, and I'd look up at his silver eyes locked on mine and let him know that as much as I loved what I was doing, I was going to demand that he take my pussy before he was done.

I came to the image of the shiny blue satin dress bunched at my hips as Hayden drilled into me from behind.

I caught my breath before I stood and headed for the closet. Who knew what would be going on come winter, when the wedding was? I mused absently. Maybe by then we would have the chance.

When I realized what I had just thought, I stopped short, my breath catching. Shock enveloped me as I realized I had just caught myself thinking nonchalantly of not being with Chris anymore. What was I thinking? That was a huge change my mind was throwing around, not some casual consideration. How could the idea have slid through my consciousness so easily?

Tears pushed up from my core as I caught my gaze in the mirror across the room. Staring at my reflection, I jumped when the door opened downstairs.

Chris was home.

I had been making omelets the Sunday morning Chris walked into the kitchen and told me he knew something was wrong.

At that moment, I knew he had known all along. Starting before I met Hayden, going back to the weeks prior when something had seemed off, when I hadn't known what it was or whether it was him or me or both of us or neither, just that it was something, Chris had known. He had always known.

He'd stood facing me, and I'd turned to him and told him everything. I told him about meeting Hayden, about the day in

the dressing room, about how guilty and uncertain and overwhelmed I felt, about how it had started even before then but I
didn't know why.

Chris had listened silently, and I found that just sharing it,
speaking the words out loud, seemed to open something in me.
A relaxation I hadn't felt for months flowed over me.

And when he said he had felt me pulling away for months
and not known why or what to do, I realized what had eluded
me for so long: what was happening in me wasn't about Chris,
and it wasn't about Hayden. Not deep down.

It was about me.

Chris and I had reached a turning point. The relationship
was asking me for something I had never given before. It was
asking me to go deeper—deeper trust, deeper authenticity,
deeper surrender.

It was asking me for intimacy.

The request was quiet, so subtle that I had only recognized it
subconsciously. And there was a part of me that was afraid of it.
That part, the part that had avoided it so many times before in
my life, was loud, and it used whatever it needed to distract me.

Enter Hayden and the incredible, magnetic sexual attraction
of avoidance.

The attraction I felt to Hayden was sincere, I didn't doubt. But
I saw then that the fixation I had experienced around him was an
unconscious redirection of my attention. It was the loud, fearful
part of me doing its best to direct my awareness away from what
it found so threatening. Ultimately, it wasn't about intimacy with
another person. It was about intimacy with myself.

Looking at Chris that day, I understood that for me, the intimacy had always been harder. Harder than leaving and starting
over again, only able to reach a certain level before I found something new that magnetically called to me. I felt that magnetic

intensity with Hayden, for sure. I had felt it many times in my life. And while at that moment I saw the pattern that had played out over and over in my past relationships when I resisted calls to go deeper inside and went after what was new instead, I saw as well that at those times, I wasn't ready for it yet. The emergence of this precise opportunity was unique—unique to here, to now, to this.

And as always, I still had the option to turn it down.

So, when winter came, the bushes outside the reception venue topped by domes of smooth white snow, I entered the room on Hayden's arm. The bridal party followed behind us as we made our way to the head table amidst the excited chatter of the hundred-plus guests.

Hayden pulled my chair out for me, and I smiled as I thanked him and released his arm. He gave me a wink and turned to find his seat on the other side of Shawn's. I watched him, recalling the various fantasies I'd entertained about the two of us on this day. The attraction was still there. Had I been at liberty to do so, I would have fucked Hayden silly every chance I got. I would have jumped him in the guest bedroom at Sarah and Shawn's engagement party, I would have sucked his cock in the dressing room of the men's formal wear store, I would have dragged him off for a quickie in one of the back rooms prior to the ceremony that had just taken place.

As it was, I was not at liberty to do that. I arranged my belongings under my chair and stood to dismount the platform, holding up my royal blue floor-length dress with one hand as I descended the steps and crossed the dance floor.

Chris met me at the edge of it. He stepped forward to kiss me, and my dress swished around my ankles as I dropped it to wrap my arms around his neck.

"I have to go back to the head table," I whispered. "I just wanted to say hi and I'll see you as soon as the first dances are over."

Chris ran a finger along my jaw, sending a shiver down my back as his hand rested suggestively on my hip. I suspected he was thinking of the new fantasy I had shared with him before he had dropped me off earlier for photos. It was cold outside, and I doubted anyone else would venture out and find us behind the building, my hands planted against the wall and Chris's cock buried deep inside me.

I had also told him, I recalled now as I kissed him a final time and turned to head back to the platform, I didn't mind if it remained just a fantasy either. I gathered my dress again in one hand as my eyes found Hayden's silver gaze across the room. I had certainly developed an appreciation for the value of fantasy, even if it was never acted out.

GETTING IT RIGHT

Teresa Noelle Roberts

Heather knelt down at her boyfriend Jesse's feet. It wasn't something she normally did—at least not outside the bedroom or wherever they happened to get their kink on—but it was a safe position from which to say what she was about to say, a safe position in which to feel small and soft and submissive, nervous and wet at the same time.

Jesse hit the remote, obviously figuring news delivered by a kneeling lover would be more interesting than anything CNN had to offer. "Yes?"

She took a deep breath, took Jesse's hands, looked into his eyes. "I want to feel the cane again. Please."

He raised an eyebrow. "Are you sure?"

"Yes…" A split second's hesitation. "I hate being afraid. The longer we wait, the more I'll build it up as a big deal in my mind. So I figure we just do it—but do it right this time. "

"That's my brave girl." He raised their joined hands to his lips and kissed hers, letting his tongue dart out to tease her knuckles. "I love you."

She grinned, a little weakly, trying to hide the way she was lurching between arousal and terror. "I love you, too, but it's not unselfish, Jesse. I need the closure. That was a weird night and I need to get past it. And besides," she added, hoping she sounded more confident than she felt, "I bet it'll be fun when we're not both being stupid."

He smiled. "Stupid's the word. We both know better than to play when we're mad."

"This time we'll do it right."

Almost a month ago, UPS had delivered the cane they'd ordered. They excitedly made plans for a lovingly kinky evening experimenting with the new toy, starting light and working up, since while Jesse had some prior experience wielding a cane, Heather knew only it sounded hot in erotica.

There must have been something nasty in the air, though. On the night they'd planned for their cane experiment, Heather came home grouchy after a bad day at work to find Jesse just as irritable. They couldn't remember, afterward, how it had started, but they got into an argument after dinner, the kind that would never reach a resolution because it wasn't actually about anything.

The only points they agreed on were that Heather had started it, and they both wanted to stop it. For some reason, at one in the morning on a weeknight, it had seemed like a great idea to use that new cane for a punishment scene and work things out that way.

Maybe it wouldn't have been such a bad idea if they'd ever done a punishment scene before, or if Heather hadn't dropped so hard, worn by pain and emotion, that she forgot to use her safeword before Jesse broke skin. As it was, it had ended in tears, and not the good, cathartic kind, but the kind that left both of them wondering if they were both crazy to be playing games with pain and power.

A few nights of attempting to be vanilla had convinced them they'd be even crazier if they didn't play those games. But the cane stayed buried deep in the toy bag, and neither of them had been sure it would come out again.

Until Heather asked.

This time they pulled out all the stops. This time the room was full of flickering vanilla- and cinnamon-scented candles, adding a medieval, almost religious air to Jesse's plain bedroom.

This time there was no anger, no exhaustion, no confusion, just lust and love and, at least on Heather's side, a lot of sexy anxiety. Under the angst and foolishness, that first time, she'd caught hints that she'd like the cane under better circumstances.

But it still scared her.

And Jesse saw her fear and helped her through it.

They necked like teenagers on the couch before moving into the bedroom and kissing and caressing some more, so Heather was wet and quivering even before she began to undress.

This time, Jesse sat on the bed and put her over his knee, as he had their first night together. Starting with light, loving smacks that sent the blood rushing, stimulating her skin, stimulating her sex, he warmed her up until she was pushing her backside up to meet his hand. Then he stepped it up a little, cupping the sweet spot of her ass with each blow, half watching the color turning from creamy to pink to almost red, half watching Heather's reaction, the pleading little yelps, the squirming, the way she parted her legs, letting loose some of her aroused musk.

"How I can resist that invitation?" Jesse stroked her vulva, then slapped it lightly, teasingly. His fingers came away wet and slick. "Now that's what I like to see," he said, his voice breathy, smoky.

He pulled her up and kissed her, lingering and deep. "Now lie on your back," he commanded. "I have a vision."

Then he started arranging her.

He arched her over so her thighs rested on her chest and told her to hold herself in place with her arms.

He tucked several pillows under her, raising her ass. "Perfect," he said. "I have a gorgeous target, but I can watch your face."

He didn't add *in case you need to safeword and can't find your voice*, but he didn't need to.

"I can't hold this," Heather said. "I'm afraid I'll move at just the wrong time."

"That's what rope's for."

Slowly, sensually, he tied her that way, ass in the air, pussy open and exposed, muscles straining. She was deliciously helpless, and the embrace of the ropes made her feel safer.

Juice poured from her pussy.

Jesse lay on the bed; buried his face in her wet, exposed slickness and took a deep breath as if the scent intoxicated him. "Yum." He began to lick.

"Jesse...what are you doing?" Heather was genuinely confused. The last cane scene had been so rough his gentleness caught her off guard.

"Making you come," he said simply, before going back to what he'd been doing.

Already wet, her pussy flooded as he tongued her, and he licked as if trying to get every drop. Of course, this just made her produce more. At first, though, he kept his attention on her lips, keeping away from her clit.

She mewled, tried to squirm to get her clit under his questing tongue, but there was only so far she could move in her current position, especially with his weight on her. He licked and licked, pausing only to take his hard cock into his hand and say, "See what you're doing to me already? I love having power over you. I don't need to hurt you to have power over you, just offer you pleasure and the possibility of more. But I want to hurt you a little. Do you want that?"

"Yes, I do. But what you're doing right now...it's so good."

"Come for me," he whispered, just before he put his tongue where she craved it.

And she did.

While she was still riding the waves of orgasm, he slipped away and picked up their favorite leather slapper.

A few good whacks took her butt from pink to red—and pushed her over to another orgasm. "That's my girl," he said, pride in his voice. "That's the good naughty girl I love. Are you ready?"

When she nodded, he reached for the cane.

Heather took a deep breath, bracing herself for the onslaught of pain. She thought she could bear it now, after all the pleasure and tenderness, but when she heard the cane hiss through the air toward her, she held her breath and tensed her muscles in fear, waiting for the fire.

First came a tap; a very stingy tap, but a tap. It felt like nothing at first, then like a long paper cut, stinging, but not too intense.

Then fire coiled through her, merged into the heat between her legs and deep inside her body.

She'd figured that after two orgasms in quick sensation, she was somewhere in the sensation Himalayas.

No, she'd only been in the foothills. Erotic energy snaked through her, setting her alight, carrying her higher. "More," she groaned, straining against the ropes that held her safe, unable to articulate clearly the strange but beautiful sensations inside her.

The next blow was harder but sweeter, pushing her deeper. The next took her even farther. "Still okay?" she heard Jesse asking, but it was as if his voice was coming from another planet. She tried to speak, but wasn't sure it worked because all her energy was turned elsewhere: to her raging pussy; to the lines of ecstatic fire on her ass.

Unable to find her voice, she smiled and nodded.

He grinned back evilly then struck her again. This time the initial reaction was downright painful, and she yelped, but it transmuted to pleasure even as she cried out, spiraled deep inside her, seemed to reach her heart and soul.

"Another?"

She meant to say something truly deep along the lines of "Oh, god, yes…" She didn't even get out that much, just a deep, throaty noise, but apparently Jesse understood.

He took her there—gave her the pain, not once, but three times in rapid succession, harder than the others. With the first two, she bit her lip, fought despite herself, despite feeling the pain transform itself almost immediately.

On the third, he ordered, "This time, come."

And she did.

They fucked after that, and somewhere along the line he untied her, maybe before or maybe in the middle—because at one point she was on top and couldn't have been if she were still tied that way—but it was foggy. Wave after wave of orgasm and what felt like a serpent exploding up her spine and Jesse's cock, Jesse's body, Jesse's beloved voice her only connection to the planet.

Afterward, when she could talk again, when the rest of the world coalesced around her again and she became aware of anything beyond the feel of Jesse, the scent of Jesse, the sound of Jesse, and later still her own vaguely aching muscles and tender ass, she turned to him and said, "Cheater."

"Whaa…?" He sounded about as vague as she felt.

"You didn't hit me anywhere near as hard as before."

"Yes, I did."

"But…but it was amazing. The other time just hurt."

He helped her stand, walked her over to the mirror, turned her around.

Her ass was a mottled mess, marked with seven distinct stripes.

"I…I…" She couldn't speak, just turned and buried her face in Jesse's chest.

"You're welcome," he said. "And thank you for trusting me to try again."

A noise somewhere between a sob and a laugh bubbled out of Heather. "Of course I trust you, Jesse," she whispered. "I know you. I love you. We both made mistakes that night, but we know what went wrong and we know better now. Thank you for believing me when I said I was ready to try again."

"Any time."

Heather stroked her tender ass and giggled. "I think we should wait awhile before any more caning. But the oral sex when I was tied up…I could stand a little more of that."

Laughing, getting hard in anticipation, Jesse reached for the rope.

THE MORNING RIDE

Delilah Devlin

With a schedule more predictable than the subway train she waited for, Sophie's chest constricted as though a cinch were slowly being tightened around her ribs. Leaving her breathless every morning as she waited on the platform beside the tracks, her odd affliction only intensified once she boarded. The journey never varied, beginning in Upper Manhattan and continuing southward. Her body had acquired the habit, which was reinforced not by some psychological disorder, but by the need for one specific miracle to occur every morning as she took her usual seat along the far wall of the car.

She sat, then rose and sat again to rearrange her skirt beneath her. She pulled at the hem and then slid it just high enough to attract attention but not so high that she looked like a slut. She ignored the low "Mmm-mm" from the college-age boy with bed-head who sat beside her.

Her attention remained focused on the stations as they were announced. "One-hundred-and-twenty-fifth Street." She straightened her back and took a deeper breath, hoping to quell the heat entering her cheeks. "Fifty-ninth Street." She unwrapped her fingers from around her purse straps because her knuckles were whitening. When the car slid to a stop at 42nd, she held her breath and averted her glance from the sliding doors, watching instead from the corner of her eye as passengers stepped inside, sought their seats and settled in for their morning commute.

She saw him, at least from the knee on down: shiny black loafers, knife-edge creases in his charcoal trousers. Sweeping her gaze upward, but still not looking directly, she eyed his tall, lean body, embracing the quickening tattoo of her heart. Dark hair, still glossy from his shower, curled close to his scalp. The scent of aftershave, spicy and fresh, followed him, and she inhaled sharply to catch it. When he took his seat along the opposite wall and two seats down, she let out the breath she'd held, the pinpricks of darkness that had narrowed her vision to a tunnel, fading back. All was right in her world again.

Never mind that she'd spent another restless night, fighting the blankets and the dreams that left her so hot and frustrated she'd retrieved the vibrator from under her bathroom sink to take off the edge. Last night had been the best, or the worst, depending on whether she wanted to sink into the dream or cry over the fact that she was tired. Even now, the potency of the dream was so strong, the details so vivid, it was easy to slide back into the moment when she'd stumbled against him as they both debarked at Chambers Street and he'd slid his hand around her waist to steady her….

He'd caught her against his chest, and she'd been forced to glance up, staring into his face fully for the first time.

"Gotcha," he said softly, the corners of his eyes crinkling.

When he didn't release her, she didn't comment, not even when people jostled past them. "I've noticed you before," she said.

"I wanted to say something, but..."

"Yeah." She pried her fingers from the lapel of his suit and backed away. His arms slid slowly from her, as though he was reluctant to let her go, and she glanced up again.

He swallowed hard. "Coffee?"

She shook her head, not understanding for a moment, then gasped. "Please."

Only when he pushed through the glass doors of the coffee shop he'd led her to, they entered a bedroom. Hers. And it was pristine for once, covers turned down, rose petals spread across the robin's egg blue cotton sheets.

He bent to pick her up, and suddenly they were both nude. Climbing onto the mattress, he lowered her slowly to the bed. He didn't give her time to savor the moment, coming over her, a knee between her thighs, opening her.

His hand cupped her pussy, and his lips pulled away from his teeth amid tight, reddened features. "Sorry, I can't wait. Been waiting so long..."

She embraced him, pulling him closer as the round knob of his cock nudged her lips. When he thrust straight toward her womb, her back arched and her breasts tightened. A long, thin moan ripped from her throat. It took only three strong thrusts before she came.

"Fuck," he muttered, then followed her, giving a muffled shout as he hammered between her legs. Even when his arousal waned, he circled inside her, hips rolling and rolling, dragging on her heated walls until she groaned and rocked against him, and he was hard again.

This time, he let his weight pin her to the mattress, bracketed her face between his large palms and held her while he rubbed his lips over hers then thrust his tongue inside.

She sucked on it, the way she wanted to suck on his cock,

and he must have read her mind because he groaned into her mouth and then pulled away, backing onto his knees. His cock pulsed, tapping his belly. He stared down at it then aimed a hot glance her way.

Sophie got her elbows beneath her. "Fuck my mouth."

He stepped over her until his knees were braced apart on either side of her chest, then he leaned over her, a hand against the wall as he guided his cock into her mouth.

Her tongue lapped at the smooth head. Her lips closed around the shaft, just beneath the glans and suctioned hard while he began to move in and out, past her teeth, along her tongue, against the back of her throat. She swallowed, caressing the head.

A hand cupped the back of her head, giving her support, and his strokes quickened. "Swallow, baby. Take it," he whispered.

Her muffled mewling cries vibrated around him, and he cried out, thick surges of cum splashing at the back of her throat.

When he pulled away, he scooted down until he could bend to kiss her mouth. "Baby, that was so goddamn hot."

The dream had ended there with his wet cock digging into her belly—before they'd shared names, before they'd agreed to see each other again. Not the sort of dream she'd ever had before—or at least not so long and detailed. It was like a scene from a smutty romance novel, rose petals and all.

Still, she'd been left wet, aching, and the dildo hadn't filled the empty space inside her. If only she had the courage to approach him. Maybe he'd be as sexy, well endowed and skilled as her dream lover—or maybe he'd be a complete dick.

Either way, she'd bring an end to this wanting.

Daniel Moore settled onto his seat in the subway car and raked a hand through his wet hair. He'd woken late and flown through his morning routine, skipping breakfast because he hadn't wanted to wait on the next train. He'd have missed her, and for some strange reason, seeing the sexy little brunette in her plain dark skirts, white button-down blouses and running shoes ensured a pleasant start to his mornings.

Danny flipped open the newspaper he'd grabbed from in front of his apartment door before he'd run down the stairs, and he pretended to read the headlines while his gaze followed the length of her pale, sturdy legs.

They weren't the longest or the sleekest, and that hint of muscle at the back of her calf wasn't all that noteworthy, but they drew his gaze up to her thighs. Her minis were modest and her thighs were rounded—not fat but feminine. And just like he did every morning, he wondered how soft the skin cloaking those luscious thighs would be.

That thought was all it took to send him straight into arousal so strong, he had to place both feet on the floor and spread his legs slightly, the newspaper the only thing shielding his interest from the other passengers crowding into the car.

The woman was an obsession, a daily good-luck charm. If her gaze fanned him once and lingered for even a moment, his whole body warmed. He hadn't approached her yet, hadn't wanted to let his anticipation tarnish his morning moments, because she'd fed every wet dream he'd had the past few weeks. Since he'd broken up with Jen, "subway girl" was the closest thing he'd had to a date. Every day when he counted down the cars until he found the one she always sat inside, he wondered if the thrill would still be there. Today, it was definitely alive.

Her legs turned to the side, and she slid one thigh over the other, the quick split teasing him. If she were his, if they'd been alone, he'd have snuck a hand between her thighs, preventing her from closing them tight, and sunk his fingers into her cunt.

Her lush mouth would open, her teeth biting into her lip, her lids sliding down her wide brown eyes to give him a dreamy sex-starved look that would have him on his knees in a second and spreading those thighs wide. Daniel breathed evenly but deeply and sank deeper into his fantasy.

The people around them faded to shadows; the rumble of the train quieted so that all he could hear were her moans and the succulent clasping of her pussy.

His hands smoothed up the inside of her thighs. She lifted her butt off the seat, and he pushed up her skirt to expose the modest white panties that covered her sex and bottom.

Rather than closing her legs to pull her underwear down, he tucked a finger under the banding at one side and pulled her panties aside to expose her folds. Then he bent close, noting the way her fingers grabbed the edge of the seat as she fell back, scooting her butt closer to the edge and her pussy against his mouth.

Her scent, baby powder and subtle female musk, ripened as he stuck his nose into her folds and swirled his mouth and chin in the moisture spilling from inside her.

Her cunt lips flared then retreated, sucking at air, and he poked his stiffened tongue inside her, fucking her while his thumb rubbed her clit.

Her breaths grew ragged, tinged with moans, and she lifted her legs, hung her thighs over his shoulders and dug her heels into his back. He rimmed her entrance then lapped upward, pulling back her hood, then fluttering the tip of his tongue against her clit while he thrust two fingers inside her.

Her sex clenched around him, and more scalding liquid surrounded the digits, easing his way as he pumped inside her.

"Please, please," she groaned.

His cock was engorged, the skin stretching painfully around it; his balls ached. He gently pushed her thighs off his shoulders and opened his pants, pushing them down just far enough so that he could reach inside and free his cock. His white dress shirt split around it; his pants framed the bottom side. The woman reached down and grabbed his shaft and scooted off the seat. Her feet parted over his spread thighs and she squatted over his cock, flexing thighs and buttocks to sink onto him, then rise and sink again.

His hands curved around her ass and bit into the soft flesh, forcing her pace faster, her downward thrust deeper. When her head fell back and her breasts scraped up and down through his chest hair, he powered upward, meeting her downward drives with sharp stabs of his cock, until she issued a short, strangled scream and came.

"Excuse me," came a voice beside him. And the man beside him rose swiftly and headed out the door as the doors slid open.

Daniel was relieved for the interruption because he'd been seconds from an embarrassing eruption. He didn't glance up to check the stops; he'd kept her in his sights the whole time he'd daydreamed about fucking her, and she hadn't moved. They shared the same destination.

When she gathered her things, he folded his paper and placed it on the seat beside him, rubbing a hand surreptitiously over his cock to make sure it stayed against his belly, stiff but aligned with his zipper and therefore less noticeable. Then he sat forward.

The train rumbled to a stop. The doors swished open. The woman took a deep breath, shouldered her tote bag and rose. He followed her out the doors a second behind, not allowing anyone else to come between them. Not because he intended to stop her today, but because no one was going to steal his view of her backside as she walked ahead of him.

Goddamn, everything about her pleased him: her baby-powder scent, the bounce of her shiny shoulder-length hair, the twitch of her firm ass. She glanced to her side and reached into her purse, then glanced up and caught him looking.

Her eyes widened, then she stumbled, going down on her knees to the concrete platform. He followed so closely he had to straddle her to keep from kicking her. Her head came back, hitting him in the groin, and he doubled over, his fingers digging into her scalp to cup her head and push it back.

"Sorry."

"Fuck."

He couldn't have said who said what, but he backed up and knelt beside her, grimacing at the ache in his balls. At least he didn't have to worry about his erection anymore.

She cupped her knee and her face screwed up in pain. "I'm okay," she said, her voice tight—rather like he'd often imagined it would sound when she was close to coming.

"You're hurt."

"Didn't mean to hit you there."

They both stared as people muttered and flowed like a river around them.

Daniel stuck out his hand. "I'll help you up."

Her hand settled inside his. Her fingers were slender, her palm warm. He grasped her firmly and stood, pulling her up with him. He didn't let go of her as she wobbled a bit. "Gotcha," he said, cupping her other arm as he held tightly to her hand.

She blinked; her cheeks filled with warm color. When she glanced down, she gasped. "Hell, and I didn't bring a change of panty hose."

"Maybe you should just take them off," he said, staring at the ladders streaking down the shredded hose. When she gave him a startled look, he felt his own cheeks heat. "Didn't come out quite right, did it?"

The corners of her mouth twitched. "Thanks for the rescue."

His heart thudded heavily against his chest. "Any time."

"I've seen you before," she said then swallowed hard.

He liked the melodic roll of her voice; not too high, but still feminine. "I've seen you, too."

She glanced away and a deep breath blew between her pursed lips. "Guess I better go. Thanks again." She pulled her hand from his, gave his face a quick but strangely poignant glance and turned away.

Daniel cursed his cowardice. "Wait a second."

The woman glanced over her shoulder.

"I've been waiting too long to meet you to let you walk away before you promise to have dinner with me." The words came out in a long, rambling growl and he felt his face warm.

Where a hint of humor curving her mouth had made his heart beat heavier, the full-blown beauty of the wide smile she gave him now took away his breath.

She reached into a pocket of her purse and pulled out a business card. "Call me?"

He glanced down at the card but couldn't take anything in, just the fact that she hadn't said no to his suggestion.

"You know," she said, hesitating for second, "I've been waiting a long time, too."

Daniel knew he was moving too fast, but his body was hot, ready to pounce, and her expression was open and she didn't pull away as he leaned down to kiss her. It was just a quick, chaste touch of his mouth against hers. Her lips were soft. Her breath minty.

Another flow of people moved around them, and he shook his head. "I'll call."

She gave him a small, tight smile and turned away.

Daniel watched her move away, not liking the leaden feeling

that weighed him down. He stepped out, unwilling to let her out of his sight. When he caught up with her, he cupped her elbow. "Promise I'm not a stalker, but would you have coffee with me?"

A gust of laughter shook her, but she quickly nodded. "I know just the place."

THE EFFICIENCY EXPERT

Portia Da Costa

Oh, no, *he's* here. The efficiency expert. He's in my favorite bar on my favorite stool, just when I thought we'd got rid of him.

I'm supposed to be here celebrating. The company's efficiency review is finally over, and I've kept my job by the skin of my teeth. I thought that hyena of a consultant or troubleshooter or whatever the hell he is would be long gone by now and good riddance. But what do I find? He's still here and drinking in the very place where I'm about to toast his departure.

Noah Stevens, that selfsame efficiency troubleshooter slash corporate carnivore. The very monster everybody's so glad to see the back of, even if he is unbearably cute and sexy in his stern, almost machinelike sort of way.

He doesn't look stern tonight, though, or even remotely mechanical. In fact, he looks as weary as hell, almost shattered somehow, as if he's been punched in the gut by fate. Could this be a pang of unexpected sympathy I'm feeling? Workwise, he's been beyond a nightmare, but somehow with shoulders slumped, his blond hair a bit ruffled and a slightly rubbed-out look about his eyes, not to mention what looks like a quadruple vodka in front of him, he looks strangely vulnerable: kind of tender and touchable; definitely in need of a hug.

Shall I run for it? Get discreetly out of here and join the festivities with the other survivors? I'm tempted, but something about the line of his body intrigues and stirs me. I must admit, I have a few types, and as a Mr. Sharp Suit Corporate, he's not really one of them. And yet, even though he's made my life a hell of uncertainty these past few weeks, I do—reluctantly—fancy him something rotten.

He turns from the bar and makes my decision for me.

"Hi, Susie. Are you drinking?" he taps the stool next to the one where I usually sit. "Have one on me.... I think I owe you one, if not three or four."

Well, ain't that the truth!

"Okay. Yes...that'd be great." I slide onto the stool. Up close, he looks quite different from the barracuda of the office. The jacket of his sharp business suit is on the stool beyond, and the shirt beneath looks deliciously soft and molds to the shape of his shoulders and chest—his broad, deep chest. I've never actually seen him out of his tailored corporate armor before, but he's a beautiful male treat, now that he's revealed to me a bit of what previously I've only speculated about.

His thighs are nice, too, strong looking as he adjusts his position on the stool slightly. As he signals to the barman, I can't help wondering what his cock is like. Is he big? He looks as if he might be, but it's difficult to get a clear view without being caught blatantly ogling him. The way he shifted in his seat just then makes me speculate that he might have a hard-on...for me? Just like that? Such wild, untamed sexiness seems totally at odds with his until-now strictly controlled persona.

I request what he's having and get a double gin, over ice. Not my usual tipple, but it's somehow both head clearing *and* intoxicating, a bit like Noah himself really.

We clink glasses and stare into each other's eyes. His look reddened by fatigue and perhaps something else, and the fact that he allows me time to note this is like a pact between us. We've barely spoken about anything but work, but now, everything seems fair game.

"Well, you look worn out...terrible, in fact...." It's a lie. For all his fatigue, he still looks fabulous. "Must be hard work threatening people's jobs and putting the fear of God into them. Surely you're not feeling pangs of guilt?" I swig my gin and watch his pink tongue sweep out and lick droplets of his own drink from his lips. My pussy clenches convulsively; shockingly. The image of that tongue sweeping between my labia makes me almost rock on my stool.

"No, not guilt. I'm not ashamed of being tough on the company, and that's a fact." His head comes up, defiant. In a flash of all-business Noah, the look in his eyes hardens and he's a warrior. "That place was full of dead wood, and it needed shaking up." He reaches for his glass, drains it, orders two more without consulting me.

"You're right there. But what is it? There's something... You look shattered. Have you had some bad news?" It seems perfectly okay to challenge him now, ask probing questions. I feel like a warrior, too, and with my pussy still throbbing, I imagine myself subduing him in bed, kneeling over him, holding down his arms while I force him to tongue me. The picture's so vivid that I have to gulp down a big mouthful of my own drink.

Noah drinks again, too. He seems to have quite a capacity for it. But his eyes are dead level and sober as he answers me.

"Girl trouble." He shrugs elegantly, his face both wry and strangely wounded as he stares back at me.

Now how come I subconsciously suspected that? He's an invulnerable hard case, but like all hard cases, he has an Achilles' heel, too. And his is a romantic susceptibility, it seems. I don't know how I knew, but clearly some woman somewhere has hurt him.

"Sorry to hear that," I offer cautiously. I lick *my* lips, suggesting solace.

He gets the message and straightens up on his stool, flaunting his gorgeousness. And the more I see, the more gorgeous he seems. "There's one way to deal with it, though." His eyes narrow in my direction.

I don't question because I don't need to.

"Hair of the dog...or should I say bitch?" He gives a little shrug and a quirk of his lips at his lapse in political correctness then slips off his stool, swoops up his jacket and briefcase and starts walking. I follow, suddenly well aware that the Royale Bar is in the lobby of a large hotel, and this is probably where he's staying.

This is crazy; unexpected and yet expected. It's been building since he first walked into the office, but we're both too professional to have succumbed to it.

I'm not wrong about his intention, or mine, and once we're in the lift together, he confirms everything I suspected. His briefcase falls to the floor with a *clop* and his jacket follows it. In one beat of my heart, he's manhandled me up against the mirrored wall and stuck his tongue in my mouth and his hand up my skirt. He kisses me hard, jabbing, and grabs my crotch through my panties and gives it a rough, possessive squeeze.

Now this is what I call an efficiency expert!

I nearly come on the spot, I'm so excited. My head whirls, full of his delicious cologne, the one that's tantalized me all the time he's been with us, and the fumes of our shared gin. I anoint my knickers with lusty juice, and his laugh of slightly tipsy victory seems to vibrate through both our bodies.

"I knew I was right about you!" He's triumphant, and he's still working me, even as he stares into my face, his eyes like stars. "I knew you were a sexy woman under all the seriousness. I knew you fancied me." Swiveling his wrist, he changes his hold on me, and his fingertips prize aside my knickers-gusset. Then he's in, right in, flicking at my clit, while with his other hand, he's round the back, squeezing my bottom cheek through my skirt. "God knows I've fancied you, Susie. It's nearly killed me."

I moan, torn between rising on my toes or bearing down hard on his fingers. He's really unstoppable. No delicate, tentative, getting-to-know-you caresses here. He grabs hold of me like a force of nature and handles me hard. I feel like collapsing and it's only the lift wall that's holding me up. Dimly I wonder why on earth we haven't reached our floor yet, but then I see that he's pressed the hold button somewhere amongst our fondling.

But we can't stay in here long, and I realize that he won't release me until I come. So bearing down it is, and as he laughs again and renews his furious efforts, I clutch my breast, tweaking my nipple through my bra.

That always gets me off, and this time's no exception. With a harsh, uncouth grunt, I give in to it, my pussy pulsating like a heart and yet more juice slithering out of me to saturate Noah's fingers.

"Good little Susie. That was nice. I love bringing a woman off. I love to feel her pleasure against my hand."

He's arrogant, domineering, quite ruthless; like his office persona, but in a thrilling new variant. He sucks the taste of me off his fingers and then releases the lift and in seconds the door's sliding open. I barely manage to straighten my skirt in time and stagger out onto his floor, convinced that the older guy who's just got into the car will smell me and know what we've been doing. I imagine him grinning and maybe touching himself as he descends.

I feel I have to assert myself and regain some ground.

"I don't normally do that, you know," I say firmly as I follow Noah along the corridor. "I'm only using you as compensation for all you've put us through, you do realize that?" It's the first thing that comes into my head, but it seems to make sense. Which is a miracle, really, because I can't stop looking at Noah's fabulous ass in his well-cut trousers. I'd like to fall on my knees, rub my cheeks against *those* cheeks and caress his masculine bum this very minute.

"No problem, I know that," he says, "and I deserve it. It's a damn sight more than a drink that I owe you." He flings me a smile and wink over his shoulder. "Do you think that guy who got into the lift just now knows I was just repaying a debt?"

I bet he did.

The moment the room door closes behind us, Noah gives me a long questioning look. He's still dominant, still a man who's used to being in charge. But he's not quite the ruthless bastard all my colleagues think he is. He wants to know that *I* want what he wants.

I nod.

He says, "Strip. All off. I want to see you naked, you gorgeous woman."

Shaking, I drop my bag into an armchair and start to obey him, even though my fingers don't seem to work right. He flings aside his briefcase and jacket and crosses straight to the dressing table. There's a bottle of Gordon's there and a glass, and he seems to consider pouring himself a measure. Golly, he can't half knock it back.

But then he appears to think twice and turns to me. The fact that he considers me intoxicating enough already makes me warm.

When my clothes are off, I've never felt more naked in my life. I'm dripping again, too, and I could swear he'll be able to see it running down my thighs.

"Show me your pussy, love. Lie on the bed. Legs open wide."

I comply, lying back and holding my knees to open myself. He comes right up to me and studies my wet flesh. Then he reaches between my labia, grabs my clit and tweaks it between his finger and thumb. I whine like a baby, but he's merciless. Within seconds I'm coming again, my pussy clenching.

I gasp for air, beached on the bed, my sex on fire with pleasure. I can't do a thing and I don't resist when he manhandles me farther across the mattress, then starts working on his belt buckle.

Within seconds he has his cock out, and it's a beauty, just as I hoped it would be. It certainly looks damned pleased to see me, hard and hot and high, glans gleaming with precome.

"I hope you've got a condom for that thing." I can't see an efficiency expert not having one, but better safe than sorry.

He narrows his blue eyes at me, but he's smiling. He reaches into his back pocket and pulls out the requisite foil package. I wonder dimly if he's been carrying one all the time he's been working at the firm. Efficiency expert, eh? Always organized and prepared for anything. I whimper, staring up into his stern, passionate face as he sheathes himself in a quick, businesslike fashion. Has he been aroused by me before now? Has he been suppressing his desire all the time he's been putting the fear of God into the workforce? His desire for me there all the time, but controlled because of circumstances and presumably his "girl trouble"?

Without further ado, he lowers himself between my thighs and with a deft adjustment, positions himself and pushes firmly into me. When he's lodged in deep, I caress him, clasping my sex around his, just as firmly.

"Yes! Hell, yes! Oh, god, yes!" he shouts, jamming himself into me, demanding more—which I'm ecstatically happy to give. Working him with my inner muscles, I'm pleasuring myself as much as I am him and, still moaning and gasping, I reach around, rummage in his clothes and grab his sexy bottom at the same time, sliding my fingers into the cleft to tickle his anus and add an extra frisson to his pleasure.

"Oh, my god, you clever, delicious bitch!" he howls, bearing down harder and riding me as if I'm a bucking bronco and he's a rodeo star. But then he kisses me, too, his lips roaming my face as we strain against each other, raining down affection, even tenderness and making me feel like a chosen handmaiden worshipping her unexpected new god.

Anxious to please, I plague the little vent of his bottom even harder whilst I still have the wherewithal to think....

He shouts and comes instantly, his cock pumping inside me, his staccato thrusts beating my aching clit and compelling me to soar with him.

Afterward, at his urging, I bring myself off again as he watches me, but this time he seems sated and just lies there, his eyes unfathomable as they follow my fingers. He doesn't even bother to touch his sex.

The orgasm satisfies me but somehow not completely. I've had this tough man on my case for nearly a month now, but after tonight, I'll probably never see him again. And that definitely induces the old postcoital *tristesse* or whatever. I shouldn't take it so hard. I enjoy the occasional one-night stand, ships that pass and all that, golden moments of seizing the day...or the night.

But somehow, Noah Stevens has gotten under my skin. I want to know more about him. I want to know who hurt him...and if there's a way I can make things better.

When we're both dressed, he hands me a glass of gin. He seems to have finished drinking now, and he's steady as a rock and apparently as sober as a judge.

"According to your personnel file you've got two weeks leave owing to you."

What?

"Yes, that's right. I have... What of it?"

"Fancy spending some of it in Sardinia, all expenses paid? My 'girl trouble' has decided she'd rather go to the Seychelles with someone else, and I never got around to cancelling her ticket."

Noah looks at me, his gaze steady. He seems superficially nonchalant, but somehow, at the back of his eyes, he's not quite pleading, but he's very definitely asking. With feeling.

"Okay, why not? Sounds fantastic!" Am I insane? I don't really know him at all. "I haven't had a decent holiday in ages."

He smiles, a wide, creamy, happy, cocky sort of smile—but from the heart.

"Okay then, it's a deal!" He takes my glass from me and sets it aside, looks at me very, very seriously. "There're no strings, Susie...but...well, if something *should* happen, well, let's say I'm open to every possibility, if that suits you, too?"

I consider the possibility of possibilities...and I like it. I like it a lot. My heart thuds in a way that's got nothing to do with sex. Well, it's a bit to do with sex but also to do with those possibilities.

There's no law that says a rebound relationship with someone you once thought you hated can't grow into something real and wonderful.

"It suits me. It probably shouldn't, seeing as you nearly lost me my job, but it does."

Ever the efficiency expert, he doesn't waste a moment.

"Okay then, get your clothes off again, and let's celebrate our trip, shall we?"

Before I can even start, he kisses me hungrily again, like a pirate king savoring his plundered booty, then he feels up my bottom and my pussy whilst murmuring sweet nothings in my ear.

Smiling against his shoulder, I start tugging at my blouse....

REKINDLE

Kathleen Bradean

'm gonna fuck you seven ways to Sunday."

Carl choked on his coffee. "What?"

"Happy birthday, hon." My light kiss left a smear of raspberry lipstick on his cheek. "Keys. Where did I put my keys?" Inside, I giggled, but outside, I kept up the act, shuffling the pile of bills on the kitchen counter.

Do I have your attention, honey?

Well into his forties, Carl was still cute. His soft graying curls swept against the edge of his white collar. When he wore turtlenecks, he looked like a jazz musician.

He dabbed his striped tie with a paper towel, but he eyed me like a conductor confronting a squeaky clarinet.

"That isn't what you said, Sara."

Plates in the sink would have to wait, but I ran a towel over the counter. A drop of coffee sizzled on the hotplate as it evaporated into steam and aroma.

Our daughter, Jenny, plopped into a chair at the kitchen table. "Wazferbreakfast?"

At least she still talked to me.

"Anything, as long as you make it for yourself, sweetie. You're catching a ride home with the Millers after your music lesson, right?"

She bobbed her head as she read the back of a cereal box.

"We're in talks to bring the Berlin Philharmonic into town. They're eight hours ahead, so I need to get to work and Skype them. Don't forget to say happy birthday to Dad," I reminded Jenny as I grabbed my purse.

"Happy birthday." Jenny squinted at Carl. "How old are you now? Like a hundred or something?"

Poor kid got the smart-ass gene from both sides. She couldn't help it. Lucky for her, she got musical talent from both sides, too. That almost made up for the attitude.

Carl followed me out to the driveway of our cookie-cutter suburban home. I missed living in the city.

"Wait. You said something..."

I made my big brown eyes go innocent. "I'm coming by your work for a little birthday lunch, so don't go into any long meetings before noon." I unlocked my red minivan and tried hard to suppress my smile as I buckled my seat belt across my ample mom hips.

He put his hand on the door so that I couldn't close it. "You never say *fuck*."

"Carl! Really. Such language." I was having too much fun. Instead of a good-bye wave, I put my fingers in a *V* over my lips and waggled my tongue between them. In the rearview mirror, I could see him standing in the driveway, clutching his World's Best Dad mug, watching me with a puzzled expression on his face.

* * *

With my imagination so worked up over Carl's birthday surprise, I had to leave my desk to take care of myself early in the day. I went into the last stall in the ladies' room. It wasn't easy, gripping that cold metal handicap rail as I worked my clit, my ears burning, my gasps muted as coworkers washed their hands and gossiped at the sinks.

I loved how wanton that made me feel. Life was too short to waste an orgasm. Besides, the only difference between good girls and bad ones was that bad girls got caught.

Using my juicy fingers, I smeared my scent across my wrists and neck like it was perfume.

People noticed the flush on my cheeks as I moved through the symphony's offices. My nipples rubbed against the inside of my white cotton bra. I could have sworn that the prickly Swedish bassoonist we had just hired smelled me as I went past him. That was the first smile I'd seen on his long, dour face.

If I was caught, did that make me a bad girl? I giggled.

I can be a bad girl if I want to.

I wriggled in my desk chair as I typed.

The first email I sent to Carl was simply the word *Black.*

Half an hour later he responded with a question mark.

Married for years, we had communication down to an art. No wasted words.

The second email said *lace.*

It took him over an hour to come back with *Did you mean to send two emails to me? I got one that said lace, and another that said black.* Carl was the sweetest man on earth, but sometimes I despaired for him.

"Work with me, hon," I muttered at my screen as I sent him *French.*

My clit throbbed in time with my pulse, sweeping out

measures of desire like a metronome.

He didn't bother to comment on that message. As I left my office to pick him up for lunch, I sent the last email.

Knickers.

"The Dallas office crashed their database, again," Carl apologized as he walked off the high-rise elevator forty minutes late. He gave me a distracted peck on the cheek as we walked through the marble lobby. "I wouldn't mind so much if it was a computer problem. That I can fix. The problem in that office seems to lie between the keyboard and the chair. It's the same damn thing every time."

He held the door for me. We stepped onto the chilly city street. The air stank of bus fumes. Gusts of wind pushed my skirt against my mons. A chill ran up my spine, but it had nothing to do with the weather.

People moved down the sidewalk with their heads down and their coats hugged tight at the neck. Their faces were portraits of unhappiness. Did they realize that they were drowning in misery?

We weren't like them. We knew about happiness. It wasn't a pursuit. It was a choice.

I could see from Carl's dazed eyes that he daydreamed of idiot-proof code. None of my birthday surprise would work unless I had his full attention.

I nudged him. "Get my emails?"

His hand was on my elbow. He stopped walking and stared down at his shoes. "Yes."

"All four?"

He ducked down farther in his jacket. I could barely hear his muffled answer. "Yes."

He was so damn cute. I vowed to always remember that about him.

I'm marking you on my heart, Carl. I've grown too accustomed to you. I want to get a fresh perspective so that I can feel every nuance over again, like a jazz interpretation of a classic song. I want to fall in love with who you are now. How have you changed in the years we've been together? Have there been shifts so gradual that I didn't notice?

"I promised you lunch. Come on." I tugged at his arm. Another gust of wind tried to lift the hem of my skirt. "It's colder than I expected."

Carl glanced up at the sky and seemed surprised to see the low clouds. "Hmmm. Well, it's spring." He shrugged.

We're not this boring. Come on, honey. Remember that night on the picnic table? We're still those people, I swear.

Carl followed me into the lobby of a downtown hotel. The glass doors slammed shut behind us, cutting off the wind. I straightened my hair with my fingers, giving him a chance to ask, but he either trusted me or didn't notice where we were.

"Let's sit here." I found us a secluded wicker couch in the lobby bar. A tall planter and a thick column hid us from the reception desk. We went through the unwrapping ritual, coats and scarves piled over a brass railing until we were down to our comfortable office layers, him in white shirt and tie, me in skirt and sky blue blouse.

The wicker couch was for two, a love seat. The slick chintz cushions were jungle green. In front of us was a small cocktail table, wicker and glass.

"I have your present, but I want to explain it first."

I dug through my big mom purse and pulled out a small container with a frosted cupcake inside. The pristine white frosting smeared against the clear plastic. I popped the top and stuck a small blue tapered candle into the stiff buttercream.

"I bet you remember when you stopped believing in Santa

Claus, but do you remember when you stopped believing in birthday wishes?"

Carl blinked at the cupcake. "Not really. No traumas or scars."

I rubbed my neck and wrists to raise a faint whiff of my personal perfume. From the movement of his thick eyebrows, I saw that Carl smelled me but doubted his senses. His nostrils flared a little.

Glancing around the lobby as if I were about to tell him a big secret, I leaned across the uncomfortable couch. "What if I were to tell you that birthday wishes are real?"

He chuckled.

"They are."

"If you say so."

I saw the smirk at the corner of his mouth. My shoulders slumped.

"Come on, honey. Play along. Please?"

"Okay."

He made it clear he was humoring me. That's all I asked for. He could be skeptical, but he had to at least pretend.

"This is no ordinary birthday candle." I did a magician's hand flourish over the taper.

"No? Really?"

"Don't be a prick, Carl."

"Sorry."

"Believe."

I struck a pose like a conductor about to launch into an overture. My hands made circles around the candle before touching my closed eyelids. I had to get into the part again.

"This, as I said, is no ordinary candle. One day, as I was walking outside the symphony hall, I found a secluded alleyway I'd never seen before. Curious, I went down it."

Carl still had a smart-ass grin on his face, but despite that, I could see he was hooked.

"At the end of the alleyway, there was a mysterious store. The windows were coated with thick dust. I peered into them, but could only see glimmers of metal and wood. The deep blue awning over the door said ANTIQUITIES AND CURIOSITIES. Well, I needed a gift for your birthday, so naturally, I went in."

"Naturally." Laughter was on his lips, ready to cascade.

"There were cases filled with junk and antique jewelry. I saw the mellow gold glint of a saxophone on the wall. There were books and occult items stacked haphazardly everywhere. At first, I thought that I was alone, but a tiny, ancient Asian woman stood at the back of the store, smoking from a long, thin white pipe. The place was so quiet that I could hear the shuffle of her bound feet across the wooden floor."

Carl's eyes glinted.

"Anyway, long story short, the old lady sold me this candle. She promised that it was good for one birthday wish."

"Did she mutter any ominous warnings?"

"You'd think so, but no." I found matches and lit the candle. "So, make your wish." I sat primly beside him, offering it up to him with both hands.

He didn't take more than a few seconds before he started forward, lips puckered.

"Wait! Put some thought into it. This is a guaranteed wish."

As he leaned over a second time, I pulled it away so quickly that the flame died. The wick was an orange-hot ember before it leapt to life again.

"What?"

"I meant to remind you of something."

Carl was losing his patience.

"Black." A smile quirked up on the side of my mouth. "Lace."

"French knickers," Carl intoned as quietly as a penitent. He tugged at his pants.

A waiter in a tuxedo vest came to get bar orders from us. I sent him away.

Carl squirmed. "What were those emails about anyway?"

"Wax is dripping on your cake, dear. Make your wish." I offered it to him again.

He caught my wrist before blowing. The flame died for about seven seconds before the trick candle relit.

"Hey! What happened to my wish?"

I set the cupcake down on the small table in front of the couch. "You don't need any more things. We have a house full of crap."

He pretended to scowl. "I suppose a refund is out of the question."

"Bear with me. I made a real wish on my birthday candles last month. I don't know if you remember, but I was able to blow out all forty with one breath. That got me thinking about wishes, and us, and me."

"I see. You get a wish and I don't."

I knew he didn't really care.

The frosting's sweet scent was too strong. I pulled out the candle and snapped the lid shut.

"Up until now, I've been the kind of person my parents expected me to be. Frankly, I'm sick of it. I don't want to be a good girl; I don't want to be responsible all the time. I hate being so much like everyone else that I can hardly recognize me anymore. So I've decided to take control of the second half of my life. From now on, I'm going to be as sexy as I want to be."

"You *are* sexy."

"And you're a god, Carl. The perfect husband. My best friend." I put my hand on his thigh. "And you're hot. I wanna fuck you. Here, now, in the middle of the day, with the lights on and the curtains open. I want to be your nasty girl."

He watched my hand crawl up his leg like it was a tarantula. The thin wool was smooth under my fingertips. Carl blushed, but his face wasn't the only place his blood raced. I could see the outline of his dick. I scooted closer to him so that our thighs touched.

"The thing about those black lace French knickers? I'm not wearing them. In fact, I'm not wearing any panties. The only thing between my bare ass and this couch is my skirt."

Admitting that got me hot. I pressed my legs together and felt squishy. Talking dirty to him in hushed tones in the hotel lobby was just about the level of naughty I could handle. It worked though. Lord, but it worked. Everything between my legs tingled.

"I was thinking about our marriage vows, honey. I promised to forsake all others, but I don't. I put my job first, music, our daughter, a million other things. So, this is my present to you. From now on, you come first. I'm going to remember every wonderful thing about you and appreciate it the same way I'd savor a piece of dark chocolate slowly melting on my tongue."

He pinched his nose as if to hold back a tear.

I took his hand. "We're already checked into a room. Come upstairs with me, honey. Let me make love to you."

We shared the elevator with faded men in suits. The poor dears looked as if all the joy in life had been sucked out of them long ago. That wasn't going to happen to us.

I slowly goosed Carl and kept my hand on his ass until we got out at our floor.

Carl let the flow take him. He didn't ask what came next. This was another thing to love about him—how much he trusted me.

The room was pleasantly warm. Earlier, I folded down the bedspread so that the tan velour blanket underneath would be against our skin. The local jazz station played something bluesy on the portable I brought from home.

I closed the door and went into action. A seductive walk would have been awkward, but I knew how to use my voice. While I loosened his tie, I growled close to his ear, "I think it's so hot that you still treat me like a lady, even though you know better." I trailed my fingers down his chest.

He stared at my hands as I tugged his belt out of the loops. It was some powerful magic, the unexpected mixed with the familiar. He was already hard.

"Saturday mornings, you could be out golfing or watching football, but you coach Jenny's teams instead. I can't tell you how very, very sexy a man is when he's being a dad."

Carl's mouth opened as I pushed him gently to the bed. I hadn't seen that look on his face in years. It amazed me that no matter how many times we knocked it out, he still had a sense of wonder about sex.

You make it spiritual, Carl. You keep sex sacred. Every time you look at my bare breasts or rounded butt, your eyes show such reverence for me that I can't think of myself as undesirable. You make me sexy.

"From now on, every time I think warm thoughts about you, and I get turned on, I'm going to let you know. You don't mind, do you, honey?" I crooned. My fingers traced his warm skin.

He shook his head slowly. Maybe it was too radical of a change for him. I never initiated anything. We had our codes, though. If I came to bed naked, he knew I wouldn't turn him down. But I never pounced on him. After sixteen years, I figured that he wouldn't mind if I made the first move.

Hiking up my skirt, I straddled his legs. My lips pressed against the pulse at his neck. "I was thinking about last night. I'd like that, but with more kissing." I let him feel the edge of my teeth.

"You think about sex the next day?" He was shocked.

"Yes. I do." How could I have hid that from him for so long? "Sometimes it makes me wet all over again."

Carl had always liked kissing, much more than I did. I brushed my lips over his and pressed closer. We were going to kiss as long as he wanted.

He got out from under me and knelt on the bed to come down at my mouth. His hands cupped my face. My hands slid under his shirt, feeling his labored breath, his hard-on, the way he abandoned himself to my game.

Carl tasted sweet and dark, like coffee.

I couldn't remember the last time we'd kissed like that. We treated our kisses with such casual disregard that they'd become sexless things, as sparse as our words. We knew each other so well that it seemed everything was distilled into staccato communication, but I wanted to slow things down. No pizzicato plucking at him like his body was a string on a violin. Nope. He deserved the long draw of the bow caressing his body so that after my touch was gone, he would still vibrate.

My thighs were wet. The scent of sex rose in the heat between our bodies. I wanted to peel away my good girl clothes and play the vixen with him, but everything was too perfect. Afraid that I'd break the spell binding us, I let him lead.

Carl lingered on my mouth. He pressed hard against my lips, as if he'd been starved for too long.

The outline of his dick showed against his pants. I rubbed my thumbnail over the head. Unzipping his fly, I groped his balls.

You're so turned on, Carl. Did you ever dream I'd do this with you? Did you want it, but were too afraid to share your fantasies? You can't disgust me. Don't be afraid to be a little rough, a little cruel, because I'll know that your heart isn't in it. I'll play any game you want. I'll make any wish come true.

"Baby," he breathed against my mouth.

I stroked his hard-on as my clit ached for attention. Shoving up my skirt, I fingered myself. I was swollen for him, ready to burst in a gush of hot, sweet juices.

I put his hand between my legs.

"This is what you do to me."

"You've got me really turned on, too," he admitted.

I moaned as his long fingers slid inside me. He knew exactly where to touch me. His fingers fucked me while his thumb worked over my clit. It was a well-practiced move and it always worked.

I stroked him through his underwear. The white cotton strained. Finding that special spot below the head, I pressed my thumb against his cock while I slowly squeezed his balls. They were hot in my hand, heavy.

"No," Carl pleaded. He pulled his hips back from me, but I grabbed his cock and pumped. "I can't—" A shudder ran through his body. Holding the note long and low, he moaned. The music of sex.

I felt the warmth spurt from him.

"I'm sorry. I came," Carl apologized as he drew back.

"Sorry? Sweetheart, that was the idea. It's so hot that I turn you on that much."

"Oh, yeah, it turned me on." He was angry with himself, as if he'd failed. "Ladies first, always, even if she doesn't think she's a lady."

I laughed as I gently kissed him. "Honey, it used to be that a stiff wind could get you off. Now it takes a lot more. It's a huge compliment that you got that turned on just by kissing me. Besides, today, it's all about you." I nibbled at his ear until he shivered.

"But it's no fun if you don't get anything out of it."

I reclined back on the mattress and twirled a piece of hair around my finger. I felt like a wicked seductress and loved every second of it. My toes pressed into his groin. "Another reason why you're the best."

I spread my legs. "If you feel that bad about it, come over and finish me off."

"My god! You really don't have on any underwear."

My hand slid down between my legs. I pinched my clit. "You're so good at rekindling fires, honey. How about stoking this?"

Before I said good-bye in the lobby of his building, I maneuvered Carl behind a marble column and roughly grabbed his collar. "You might want to take a nap in your office this afternoon, baby, because I expect you to put out tonight, too."

He laughed, but I could see it turned him on.

"Oh, damn! We left my special candle and the cupcake in the lobby of the hotel." He pretended to be disappointed. "And I'll bet that if we look for that mysterious shop, it won't be there anymore."

"Those mystical places come and go so unexpectedly," I agreed ruefully before a grin spread over my face. I couldn't stop my giggle. We were coconspirators. He made life so fun.

His eyes twinkled. "Thanks, babe. I—" He couldn't seem to think of a way to end that, but I already knew what he meant.

Words were unnecessary. He was my oxygen. He was all I needed to keep the spark glowing.

Any long-term relationship took work, but keeping the magic between us felt more like play. The real trick was remembering to take time to do it.

Before he could step into the elevator, I touched his arm. "If you don't mind me asking, what was your wish?"

Carl gave me his sappiest grin. "Nothing. I'm smart enough to know that I already have everything I could wish for." He gave the lobby a quick glance before whispering, "Dirty girl."

ABOUT THE AUTHORS

JACQUELINE APPLEBEE (writing-in-shadows.co.uk) is a black bisexual British woman who breaks down barriers with smut. Jacqueline's stories have appeared in various anthologies including *Best Women's Erotica* and *Best Lesbian Erotica*. Jacqueline has recently penned *Erotic Brits*, a sexy tour around the United Kingdom and Ireland.

WICKHAM BOYLE has been writing erotica for women and occasionally couples since 1983. Her work has appeared in collections and online. She is also a mother, theater producer, financial arbitrator on Wall Street and travel writer. Her closet is full of many hats.

KATHLEEN BRADEAN's stories (KathleenBradean.Blogspot. com) can be found in *The Sweetest Kiss: Ravishing Vampire Erotica*; *Where the Girls Are*; Zane's *Caramel Flava II*; *Coming Together: Against the Odds* and many other anthologies. Be seduced by her 140 characters at a time on Twitter.

ANGELA CAPERTON's eclectic erotica spans many genres, including romance, horror, fantasy and what she calls contemporary-with-a-twist. Look for her stories published with Cleis, Circlet Press, Drollerie Press, eXtasy Books and in the indie magazine *Out of the Gutter*.

LIZZY CHAMBERS is a previously unpublished college student from the great Midwest. She is currently pursuing a BA in English, with a minor in gender and women's studies. In the future she hopes to teach and continue writing steamy stories about hunky men and the bold women who capture them.

PORTIA DA COSTA pens both romance and women's erotica and is the author of over twenty novels and a hundred-plus short stories. She's best known for her Black Lace titles, but now writes for a variety of publishers, including Harlequin Spice.

MONICA DAY is founder of the Sensual Life and hosts *Living the Sensual Life: An Evening of Erotic Open Mic* in Manhattan. She holds a degree in creative writing from Mills College and uses writing as a tool of sensual freedom in her courses, workshops and her own everyday life.

DELILAH DEVLIN (delilahdevlin.com) is an author with a rapidly expanding reputation for writing deliciously edgy stories with complex characters, creating dark, erotically charged paranormal worlds and richly descriptive westerns that ring with authenticity.

JUSTINE ELYOT has written extensively for Black Lace and Xcite. She lives in the United Kingdom.

EMERALD's erotic fiction (thegreenlightdistrict.org) has been published in anthologies edited by Violet Blue, Rachel Kramer Bussel, Jolie du Pre and Alison Tyler as well as at various erotic websites. She currently lives in Maryland and is an advocate for reproductive freedom and sex workers' rights.

LANA FOX's erotica (lanafox.com) has been published in Clean Sheets and numerous anthologies by Xcite. She also has a story published in *Alison's Wonderland*, edited by Alison Tyler. "The Silver Belt" is inspired by the erotica of Anaïs Nin.

ISABELLE GRAY's writing (pettyfictions.com) appears in numerous anthologies and her alter ego (or is it the other way around?) is the editor of the Cleis anthology *Girl Crush*.

A. M. HARTNETT (amhartnett.com) published her first erotic short story in 2006. She lives in Atlantic Canada and has set most of her work in this locale.

ANNABETH LEONG (annabethleong.blogspot.com) is the pseudonym of a journalist and short story writer. Her erotica has appeared on the Oysters and Chocolate website and in several anthologies, including *Girl Crush* from Cleis Press.

TERESA NOELLE ROBERTS writes romantic erotica and erotic romance about loving people who aren't necessarily vanilla or monogamous. Look for her paranormal romance novels (kinky and/or poly) from Samhain and Phaze and her BDSM-oriented erotica in more anthologies than you can shake a riding crop at.

SUZANNE V. SLATE is a librarian who lives in the Boston area with her longtime lover. She has published a variety of nonfiction articles and a book and has recently begun writing fiction.

DONNA GEORGE STOREY (DonnaGeorgeStorey.com) is the author of *Amorous Woman*, a steamy, semiautobiographical tale of an American woman's love affair with Japan. Her short fiction has appeared in numerous journals and anthologies including *Penthouse, Best American Erotica* and *The Mammoth Book of Best New Erotica*.

CHARLENE TEGLIA's work (charleneteglia.com) has garnered several honors, including the prestigious *Romantic Times* Reviewer's Choice Award for Best Erotic Novel. Her work has been excerpted in *Complete Woman,* and selected by the Rhapsody, Doubleday and Literary Guild Book Clubs.

SASKIA WALKER (saskiawalker.co.uk) is a British author whose short fiction appears in over sixty anthologies. Her erotic novels include *Along for the Ride, Double Dare, Reckless, Rampant, Inescapable* and *The Harlot*. Saskia lives in the north of England close to the Yorkshire moors, where she happily spends her days spinning yarns.

ABOUT
THE EDITOR

RACHEL KRAMER BUSSEL (rachelkramerbussel.com) is a New York–based author, editor and blogger. She has edited over thirty books of erotica, including *Fast Girls; Smooth; Orgasmic; Bottoms Up: Spanking Good Stories; Spanked; Naughty Spanking Stories from A to Z 1* and *2; Fast Girls; Smooth; The Mile High Club; Do Not Disturb; Tasting Him; Tasting Her; Please, Sir; Please, Ma'am; He's on Top; She's on Top; Caught Looking; Hide and Seek; Crossdressing; Rubber Sex* and *Bedding Down.* She is the author of the novel *Everything But...* and the nonfiction book *How To Write an Erotic Love Letter, Best Sex Writing* series editor, and winner of three IPPY (Independent Publisher) Awards. Her work has been published in over one hundred anthologies, including *Best American Erotica 2004* and *2006,* Zane's *Chocolate Flava 2* and *Purple Panties, Everything You Know About Sex Is Wrong, Single State of the Union* and *Desire: Women Write About Wanting.* She serves as senior editor at *Penthouse Variations* and wrote the popular "Lusty Lady" column for the *Village Voice*.

Rachel has written for *AVN, Bust,* Cleansheets.com, *Cosmopolitan, Curve,* the Daily Beast, Fresh Yarn, TheFrisky.com, Gothamist, Huffington Post, Mediabistro, *Newsday, New York Post, Penthouse, Playgirl, Radar, San Francisco Chronicle, Time Out New York* and *Zink,* among others. She has appeared on "The Martha Stewart Show," "The Berman and Berman Show," NY1, and Showtime's "Family Business." She has hosted In the Flesh Erotic Reading Series (inthefleshreadingseries.com) since October 2005, and she blogs at lustylady.blogspot.com. Read more about *Passion* at passionromance.wordpress.com.

More from Rachel Kramer Bussel

Best Sex Writing 2010
Edited by Rachel Kramer Bussel

The erotic elements of *Twilight*, scary sex laws, the future of sex ed, the science behind penis size, a cheating wife's defense of her affair, and much more make it under the covers of *Best Sex Writing 2010*.
ISBN 978-1-57344-421-7 $15.95

Please, Sir
Erotic Stories of Female Submission
Edited by Rachel Kramer Bussel

These 22 kinky stories celebrate the thrill of submission by women who know exactly what they want.
ISBN 978-1-57344-389-0 $14.95

Please, Ma'am
Erotic Stories of Male Submission
Edited by Rachel Kramer Bussel

Bestselling erotica editor Rachel Kramer Bussel has gathered today's best erotic tales of men who crave the cruel intentions of a powerful woman.
ISBN 978-1-57344-388-3 $14.95

Fast Girls
Erotica for Women
Edited by Rachel Kramer Bussel

Fast Girls celebrates the girl with a reputation, the girl who goes all the way, and the girl who doesn't know how to say "no."
ISBN 978-1-57344-384-5 $14.95

Do Not Disturb
Hotel Sex Stories
Edited by Rachel Kramer Bussel

Do Not Disturb delivers a delicious array of hotel hook-ups where it seems like anything can happen—and quite often does.
ISBN 978-1-57344-344-9 $14.95

Women's Erotica from Violet Blue

Lust
Erotic Fantasies for Women
Edited by Violet Blue

Lust is a collection of erotica by and for women, a fierce and joyous celebration of female desire and the triple-X trouble it gets us into.
ISBN 978-1-57344-280-0 $14.95

Just Watch Me
Erotica for Women
Edited by Violet Blue

Intended as inspiration for bedroom adventures, this heady collection of erotic stories is filled with hair-raising and relatable encounters.
ISBN 978-1-57344-417-0 $14.95

Best Women's Erotica 2010
Edited by Violet Blue

From the sparks between strangers to the knowing caresses of longtime lovers, the characters in these steamy stories revel in erotic adventure.
ISBN 978-1-57344-373-9 $15.95

Best of Best Women's Erotica 2
Edited by Violet Blue

Lovingly handpicked by Violet Blue, those erotic gems have been polished to perfection by the bestselling editor in women's erotica.
ISBN 978-1-57344-379-1 $15.95

Girls on Top
Explicit Erotica for Women
Edited by Violet Blue

"If you enjoy sexy stories about women with desirable minds (and bodies and libidos that match) then *Girls on Top* needs to be on your reading list."—Erotica Readers and Writers Association
ISBN 978-1-57344-340-1 $14.95

Read the Very Best in Erotica

Fairy Tale Lust
Erotic Fantasies for Women
Edited by Kristina Wright
Foreword by Angela Knight

Award-winning novelist and top erotica writer Kristina
Wright goes over the river and through the woods to
find the sexiest fairy tales ever written.
ISBN 978-1-57344-397-5 $14.95

In Sleeping Beauty's Bed
Erotic Fairy Tales
By Mitzi Szereto

"Classic fairy tale characters like Rapun-
zel, Little Red Riding Hood, Cinder-
ella, and Sleeping Beauty, just to name
a few, are brought back to life in Mitzi
Szereto's delightful collection of erotica
fairy tales." —Nancy Madore, author of
Enchanted: Erotic Bedtime Stories for Women
ISBN 978-1-57344-376-8 $16.95

Frenzy
60 Stories of Sudden Sex
Edited by Alison Tyler

"Toss out the roses and box of candies
This isn't a prolonged seduction. This is
slammed against the wall in an alleyway
sex, and it's all that much hotter for it."
—*Erotica Readers & Writers Association*
ISBN 978-1-57344-331-9 $14.95

Afternoon Delight
Erotica for Couples
Edited by Alison Tyler

"Alison Tyler evokes a world of heady
sensuality where fantasies are fearlessly
explored and dreams gloriously realized."—Barbara Pizio, Executive Editor,
Penthouse Variations
ISBN 978-1-57344-341-8 $14.95

Can't Help the Way That I Feel
*Sultry Stories of African American Love,
Lust and Fantasy*
Edited by Lori Bryant-Woolridge

Some temptations are just too tantalizing
to ignore in this collection of delicious
stories edited by Emmy award-winning
and Essence bestselling author Lori Bryant-Woolridge.
ISBN 978-1-57344-386-9 $14.95

Ordering is easy! Call us toll free or fax us to place your MC/VISA order.
You can also mail the order form below with payment to:
Cleis Press, 2246 Sixth St., Berkeley, CA 94710.

ORDER FORM

QTY	TITLE	PRICE

SUBTOTAL	
SHIPPING	
SALES TAX	
TOTAL	

Add $3.95 postage/handling for the first book ordered and $1.00 for each additional book. Outside North America, please contact us for shipping rates. California residents add 9.75% sales tax. Payment in U.S. dollars only.

★ Free book of equal or lesser value. Shipping and applicable sales tax extra.

Cleis Press • Phone: (800) 780-2279 • Fax: 510-845-8001
orders@cleispress.com • www.cleispress.com
You'll find more great books on our website

Follow us on Twitter @cleispress • Friend/fan us on Facebook